Honor in the Blood

To Vickie-Ann
you're the best!

Honor in the Blood

a novel

s. h. montgomery

S h montgomery

Published by Mammoth Star Publishing

This is a work of fiction. Any references to real people, events, establishments, organizations, or locales are intended only to give this novel a sense of reality and authenticity and are used fictitiously, with the exception of historical dates and events. Incidents, characters, and dialogue are from the authors imagination, and any resemblance to real persons living or dead is entirely coincidental.

Cover Design by James Kelly

ISBN 978-1-886726-29-1

PRINTED IN THE UNITED STATES OF AMERICA

IN MEMORY

of

Nick

Who knows what will come out of the soul of man?

The soul of man is a dark forest, with wild life in it.

Henry Miller

1

Chicago - 1947

Francesca snuggled close to Fin who was snoring peacefully beside her. She had been Mrs. Finnegan Callahan for five months. The wedding vows still fresh in her mind had gone off without a hitch. Despite the rebellion brewing, her family had been at their best ... Angeline, her sweet sister and nun acolyte, had been her maid of honor. Dominic, her brother, already acting like the priest he would soon become, so capably helped Father Joseph perform the ceremony. Mama and Papa decked out in their Sunday best, portraying happiness for her sake because she was so excited.

Even Meghan, Fin's mother, was on her good behavior. Granted she looked disapproving, but when Father Joseph asked if there were any objections to the union, she didn't oppose, as Francesca knew she wanted to. Yes, the ceremony had been perfect. But the reception ... it hadn't been amusing then, but now a smile crossed Francesca's face as she reflected ...

The Savios' backyard had been decorated that morning by family members. When the happy couple arrived from the church for the reception, Francesca was too elated to notice that the flowers her mama had woven with arbor leaves were growing limp from the heat and that the band members continued to wipe sweat from their faces.

Francesca danced the first dance with Fin, the next with her papa, then took turns dancing with all of her brothers, Gino,

Pietro, and Carlo. She had not, however, danced with Dominic, who never passed up a chance to take the microphone and belt out a song, which he did with gusto. The dance floor was crowded. Even Vito had thrown down his cane and taken Maria in his arms. Francesca waved at them, glad her parents were enjoying themselves.

She scanned the dancers and realized Fin wasn't there. By the time she returned to the head table and found him, she sensed something was amiss. He was acting strangely. She'd thought the reason might have something to do with his parents, but Meghan had been seen wandering to the far corner of the yard toward the shade tree. Perhaps trying to find relief from the sun, or was she engaging in her usual snobbery? It didn't matter to Francesca. This was her day, and she didn't care the reason. Papa and Michael, her new father-in-law, were deep in conversation at one of the tables. Too bad such niceness didn't exist between her mother and Fin's instead of the iciness they exuded.

Francesca liked Fin's father and felt that he approved of her. She wondered if Meghan ever would. Fin's parents were such an ill-matched couple. Francesca decided Michael must have the patience of two saints in order to love and put up with cold, overbearing Meghan when he showed so much warmth. The two sets of parents were as different as circles and squares because Francesca's mama and papa adored each other.

Francesca plopped down beside Fin, trying to catch her breath from the Tarantella that she and Gino had been dancing. "Is something the matter?"

"Naw, guess I'm just tired. After all, I think I've danced with every woman here."

"All except your mother. Why won't she dance with you? It's your wedding day. What's her problem?"

"What do you think? Me. I've always been her problem."

"Oh, Fin, I'm sorry, I just thought today of all days, but I should have known.

"Never mind her. Look at all the money I got." Fin laid a crumpled wad of bills on the table in front of him.

Francesca took some money from her waistband and added to the pile. "As you can see, I've also done my part. Boy, I thought I was doomed to be crippled by the way Mr. Rollosi stepped all over my toes. Glad I survived because he gave us five dollars. I don't care if your mama does think that the Italian custom of having a money dance is for peasants. Thanks to all this cash, we now have some extra to help set up our apartment."

Fin seemed preoccupied. "How long before we can leave?"

"Leave? This is our party. Aren't you having fun? Come on, let's dance some more. We're not going anywhere until after the cake is cut. And wait until you taste it. It's luscious."

"I'm sure," Fin mumbled.

"Well, don't sound so enthusiastic. Come on, let's dance."

"You know I'm not a good dancer. Drag one of your brothers out there again."

"It's not the dancing, I just want to be in your arms." Francesca caressed Fin's cheek.

"Don't worry about that. You'll be in them as soon as we get to that fancy hotel room your papa's friend gave us as a present."

"Yeah, that was really nice of Mr. DeCassio." Francesca noticed the empty wine glass in front of Fin. "How many of those have you had?"

"Not enough to make me want to dance."

Fin's face was flushed, and Francesca sensed it wasn't from the sun. Early in their courtship, she'd smelled liquor on his breath but never thought much about it. Wasn't that what young boys did? Especially Irish and Italian ones? Besides, it probably gave Fin a bit of courage to face his shrew of a mother.

Sneaking around behind his parents' back to court her hadn't been any easier for him than it had for her. Now being a married man, Fin didn't need to obey or listen to his mother anymore. He could stand up to her.

Abruptly, the band stopped playing. "What's going on?" Francesca looked up and saw a scuffle in the middle of the dance floor.

"Oh, no, what's Carlo doing? He's fighting with Tommy Henley that nice friend of yours."

"Most likely one of those Italian hates a mick fight." Fin reached for the wine bottle, in the middle of the table, and poured the last of its contents into his glass.

"Well, go stop them."

But Francesca's papa was already there. Vito banged his cane first on Carlo's head, then on Tommy's.

"Basta! Basta! Break it up."

A couple of Vito's goombas appeared and pulled the fighters apart. Carlo wrested himself away and lunged for Tommy. But instead of reaching his goal, he stumbled, diving headlong into the table at the edge of the dance floor where the Mille Foglie was displayed. Carlo ended up sprawled on the ground, covered with wedding cake, the bride and groom centerpiece from the top perched on his head like a hat.

"Oh, no, my beautiful cake. It's ruined! I'm gonna kill Carlo." She rose to go to the disaster, but Fin grabbed her arm and laughed heartily.

"Sit down. The cake's gone and now Carlo's going too"

A couple of DeCassio's henchman, who until now had stayed in the background, came forward, picked up Carlo, and ushered him into the Savios' house. Except for several of Maria's friends, who now cleaned up the mess, the reception resumed as if nothing had happened. The band played and couples danced.

"Oh, so you think it's funny?" Tears coursed down Francesca's cheeks.

Fin wrapped his arms around her. "Don't cry. It was just a dumb old cake."

"It was not dumb. It was special. Just for us." Anger replaced Francesca's tears. "This is our once-in-a-lifetime day. Doesn't it mean anything to you?"

Fin, seeing her distress, pecked her cheek. "Of course, of course it does. But, honey, look there's still the groom's cake. And if we have only one cake to cut, we can start the honeymoon sooner."

The room Sigari DeCassio arranged for their wedding night was at the magnificent Drake Hotel, which sat at the end of Michigan Avenue in front of Lake Shore Drive. Until he committed suicide, gangster Frank Nitti, Al Capone's successor, had operated from a suite of rooms at the Drake. Now, another top mobster worked there, and at Sigari's request had upgraded the couple from a regular room to the Honeymoon Suite.

It was better than any dream when Francesca and Fin exited Sigari's limo, proceeded through the round carved door off Walton Place, and climbed the steps to the lobby with its checkered Bottacino marble floor. Lush flowers burst in greeting from an urn sitting on a round table in the middle of the lobby. Francesca tucked her arm through Fin's. "I feel like a princess."

The bellman directed the way to an elevator and with trepidation Francesca passed carefully over the small empty space for her first ride. When the operator in his military-like uniform and white gloves slid the inside brass gate and the elevator doors closed, and the car began its ascent, Francesca gripped Fin's arm tighter. Her stomach heaved when the car lurched to a stop on the tenth floor.

The bellman unlocked a double door, and Francesca and Fin followed him into a plush gold and white suite of rooms. They were in awe when they viewed the sparkling waters of Lake Michigan visible through the windows before them. Pulling their eyes away, a living room with elegant silk moiré-covered furniture and highly-polished mahogany tables greeted them. Through French doors, a bed beckoned. A vase of white lilies, champagne on ice, and strawberries dusted with powdered sugar sat on a table nearby.

"Oh, my, have you ever?' exclaimed Francesca, smelling the flowers, then twirling around, feasting her eyes on the grandness that surrounded her.

"It's pretty darn swanky," said Fin, bouncing on the bed, excited at the thought of what would soon take place beneath the sheets.

"It's glorious." Francesca squealed in glee.

If only Fin's battle-ax of a mother could see them now.

"Well, we might as well break open the champagne and toast to this good luck. Your papa seems to know the right people."

"I guess so," said Francesca. She bit into a juicy strawberry. "Oh, here take a bite, this is the sweetest ever." She held out a plump berry to Fin.

"Not as sweet as you," said Fin. He grabbed the hand that held the strawberry and pulled her down on the bed beside him. After a few lingering kisses, Francesca jumped up.

"Why don't you undo the bed and open the champagne, while I get out of this dress." She picked up her valise and went into the bathroom.

Before long, Francesca heard the the pop of the champagne's cork and knew that Fin was waiting for her. She became nervous as she slipped on the lacy, white nightgown she'd splurged her last penny on. She wanted everything to be just right for their first night together. After running a comb through her ebony hair and brushing her teeth, she grinned her lop-sided smile at the mirror over the sink. She felt ready. Opening the bathroom door, she was about to say something when she heard a noise.

Fin lay stiffly on his back snoring, looking like a dead man. One hand on top of the other protecting his manhood. Beside the bed on the floor was an empty champagne flute.

Francesca watched Fin sleeping now as she had on their wedding night. No longer snoring, his lips made little popping sounds. She regarded the ceiling. The cracks in the plaster looked like a map of the world, and she wondered when China might fall on their heads. The plink, plink, plink drip of the bathroom faucet grated on her, and the moldy smell of age caused her nose to wrinkle. These things wouldn't bother her so much if she knew Fin was happy, but he wasn't.

Searching for a place to live hadn't been easy. Fin didn't want to live in the Italian area, but rent was too high in Irish Bridgeport, and too far from the post office where he went every morning to sort the mail and walk his route. After days of searching, they'd finally settled on a second-story walk up off Taylor Street. With Fin's job and hers clerking at Briscom's Department Store, where she'd worked since leaving high school, they could afford it.

After settling in, Francesca, wanting to be a good daughter-in-law, had extend an olive branch and invited Meghan to lunch on a Saturday when Fin was working. By the time Meghan scaled the flights of stairs to their two-room apartment, she was winded and in bad temper. Then when she saw the sorry state in which they lived, despite Francesca's attempt to create a homey feel by placing a colorful afghan over the used sofa's worn places and hanging sunlit yellow curtains at the windows, Meghan sniffed like a hound following a bad odor. She ran a white-gloved finger across one of the scratched end tables, holding up the finger, inspecting it. She acted surprised at finding no dust, straightened a picture, then focused her attention on the table that Francesca had set with care.

"For your information, I'm allergic to marigolds," said Meghan, spying the arrangement in the middle of the lunch table.

"Sorry, I didn't know," said Francesca, swiftly removing the offenders to an empty cupboard in the kitchen.

After a few more critical glances around the room, Francesca thought Meghan was going to leave. Instead, she parked herself at the table, waiting to be served as if she was the Queen of England. She took a couple of nibbles of the Pasta e Fagioli and moved the expensive spinach salad with figs around on her plate, taking bird bites here and there, while Francesca made awkward conversation. Neither the weather, Fin's job, nor inquiring about Meghan's health brought more than two word responses.

Afterward, Meghan hurried away, but not before complaining about all the steps she had to descend. Francesca guessed it would be her mother-in-law's first and last visit and questioned why she'd tried to be nice to the woman at all. Or why Meghan, for that matter, had accepted the invitation. The woman was a bitch and an enigma.

Attitudes weren't much better on the part of the Savio's toward Fin, at least the men's. Her papa, whom Francesca thought accepted Fin, hadn't. He told Francesca after her marriage, he had no use for the Irish or for Fin and thought him a *spostata*, a real jerk, and that he would never be good enough for her. Yet, Vito had added that he loved her and hoped she was happy.

Dominic was the only one of Francesca's brothers who welcomed Fin. The other three, echoed Vito's sentiments. They only appeared to be resigned to their brother-in-law because they adored their sister. Still, they were as friendly to him as a couple of cheetahs making a kill. After a couple of uncomfortable visits for Fin at the Savios', Francesca visited her parents without him.

This suited Fin just fine because he returned the Savio men's rancor. Before marrying, he had delighted in going to the Savios' and wolfing down Maria's delicious food. Although he missed Maria's cooking, he detested everything else. Fin and the Savio men had done a U-turn regarding civility.

Italian and Irish prejudices had been discussed several times before their marriage. Both Fin and Francesca pronounced them absurd. But now, Francesca discovered Fin's thinking equaled his mother's biased view. He talked about dagos as if he wasn't married to one. He came home after work, complaining to Francesca about their stupid accent, the way they used their hands when they talked, and how the strong smell of garlic knocked him over when he stepped on the stoops to deliver letters.

Francesca was stunned. She asked Fin why he had married her, if he despised Italians so. Fin shrugged, saying she was different. After he had saved her from being raped by Masimo when they were teens, she had called him her hero. That's when he'd fallen for her.

Francesca found it all confusing. "If you feel as you do, how can you consider Dino your best friend. He's Italian."

"Dino's an exception to the rule."

Francesca couldn't believe that she had been so blind and hadn't been able to sense his feelings. Was the reason he loved her because she had called him a hero after he'd rescued her? It puzzled her. Fin and his mother had never gotten along. Why now did his mother's beliefs hold more sway than Michael's, who had never been a bigot?

Francesca finally concluded she must have been a conquest, and once the mountain had been explored Fin's true colors came through. She couldn't decide if she was angry, sad, or both. Sex and the church seemed to be the only thing keeping their marriage from completely crumbling like an old brick wall.

She rolled over, her back to Fin, and wondered where it would all lead.

2

Fin grew irritable when Francesca told him that Christmas would be spent at the Savios'.

"You know I don't give a rat's ass about going there with all those damn dagos."

"Too bad. Besides, you won't be the only Irish person there. Pietro's Sylvia is a mick just like you." Inwardly, she laughed at her zinger. " I know you don't want to spend the holiday with your mother. And she certainly doesn't want to spend it with me. You need to realize that Christmas is an important time for my family. I'm giving up some of Mama's traditions as it is." She glanced at their lone decoration, a dismal tree with a crooked trunk, already dropping its needles.

"Well, you met her for midnight mass last night, didn't you?"

"Of course, I'm not giving up the church, but I'm also not relenting about spending our Christmases with my family. Did I tell you the new rule? From now on, only children in the family will be given presents."

"Well, it's a good thing. No one would get anything from us, anyway. We can't even afford to give each other a gift." For a moment, Fin seemed sad.

Francesca hugged him. "I don't care. You're the only gift I want."

The Savio's little house brimmed with people by the time Francesca and Fin arrived. A lighted nativity scene welcomed from a window, and the minute they opened the front door and stepped into the foyer, confusion burst forth as if a *pignatta* had been broken. Laughter and voices, the screams of children chasing each other up and down the stairs, and cigar and cigarette smoke infused with food aromas spilled out to meet them. Vito, some neighborhood goombas, and the Savio sons were in the living room smoking and visiting. When the rowdy children saw Fin and Francesca they ran to meet them, nearly knocking the couple down.

"Hey, Auntie Francesca, look what Santa Babbo Natale brought me." Pietro's son, Tommy, held up a bright red fire truck.

"That's nice. Why don't you go play with it and quit running?" But Tommy was off after a neighbor boy.

Colin pulled on Fin's arm. "Come on. Come play with me."

"Not right now." Fin shook him away.

"Come on kids, quieten down," said Francesca unwinding Valentina's arms from her legs so she could move.

In the distance, Simona was crying, and Sylvia shouted for Pietro to control the running hellions because she was busy feeding the baby.

"I know it's a madhouse, but this is our Christmas," said Francesca, seeing a sour expression cross Fin's face. "Get used to it."

They walked into the living room and all the men hugged and kissed Francesca and wished her, *Buon Natale*.

The only brother greeting Fin was Dominic, who was visiting from Wisconsin where he was now a new priest with his own parish. Pietro and Gino nodded in Fin's direction, Carlo raised a finger in recognition, but Vito ignored him.

The extended table, filling the dining room, had been laid with Maria's best tablecloth. Unmatched crystal wine glasses and china plates, which Maria had purchased through years of shopping at the Maxwell Street market, danced with color from the reflected Christmas tree lights. A sideboard laden with all kinds of sweets, including Vito's favorites Buccillati, Cassata, and Panettone awaited the meal's finale.

"Go. Join the men," whispered Francesca, "while I go down to the kitchen and help Mama."

Reluctantly, Fin headed for a corner of the parlor and the only empty chair in the crowded room. He felt like a sixth finger, useless and unwanted. Joining into the conversation with the men wasn't an option, so he stared at his surroundings.

The house was decorated with gaudy chains of red and green construction paper strung over the top of all the windows, and a second crèche, with plaster figurines, sat on a side table. An ox and an ass hovered around Mary and Baby Jesus while Joseph looked on. Fin had questioned Francesca when they were dating as to the reason there were no cows or sheep in the manger. She told him that according to Italian legend, the ox and ass warmed the newborn with their breath. It seemed to him that other livestock could do the same, but he'd kept quiet.

The Christmas tree dripped with silver tinsel which he knew Maria carefully removed each year and reused. An angel topped the tree. Instead of a figure of Santa Claus sitting nearby, Fin saw Le Befana, the old witch on her flying broom dressed in a colorful patched coat and worn out shoes. On January 6th, Epiphany Day, Italian tradition called for her to leave gifts and fill stockings with candy for the good children and coal for the bad.

Combining the old with the new, Santa brought presents to the Savio children on Christmas morning, but Le Befana filled stockings on the Epiphany. Listening to all the noise and running feet, which Pietro hadn't succeeded in curbing, Fin decided this year the brats would be sure to receive the icky, black sugar pieces, emulating coal.

He turned his attention back to the tree with its stars and gleaming balls and the new-fangled bubble lights. Watching the gurgling liquid his mind percolated with thoughts of another Christmas. He and his mother had gone to the forest preserve and gathered mistletoe, and how his parents had kissed after hanging the greenery. It dawned on Fin, that had been the only time he'd ever seen them in a loving moment. That same holiday, Meghan had presented him with a bow and arrows and had taught him to shoot.

He shuddered remembering the helpless bird his mother insisted he kill to see if he was worthy of learning her Druid ways. Even now, he felt sick thinking of the nauseating sight---the poor bird lying lifeless in the snow. It had been the end, if there had ever been a beginning, to his relationship with his mother. To this day, he knew he was her biggest disappointment.

When Francesca entered the kitchen, she was surprised to find squinty-eyed Arriana Gabbelli, among the women. Arriana's father, Lonzo, had given Gino his cushy city job.

Once in passing, Gino mentioned to Francesca he'd made a pact with the devil for the employment because his end of the bargain was to be nice to Arriana and take the guitar-shaped woman out every week. It seemed to Francesca, that Gino inviting Arriana for Christmas was going way beyond keeping his part of the deal. She decided it was better than him bringing Rosie from the Chez Paree or one of his other floozies, but she made a mental note to ask Gino what was going on with him and Arriana.

"Buon Natale," said Maria, leaving a pan of Tortellini Bolognese, wiping her hands on her apron before welcoming her daughter.

"Buon Natale, Mama" Francesca held out a heavy dish and smiled. "Meatballs. Made your favorite way."

The other women gathered round to welcome Francesca, all talking at once, wishing her a Merry Christmas.

Mrs. Giocomelli, pinched her cheek. "Are you pregnant yet, cara?

"Your mama wants to hear the footsteps of a bambino," chimed in Lillian Grillo.

Mrs. Fratini guffawed like a man. "Should I start knitting *la comerta* to keep the little one warm?"

Francesca welcomed the chaos and silently thanked Fin for making her late. Since he hadn't wanted to come, he'd dragged his feet. They'd arrived after the food preparation was finished and it was already time to carry the dishes upstairs to the table, so Francesca was able to avoid answering all the women's questions.

Maria pushed some straggling gray strands of hair into her braided bun. "Sylvia, after you finish feeding Simona get the other children seated at their table down here. Then come up pronto. You know your papa. He won't wait too long before he starts clamoring to eat. I've talked him into sitting through Dominic's blessing this year."

Early in their marriage, Vito announced that giving thanks to God before meals was not to be said aloud because he wanted to eat immediately and not hear their rigmarole. This year, bowing to Maria's wishes he had conceded to listen to Dominic's words of thanks. Now he suffered in silence with a slightly bowed head, eager for the food in front of him.

With half-closed eyes he slyly stole a look to see if anyone else was bored with his son's long-winded appeal to God. Vito was prepared to dig in the minute amen was said, but Maria shot him her, *I dare you* look. He paused grudgingly as she tapped a spoon on her glass.

"Since we have only a small family, I welcome our friends to our table to help us celebrate this special day." She nodded to Vito. At last it was time to eat.

Between each *portate*, everyone sat back to rest, digest, and share stories of past Christmases. The hubbub and vast amounts of food and wine was a contrast to the quiet Irish celebrations that Fin had known.

He guessed his parents would be enjoying the same kind of holiday this year. Except for missing his father, he did enjoy the wealth of Italian food, particularly the wine, which he swigged down. He wanted to be ready for a refill, when Carlo, in charge of pouring, offered more. Otherwise, Fin was bored silly with all the Italian nonsense of everyone chattering at once. So when Maria started reminiscing after the pasta course, it was a welcome change.

"Back in Benevento, there was always a live Presepe at Cathedral of Santa Maria Assunta. One year, my brother Gian was Joseph, and I was Mary."

Maria had a far away look in her eyes. "After our midnight mass on Christmas Eve, the congregation always flocked to the town square with lighted candles to wait for the zampognari and the pifferai. I loved listening to these bagpipers and flute players, who traveled from the mountains to play their instruments wearing sheepskin vests, long white stockings, and dark cloaks. It was the perfect evening before our Christmas feast the next day."

Long before the languorous meal had ended and the sweets on the sideboard devoured, the children had fallen asleep downstairs.

The men, rubbing their sated bellies, left the table for a game of poker in the living room and grappa. The women cleared the table.

Not wanting to leave one drop of wine undrunk, Fin drained his glass. In returning the goblet to the table, he knocked it over, and it hit the edge of a plate. The glass broke at the same time taking a chip out of the edge of the dinnerware.

Francesca was thankful Vito had left the room because the incident would give him more cause to dislike Fin. When the accident occurred, some of the women inhaled, but Maria smiled, taking it in stride.

"Don't worry, Fin. It's not as if it's the best china and glassware," said Maria.

Yet, Francesca knew that in spite of the dishes not matching, her mama cherished each odd piece that she'd scrimped to buy, and that the accident was upsetting to her. But that was Mama, kind to everyone. Still, Francesca was aware that those who had witnessed the mishap wouldn't be as generous. They would bring up Fin's clumsiness every Christmas for years to come. It was the Italian way.

3

Then it was the day before New Year's Eve. Since Francesca had discovered Fin's strong dislike for Italians, she resolved to try and change his thinking. Maybe a nice romantic dinner with some of her papa's homemade wine would be a start. But she had something else in mind too. She mustered her courage, got on the bus, and went to see her mother-in-law.

She hadn't been to the Callahans' house since the day she and Fin had announced their marriage plans. Meeting Fin's haughty mother, who had looked down her nose at Francesca, had been the worst day of her life. She had no expectation that today would be any different.

There had been no contact with Meghan since the frightful day that she had invited Meghan to lunch shortly after the wedding. Francesca quivered with rage remembering how horrid and rude her mother-in-law had been. She collected herself for a few minutes in front of the Callahans' imposing front door before lifting the brass knocker.

Meghan was taken aback and struck mute when she opened the front door to find Francesca standing there.

Francesca shifted from one foot to the other. "Hello, Mrs. Callahan. I'm sorry to bother you, but I have a question."

"Ye came all this way to ask something? That's what the telephone's for," said Meghan, finding her voice, closing the door, as if Francesca was some unwanted door-to-door salesman.

Francesca was determined not to let Meghan get to her, even though it seemed that the door was about to be slammed in her face. "You know we don't have a phone. That's why I'm here."

"Who is it, Meghan?" A voice called from inside the house.

"It's just Fin's wife, Aunt Kitty."

Fin's great-aunt appeared at the door. "Well, don't just stand there, Meghan. Invite Francesca in."

"It's okay. I'm fine here."

Kitty opened the door wider and stood in front of her niece. "Get yourself in here. You'll catch your death out there in the cold."

She took Francesca's arm and led her inside. Kitty indicated a wingback chair by the fireplace. "Sit down and warm yourself. Can we offer you a spot of tea?"

Meghan followed Kitty and Francesca into the living room, glaring daggers at her aunt, who would have been dead by now had the projectiles been real. The look didn't go unnoticed by Francesca.

"No, thank you, I don't want to miss the next bus back. I'm planning a New Year's Eve celebration for Fin, and I stopped by to ask if there are any special Irish traditions that I should observe for our first new year's together? I thought I'd surprise Fin by combining traditions from both our families."

Kitty took a seat in the wingback across from Francesca. Meghan, standing behind Kitty's chair, clenched her jaw at Francesca's statement.

"That's a sweet gesture, my dear, but I can't think of a thing," said Kitty. "I certainly doubt you want to bake a Bairin Breac, have Fin take a few bites, and then throw it at your front door."

Francesca's eyes widened. "Certainly not. What's the reason for that?"

"Well, it's what we did back in Ireland to ensure there would be food in the coming year. Silly custom, now that I think about it. Here in America, we Irish have only small parties or dinners in our homes with a bit of drinking. You know how we love our whiskey." Kitty's round face glowed in the firelight. "All except Fin's father who doesn't touch a drop, of course. Not a typical Irishman in my book, but I love the dear man."

"Since coming to America, we do sometimes bake the cake, but we eat it all on January first, which is called Day of The Buttered Bread. In the old country, we made sandwiches with the sweet bread and placed them outside the door, another ritual to ensure that food will be ample. I'd give you the recipe, but Fin's not fond of it."

Meghan moved to stand between the two chairs, her back to the fireplace. "Well, Francesca, ye might put clean sheets on yer bed and stock the pantry."

"I could what?"

"Er, yes," said Kitty, giving Meghan a piercing look. "That's another old practice of ours. Not exactly what you had in mind is it, my dear?"

"No ... no, it's not, said Francesca, squirming in her chair under Meghan's disdainful stare. She'd had quite enough of these foolish Irish suggestions and of Meghan's usual arrogance. Aunt Kitty, on the other hand, was a delight.

"Fin and I won't be having a party. It will be a nice, quiet dinner for the two of us. I just didn't want Fin to feel uncomfortable by only celebrating like an Italian if there was something that he's used to doing."

"What a ridiculous idea," blurted Meghan.

Kitty interrupted her. "Francesca, I'm sure being with you is all Fin needs. I'm so sorry that we couldn't be of more help. Perhaps you should create your own traditions."

"Well, it was worth a try. Thank you so much. Was nice to see you." The last comment was directed at Kitty. "I really need to be going."

"Happy New Year to you and Fin," said Kitty, giving Francesca a hug and showing her out.

"Happy New Year to you, Aunt Kitty. And to you, Mrs. Callahan. Please give my regards to Michael." Meghan had turned toward the fireplace on the pretext of warming her hands and made no reply.

On the bus ride home, Francesca reflected on the Italian new year mores that Maria had told her were observed in Italy, such as wearing red underwear and throwing old and no longer useful items out the window. Francesca giggled. Just as the Irish, the

Italians had some pretty ridiculous customs. Although, maybe the red underwear thing wasn't. If she had any extra money, which she didn't, she would buy some scarlet panties. That might really please and surprise Fin.

Bumping along, she planned the coming evening. Since there were no Irish traditions to observe, she would go ahead with the one her family practiced, that of having lentil and sausage stew for dinner. Then at midnight when the bells of Our Lady of Pompeii rang out the old year and rang in the new, she and Fin would take a bite with each toll.

She wasn't superstitious, but anything was worth a try if it might bring extra money to their meager coffers and happiness to their marriage as the ritual was supposed to do.

Francesca was finalizing preparations for their romantic dinner when Fin arrived home after meeting his father for a new year's libation. Even though Michael didn't drink, he never hesitated buying others a whiskey, and tonight had been no exception. The holiday had been a good excuse for Michael and his son to see each other without the uncomfortable air that Megan produced when Fin went to the house.

"So how was your father?" Francesca gave Fin a welcome kiss as he came through the door.

"In especially high spirits. Better than I've seen him in a while. Seemed a bit distracted. We had a nice visit, though. Was fun to see him without Mother breathing fire at us."

"I'm sure. Too bad, your mother's that way."

"Yeah, well, no need to talk about that. Dad was so happy, I'm wondering if things are better between Mother and him. Maybe with me out of the house they're happier."

"Perhaps your mother is, but I know your dad misses you a lot. You two have always been in each other's corner."

"I miss Dad but now I have you," said Fin, presenting Francesca with a single red rose, which he had been hiding behind his back. "For you, madam. Happy New Year."

"Oh, what a nice surprise." Francesca gave him another kiss before going to the kitchen to find her pickle jar vase. Fin realized that his father had been wise in urging him to buy the flower.

He noticed the set table. "What's this?"

"A romantic dinner, of course," said Francesca, placing the rose in the middle of the table between the candles. "This is our first New Year's Eve as husband and wife. It should be special."

"Yeah, babe, it will be. But right now, I want you to go in there and change those sheets." They hooted, just as they had when Francesca told him about her trip to see his mother.

"On second thought, maybe I should help you." With that, Fin scooped her up, carried her into the bedroom, and made passionate love to her.

Though there had been no lovemaking on their wedding night, Fin had learned exactly how to curl Francesca's toes, and tonight was no exception. They decided to scrub the romantic dinner and satisfy their appetites by staying in bed. Shortly before midnight, Francesca padded to the kitchen, heated up the lentil stew, and they fed each other as Italian protocol dictated. After the twelfth bite, once again, they fell on each other midst the dirty dishes.

Michael's arrival home was different from his son's. He knew Meghan had been working for days cleaning the house, getting rid of non-essentials. When he opened the front door, it was obvious she had performed her smudge ceremony, ridding the house of negative energy and blessing their home for the coming year. The scent of frankincense, myrrh, and lavender saturated the air. At one time, the aroma had been comforting, but tonight it annoyed him as he hung his hat and coat on the hall tree.

He found Kitty sipping a whiskey with Meghan and was glad she was there because conversation always flowed with a third party present. Otherwise, like many other New Year's Eves, he and Meghan would sit across the table, eat in silence, listen to the countdown of midnight on the radio, and then succumb to sleep in their separate beds.

Tonight, dinner was replete with chatter and merriment. Afterward, the women adjourned to the living room for another libation and to wait for midnight. By the time Michael joined them with his tea, they were mired in discussion. The women acknowledged him, then continued their conversation. This presented Michael time to his thoughts.

Earlier in the day, not having reason to be home, Michael decided to work a few hours before meeting Fin. He stopped at the coffee shop on the ground floor of his office building for a cup of coffee before going upstairs. He was shaken when he walked in and spotted Ireland sitting at the counter, her back to the door. Michael stopped dead in front of the cash register and caught his breath. He hadn't seen Ireland since they'd made love on the lawn of the Adler Planetarium months before Fin's wedding. Now there she sat, her familiar sable bun mocking him.

On that memorable night when he and Meghan had locked horns over Fin's upcoming marriage, he had left in a huff and had driven down Lake Shore Drive, ending up at the northeast tip of Northerly Island and the planetarium. The star-filled sky had a calming effect on him. He had sat on the car's fender reveling in the beauty that cast a glow over Lake Michigan, reflecting on his life. For some unknown reason he had passed out and fallen from the car.

He regained consciousness to find Ireland, who had worked for him as a temporary secretary, and whom he had lusted after in his mind, bending over him. He had never considered having an affair with her except in his dreams. But that night, just when he needed someone, Ireland had appeared. Remembering the unexpected encounter and seeing Ireland now gave him a hard-on. He couldn't stay. He had to leave before she saw him. But it was too late.

"Michael, is that you? Are you leaving?"

He spun around. Ireland, money in hand ready to pay her bill, was so close he could see the pinhead-size mole at the corner of her mouth. Her familiar scent aroused him beyond belief. She wore one of her ill-fitting umber suits, which did nothing for the body that he knew lay beneath. Right here in the coffee shop he wanted to rip the ghastly thing off her, reach up and release her hair from its staid bun, and ravish her. Such brazen thoughts alarmed him.

"Er ... Ireland, hello. Yes. Good to see you. Please excuse me. I forgot something in my office. I've got to go back up."

Ireland's eyes shown with amusement behind her horn-rimmed glasses, a knowing grin on her face. "Can't it wait a few minutes? Surely, you're not working today. I was leaving, but I have plenty of time for another cup of coffee. Come. Let's catch up."

Catch up? What the devil was there to catch up about? How he melted at the touch of her lips? How her downy skin felt beneath his caressing fingers? How she sent him to heights he'd never traveled before?

"I really can't. I'm meeting Fin soon. Maybe some other time. Happy New Year." Michael escaped, hastening for the elevator to take him up and away from temptation.

As he waited for the elevator door to open, temptation's high heels clicked on the marble floor behind him. He entered the elevator, and when the door closed he wasn't alone. A jerk and the car halted between the second and third floors because Ireland had pushed the stop button.

Then she had him pinned against the back wall of the car. He didn't fight it, nor did he want to. Her musky scent was irresistible. Their lips fused in urgent passion, and Michael's hand found its way under her skirt, his hand skimming her silken body, finding her fiery wetness. She fumbled with his belt and zipper and stroked him. Long legs straddled him as he lifted her---filling her. Moans of ecstasy shook the car as they became lost in each other. After a while the car ascended to the ground floor.

"Auld Lang Syne" blasting from the radio and Meghan's voice calling his name snapped Michael back to the present.

"Happy New Year, darling. Here's to 1948," said Meghan, raising her whiskey glass.

Michael tipped his teacup toward her. "Happy New Year, Meggie."

And yes, it will be.

4

Chicago - 1950s

It was a crisp October day in 1950 when Kane Joseph Callahan was born. It was the kind of fall day when leaves still crackled underfoot and ominous gray clouds scudded across a steely sky announcing an impending storm.

Inside Fin and Francesca's tiny apartment the atmosphere was sunny and happy when they saw their son's scrunched-up face. Dr. Cipriano gave the baby's bottom a good smack, then another, yet the eight-pound baby boy didn't make a whimper. Dr. Cipriano appeared mystified.

"The baby seems to be breathing well, but this is, indeed, strange." Dr. Cipriano's hand hit the child's backside again. "I've never seen a newborn not cry when it entered the world. I predict your new son is going to be an unusually strong child."

At home, Meghan was jubilant when she heard this news. It was a good sign, as was the Celtic name of Kane, which meant warrior. It thrilled her that an Italian name hadn't been chosen.

Gathering her coat around her to ward off the screaming wind, Meghan went outside to the birdbath that she used as an altar for her Druid activities. Shivering, she finally warmed after sitting in front of it for a few minutes. Rubbing the beryl stone hanging from her neck, her mind traveled to a place where few were able to go. She foresaw that this grandchild would be hers to teach the Druid ways that would make him strong as he grew into manhood. And perhaps, unlike her son and husband who had disappointed her, this boy would one day become a high-ranking political figure. There was still a chance for her to be part of the social strata she'd always dreamed.

When Michael heard he had a grandson, he immediately quit the law case he was working on, left the office, and headed for his son's apartment. On the way, he relived the day Fin was born. How he'd come into the world too early and if he had not had the constant nursing of Dr. Finley and Aunt Kitty wouldn't have survived. Michael felt remorse remembering Fin's twin who was stillborn, and how he and Meghan had buried the child without a name. He wondered how Meghan would feel about her grandson. Since she had never been loving and warm toward Fin, would she act the same with this baby?

The Savio household was excited with the announcement of Francesca's first born. Father Dominic and Sister Angeline sent congratulatory telegrams to their baby sister, saying they were eager to see their new nephew. Dominic, of course, would officiate at the christening. Maria thrilled by the birth left home to go help Francesca. The Savio brothers toasted the family's newest addition with Vito's homemade wine and smoked big, black cigars in honor of the baby. Pietro, despite having three of his own, was delighted for his little sister, as was Carlo.

Gino, who had always shared a special bond with Francesca, hoped his new nephew would love baseball as much as he and Francesca did. In his mind, he was already taking him to the games, educating him about the wiles of women, and instructing him on the ins and outs of gambling.

While Vito's sons were toasting and chin wagging, Vito sat in his chair knowing in his heart that this new grandson would be special, just as Francesca had always been special to him. He had never felt this with Pietro's sons, but this boy, when he became older, Vito would take under his wing and teach him how to be a man with honor. A man whose will could never be broken.

Three weeks later at the christening, Vito and Meghan had yet to see their grandson. After the dreadful lunch with Francesca, Meghan had vowed never to visit the apartment again and had stuck it it. Even for the boy who Meghan knew was to be hers to mold, she made no concession. Vito, on the other hand, wanted to climb the stairs to see his new grandson, but it was too difficult for him with his arthritic legs.

Now at the church, prior to the ceremony, Meghan and Vito vied for a first glimpse of their grandson. They elbowed each other in order to get a good view of the chubby baby lying in Fin's arms. Dressed in a long white christening gown, Kane's walnut-brown eyes seemed to be gazing at both grandparents as they fought over him. What looked to be a smile, though obviously gas, crossed the cherub's face.

"I think the little bambino already recognizes me," said Vito.

"Don't be ridiculous." Meghan nudged him out of the way for a better look.

Vito ground his cane into her foot and edged in front of her.

Ouch!"

"Come on. Behave you two. You'll scare him. If he cries Francesca will have my head." Fin glared at his mother and snuggled the baby closer, protecting his son from the contention.

"Nothing can scare me *a stór*." Meghan tried to peer over Vito's shoulder.

But Vito had now positioned his burly body in order to bar her advancement. A shadow of confusion crossed Vito's face at Meghan's Irish word.

Then in the background, he heard Michael mutter, "Her treasure?"

Vito growled, "He ain't your treasure."

Meghan had just raised her handbag to bop Vito on the head when Francesca stepped into the narthex.

"Dominic is ready to begin the ceremony." Francesca smoothed the top of Kane's head. "Isn't he just the sweetest thing."

"Mrs. Callahan." Francesca nodded, acknowledging Meghan, then kissed Vito's cheeks. "Glad you made it. Mama's waiting for you in the front pew."

The godparents were already in place at the baptismal. It had been a given that Angeline and Sylvia would be the godmothers, but Francesca and Fin had debated on the godfathers. Fin had wanted Dino. Francesca wasn't sold on Fin's best friend, but in the end, he and Tommy Henley from Fin's old neighborhood were chosen. This made the families happy since the Irish and Italians were both represented, and they were all good Catholics.

Michael's heart was gladdened when he heard Meghan accept Maria's invitation to an after christening celebration at the Savios'. Neither Vito nor Francesca knew the invite had been extended, so when the Callahans walked in the door, Vito shunned Meghan with obvious scorn, yet warmly hugged Michael, kissing his cheeks and leading him into the living room where everyone was gathered. Meghan had no choice but to follow like a puppy. An uncomfortable position she seldom found herself.

But she hadn't come for comradery or acceptance. She was here to be near her grandson who was sleeping soundly in his bassinet, despite the clamor in the room. Meghan headed for the corner where the baby lay.

Francesca and the other women were busy bringing up food from the basement kitchen when Michael and Meghan arrived. It surprised Francesca to see them. She ignored Meghan and continued helping with the food. She would speak to Michael later.

She was just glad her sweet Kane was quiet and not causing a disturbance for once. Already, he seemed to have a mind of his own, announcing the fact with his loud cries. At the christening, she had dreaded hearing him scream and held her breath when Dominic placed his wet hand on the baby's head. But Kane hadn't made a sound. He had only observed his uncle with interest, waving his arms.

Soon everyone gathered around the table filling their plates with Maria's culinary delights, sitting wherever they could in order to partake.

"Well, my dear," said Michael, wrapping his arm around Francesca who was arranging her mama's homemade desserts on the sideboard. "You've given me a magnificent grandson. I know he's sleeping, but would you mind if I held him?"

"Of course not. He'll be awake soon anyway because he never misses a feeding. He's a ravenous little one. Come."

Francesca's face turned ashen when she went to the bassinet and found Kane wasn't there. "Oh my god, where is he?" She looked over the room and saw everyone's hands filled with plates of food. No arms cuddled her son. "Michael, I don't see Meghan. Do you think she has Kane?"

"Well, I don't know." Michael did not seeing his wife either. "She must have him, but where?" A mystified look crossed his face. Why would Meggie have taken the baby when she had no affinity for them?

"Maybe she's with him upstairs." Francesca raced up the steps.

She returned and shook her head. "The kitchen. They must be there."

Michael followed Francesca as she ran downstairs. The kitchen was unoccupied. Francesca darted here and there in a panic, not knowing what to do.

"Where are they? Where has she taken my Kane?"

Michael grabbed her arm. "Listen."

A faint singing came from the backyard which grew louder when they opened the door.

Francesca was about to rush outside.

"Wait." Michael held her back.

Francesca saw Michael's eyes tearing. "It's a miracle. She never sang to Fin or even held him."

Miracle or not, Francesca wanted her baby. She left Michael's side and hurried out to the grape arbor to rescue her son.

"Too-ra-loo-ra-loo-ral. That's an Irish lul-la-by."

5

After Kane was born, married life began to go downhill faster than a sled on a snowy slope. Francesca returned to clerking at Briscom's Department Store while Maria watched Kane, but the job didn't last long. Francesca found she was pregnant for a second time. When her stomach started to show a bulge, publicizing her condition, Mr. Briscom said that he could no longer keep her on.

The idea of another child so soon didn't please Fin. He needed Francesca's salary to help make ends meet and berated her for being so careless. She reminded him they were both good Catholics, and he was as guilty as she in creating the child. She also reminded him how much he had delighted in the creation process. This shut Fin up and he didn't mention it again, unless he came home drunk, a condition that was becoming more and more frequent.

The fact was, he nipped from a pocket flask during work, and by the end of the day was sloshed and obnoxious by the time he arrived home. Francesca told herself she had no choice. Marriage lasted until death and besides she really loved Fin. She hoped his over indulging was just a passing fancy caused by her pregnancy. However, unlike Francesca, his boss at the post office wasn't married to Fin and fired him.

The night after getting the axe, they were getting ready for bed when Fin, on the edge of being sober, told Francesca that he had lost his job.

Her voice rose three octaves. "Are you kidding? I can't believe this."

"Shhh ... Quiet, you'll wake Kane." Fin glanced at the crib where the baby slept.

"Don't shush me." Francesca shrieked even louder. "What are we going to do? The rent is due. We have to eat. Soon there'll be another mouth to feed. With the new baby we'll need more space. As it is, we're struggling to make ends meet. Tell me, what's your plan? Or have you even thought further than the liquor bottle?"

"Uh ... Uh ... I don't have a plan. I haven't had time to think. I just got fired today."

"You need to grow up, Fin. Be a man. You have a family to take care of. You better come up with something by morning." Francesca's voice cracked when she issued the ultimatum. "If you don't. I'm moving back to Mama and Papa's with Kane."

"That's not a damn option." Fin rolled over, his back to her. "I'll think of something. You're not living with your parents. Go to sleep."

Francesca punched his back with her fist. "Don't ignore me, you coward. You'd better come up with something, or that's exactly what I'll do."

Fin lay awake all night mulling over his predicament. Vito's warning before he and Francesca had married reverberated in his head. *You better be fuckin' good ta her. Anybody hurts my baby answers to me.* No way would Fin let Vito Savio know he couldn't take care of his family.

Francesca relented the next morning, giving Fin leeway until the end of the week to come up with a job and a place to live. Fin had no choice but to talk to his father, his best ally. Gathering his courage, he went to his father's law office and divulged his dilemma.

Michael put his arm around Fin's shoulder, unaware that drinking was the cause of him being fired. "What a lousy break, losing your job. Don't give up. You'll find something else soon. In the meantime, come stay with your mother and me. We have plenty of room. Besides it'll give me a chance to spoil my grandson."

"Gee, Dad, that sounds perfect except for one thing, well maybe two ... namely, Mother and Francesca. Do you really think putting them under the same roof is a good idea? Then there's Kane. He'll drive Mother nuts."

"Don't worry about your mother. She'll do it at my behest. In fact, since the christening, she's even talked about Kane a couple of times. I think she's developed a unexpected softness for him."

"You must be joking." Fin pondered whether there was someone else he could ask for help. He slumped into one of the chairs in front of his father's desk, realizing there wasn't.

"It's the truth. Didn't Francesca tell you how your mother kidnapped Kane from his bassinet at the christening party? We found her outside in the grape arbor singing to him."

"For real?" A tinge of jealousy coursed through Fin. His mother singing to his son? She'd never sung a note to him.

Michael placed a hand on Fin's shoulder. "It's the honest truth. I think Kane may be the thread that will connect you and your mother. Why not come live with us and give it a chance?"

"I think it's too late for Mother and me to find a connection. But even if Mother agrees, I'm not certain Francesca will. Besides her old man's going to get plenty upset over this. I was hoping maybe you could just loan me money for housing until I found work. Then he'd never know."

"No, Fin. I'm not going to fund you. But don't worry. Vito won't find out unless Francesca tells him, which I doubt she will. She knows her father's temper about us Irish, and I have no disillusions about his feelings for you. I don't want to jeopardize your marriage. Besides, your mother won't breathe a word since we never see the Savios. By the time the new baby comes along, you'll have a job and be out of the house living in your own place."

Talking Francesca into moving into his parents' home was a tough sell.

"You've got to be out of your mind. How in god's name do you think that your mother and I could ever live in the same house?"

A screaming match ensued until both became hoarse and dropped from exhaustion. Francesca knew going to her parents wasn't a viable option. She didn't want them to know that she and Fin were having problems because her papa would say he told her so, as would her brothers. With their fiery tempers she wasn't sure what they might do to Fin. Oh, they wouldn't kill him, but they'd probably come up with something that would cause him to wish they had. Since her parents never ventured to see her, she decided she would be able to avoid their knowing of the living arrangements.

Francesca conceded she hadn't a choice other than to move in with the Callahans. Temporarily. It wouldn't be easy. She'd have to steer clear of Fin's mother best she could. In fact, ideas were already forming in her mind as to how she could do so.

The baby and she would stay in the bedroom a lot, go for strolls in the park, and she could visit her mama and papa more. She decided that the one bright spot was that Fin's drinking would be certain to taper off since he wouldn't want his parents to know the extent of his habit. Until they got back on their feet, she promised herself she would endure.

On the south side of Chicago, Michael had as difficult time convincing Meghan as Fin had when he broached the subject to Francesca.

"Fin made his bed, now let him lie in it. That Italian wench has ruined his life just as I knew she would. And now you tell me that she's pregnant again. What's the matter with Fin?" Meghan threw the political paper that she was reading across the room.

"Come on, Meggie, be kind. That wench as you call her has given you a beautiful grandson whom I believe you rather like. With them living here it will give you a chance to see more of Kane. The arrangement won't be forever. Can't you tolerate it for a short time despite your feelings?"

Meghan calmed down. This really might might be a perfect time to get closer to her grandson. He was five months old, and she'd read that the first few years of a child's life were the most important in its development. She could launch her campaign to bind him to her.

She already knew he had a strong mind. That had been proved when the child had screamed like a banshee at the christening party after Francesca had taken him away from her. Meghan grinned remembering Francesca's disgust in finding Kane had liked her singing. Strange, unlike when Fin was a baby, Kane felt right in her arms.

Three days later Francesca, Fin, and Kane moved in with the Callahans.

6

Crubeens and black pudding. Boiled pig's feet and anything made with blood was more than Francesca could handle. She gagged and ran from the table when she was faced with these Irish delicacies. After the third of such dinners, Michael suggested that Meghan refrain from making these kind of dishes until they were alone again.

Despite the strange meals, Fin and Francesca's living arrangement with the Callahans was working better than expected, even though tension was thicker than a London fog. Meghan was cordial to a degree and that was it.

Francesca volunteered half-heartedly to help with the household chores. Through gritted teeth, Meghan suggested she take it easy because of her pregnancy. Francesca knew that Meghan wasn't being nice. She just didn't care to interact with her. This was fine with Francesca. She didn't want to be in Meghan's home any more than Meghan wanted her there.

The cleaning lady came twice a week, and Meghan did the cooking which still did not please Francesca's palate or pregnant stomach, but at least the blood-type meals had ceased. Francesca said nothing and ate what she could of the food set before her and was thankful Michael had curtailed Meghan's cooking of her Irish favorites.

A daily routine was established. At Michael's urging, Francesca allowed Meghan to feed Kane his morning cereal, and when morning sickness overcame Francesca, Meghan wheeled

Kane in his stroller to the park down the street. Still, the usual routine for Meghan was going off to political meetings or having tea with Aunt Kitty.

After Michael left for his office, and Fin departed on the pretense of job hunting, then Francesca had alone time with Kane. When Kane awoke from his afternoon nap, Francesca boarded the bus and they would return to the Italian area to see the Savios, or she would pushed his buggy around the Bridgeport neighborhood. Sometimes they went to the church where the two of them sat in a back pew until dinnertime.

At the end of the day, Fin returned with Ginseng on his breath masking the smell of liquor. This didn't sit well with Francesca, but as long as he was nice to everyone and his parents were none the wiser, she kept quiet. She hoped in between bar stops he was seeking employment.

In the evening, everyone adjourned to their individual quarters, although some nights Michael and Fin played with Kane before bedtime, or had father and son time talking in Michael's study. So it went.

One night, when the house was quiet and everyone slept, Meghan tip-toed into Fin and Francesca's bedroom and lifted Kane from his crib. Creeping down the stairs, careful to avoid the creaking ones, Meghan made her way into the backyard.

A huge, golden moon at perigee dangled in the sky. Kane continued sleeping soundly as Meghan laid him gently on the birdbath altar. The moon glowed on his face with an ethereal light and shimmered over him like a silken blanket. Meghan sat for a while feeling the force of the night and the moon's power, reveling in the air filled with the scent of summer's late-blooming roses, and listening to a catbird in a far-off tree.

Kane stirred, opened his eyes, looked at his grandmother, and kicked his legs into the air. He babbled softly. It was as if he knew something special was happening. He reached out toward his grandmother. She held up a finger. He caught it in his chubby hand and held on. They remained attached while Meghan rubbed her beryl necklace, waiting for whatever images might appear to her.

She whispered, "This me dear boy is yer first visit to me sacred place. From the moment I heard of yer birth, I knew that ye had been born for me to teach. Tonight I've confirmed it. One of these days ye will understand all that I'm about and me kinship with nature. We will be simpatico."

Kane began to wriggle. Meghan lifted him into her arms and tenderly began to sing the Irish Lullaby, rocking him.

The peaceful moment shattered like breaking glass when Francesca's voice split the air in an ear-piercing scream as she flew across the yard, her ebony hair streaming behind her.

"What in the hell do you think you're doing?"

"Hush. You'll wake up everyone." Meghan cuddled Kane closer, shielding him from her wild-acting daughter-in-law.

"I will *not* be quiet. I hope I wake the whole damn neighborhood. Give Kane to me." Shaking with rage, Francesca seized the baby from Meghan's arms. The confrontation woke Kane, and he wailed.

"Now see what you've done. If not for me, at least calm him down."

"Don't tell me what to do." Situating Kane on her shoulder, Francesca swayed back and forth, stroking his back to quieten him. "You frightened me. I awoke and saw Kane's crib empty. You're looney. What are you doing with him out here anyway? Making him into a witch like you? I knew that staying in this house was a mistake." She bent over Kane in a flood of tears.

Michael and Fin roused by the shouting appeared at Francesca's elbow.

"Francesca, what's going on?" demanded Michael.

"Michael, oh Michael. She took Kane. I can't tolerate this anymore. I've got to get out of here." Francesca pulled on Fin's' arm. "Come on. Let's go."

"Wait, Francesca. Let's get to the bottom of this. Why did you take Kane, Meggie? Explain yourself this instant."

Fin put a comforting arm around Francesca and pulled her and Kane close.

Meghan flipped her flaming hair. "I couldn't sleep and was on my way downstairs when I heard the baby whimpering. I picked him up so that he wouldn't wake Fin and Francesca and brought him outside. It's such a lovely night. I thought I'd sing him to sleep here."

"You're lying. I would have heard Kane. I always hear him. That's what mothers do. But then, you wouldn't know about that would you, Mrs. Callahan?"

"Francesca." Michael's voice was stern. "You and Fin go back into the house now. Let me talk to Meggie alone."

Fin tried to lead Francesca away, but she resisted. "She's lying, I tell you." Francesca's eyes blazed at Meghan. "She's ..."

"Come on. Let's do as Dad wants." And this time, Francesca went with him.

When they were out of earshot, Michael's temper flared. His temples throbbed and a blue vein in his forehead distended. Meghan hadn't seen him this angry since the day they had met with Francesca's parents to talk wedding plans. On that day according to Michael, she had been a haughty bitch.

"Francesca's right. You're lying. You're not fooling me. I know you brought Kane out here for some stupid ritual of yours. For god's sake, Meggie, he's just a baby. Quit this nonsense. Listen and listen good. You are not to touch that baby ever again unless Francesca gives you permission. Do you understand me? If you don't apologize and be nice to her, that will never happen. It might not even then."

Michael's blistering words frightened Meghan to the point that she promised on her mother's grave that she would do as he asked. She felt she'd done nothing wrong, but in order to be near Kane she'd lower herself to say she had been in error and was sorry. She would attempt to be nice. At least, a wee bit nicer.

Next, Michael had a private talk with Francesca. "Meggie committed a wrong, and she understands that she did. You must know, she wouldn't hurt Kane. In fact, she loves him the way I've always wanted her to love Fin. It amazes me how much she's taken to our grandson. I'm hopeful that he might be a factor in bringing accord to all our lives. Please. Let's try to live civilly. I know you're not a vengeful person. Meghan promised she wants to get along. I'm sure you'd like that too."

Francesca agreed that she would try if Meghan did. She knew in her heart that her mother-in-law would not change, but she vowed to make an effort. However, she would need to see a big transformation in order to give Meghan time with Kane again.

The next morning, Meghan gave a half-hearted apology with Francesca nodding in acceptance. The Callahan household was back on a listing keel.

Finally, Fin came home with a job. Neither Michael nor Meghan exuded happiness with Fin's new employment when they heard it was bartending at an establishment called Bruno's Bar on the near West Side. Their son was better than that. But, at least, he would be standing on his own.

Fin couldn't stop talking about the incredible deal he'd made. They would be living, rent free, in the upstairs apartment over the bar as long as he worked there. He could barely contain his excitement. Francesca didn't share his enthusiasm, but anything would be better than living under the same roof with Fin's mother. Or would it?

7

"Aunt Kitty, it's so good to see you, but I'm surprised too. No one ever wants to climb the stairs to visit." Francesca was nursing Chiara, and Kane was toddling through the two-bedroom apartment when Kitty knocked and stuck her head in the door.

"Well, these steps aren't as bad as at your last place. But I would've tackled even those because I wouldn't miss seeing my new grandniece for anything. I'm so sorry to have missed her christening." Kitty fell gasping into the nearest chair. "Let me catch my breath before I look at the wee colleen. "Whew! Not as young as I used to be."

Francesca watched as Fin's aunt settled her matronly frame into the only arm chair. Her amber eyes sparkled over the top of the ivory fan that she produced from her handbag and was now waving madly in front of her round, flushed face. After having cooled down, she brushed strands of gray hair away from her face. Kane came running into the room at the sound of Kitty's voice and tugged at her skirt.

"Nat Kiddy, Nat Kiddy."

"Here's my darling boy." Kane climbed uninvited into Kitty's lap.

"Get down, Kane. Aunt Kitty needs to rest for a minute."

"He's all right. That's what I'm here for, right Kane?" He tugged at Kitty's pearl necklace.

"Kane, stop it. Leave Aunt Kitty's pearls alone." Finished with nursing Chiara, Francesca laid the baby in a nearby buggy. "Did you hear me, Kane? I said, get down."

"No! Like it here."

"Don't no me." Francesca pulled Kane from Kitty's lap.

"No! No." Kane kicked his feet and took a swing at Francesca. She swatted his rear end. "Go play, and let us talk."

"Hate ju," he cried, running from the room.

"It seems as if he's going through the terrible twos. If I live through this stage it'll be a wonder. Then I'll have to go through it again with this one," Francesca retrieved her newborn and placed the baby in Kitty's arms.

"What a little doll Chiara is. How did you pick her name?"

Francesca scurried into the adjoining kitchen and set the tea kettle on the stove. Kitty was glad because she needed her afternoon spot of refreshment. It was thoughtful of Francesca to make tea since it wasn't a drink Italians usually enjoyed.

"Chiara was my grandmother's name." Francesca took the seldom-used teacups from the cupboard and filled them. "Fin doesn't care for it, but it made him a bit happier when we discovered it's an Irish name too. Strange though, the meaning of Chiara means light in Italian, but dark in Irish."

Kitty laughed, caressing the baby's rosy cheek. "Seems even in names our cultures are at opposite poles, huh, little one?"

Francesca set down a steaming cup of tea for Kitty and one for herself.

" It's sweet of you to fix me tea."

"Well, I'm not a total social misfit as Meghan thinks I am." Francesca still found it difficult to call Fin's mother by her Christian name. In apologizing after their blowup, Meghan had made the half-assed request. *Please call me Meghan," she had said. "Mrs. Callahan makes me feel so old.*

"Oh, my dear, of course you're not socially inept. You're a perfect hostess. You know, I'm so glad you and Meghan have made peace. It warms the cockles of my heart that she's trying to get along."

Francesca ignored Kitty's comment. "More tea?"

"No, my dear, I must be going."

"So soon? Fin should be up from the bar soon. Why don't you wait and see him? Or you could stop down on your way out and stick your head in."

"Don't want to bother him while he's working. You know me, my dear. I like to be home before evening sets in. I'll see him next time round. Nice, though, Fin working just downstairs. Gives him a chance to spend more time with all of you. He can even partake of a free beer on the way home." Kitty chuckled.

If you only knew how many free beers he enjoys. "Here let me take Chiara." Francesca crossed the room and returned the baby to the buggy. She turned to see Kitty in the kitchen. "Oh, don't bother with the dishes, I'll clean up after you leave."

"No, problem." Kitty had already placed the cups in the sink. Finishing in the kitchen, she prepared to leave. "It was lovely being with you and little Chiara. At least, it's easier going down than coming up." Kitty descended to the door that opened onto the gangway. At the bottom of the steps, she waved at Francesca who watched from the head of the stairs.

On the way to the bus stop, Kitty kicked herself. Would she ever learn? Why, oh why, did she need to read those blasted tea leaves at the bottom of Francesca's cup? What she had seen midst the dregs had indicated future problems for the girl. Some things were better left unknown. All the way home, Kitty pondered why she had such an obsession. Now she would worry as to what might happen in Francesca's life.

8

A bolt of lightning crisscrossed the sky behind Michael, who engrossed in work at his desk, looked up when Madge Dowd, his secretary, stuck her head in the door and announced a visitor.

"I didn't realize I had an appointment this afternoon. I'm very busy." He swiveled his chair, watching rain pelt the window behind him. "Tell whomever it is, that this isn't a good time. Make an appointment for another day."

"I can try, Sir." Madge glanced over her shoulder at the young woman in the waiting room, "but she seems pretty adamant about seeing you. Indicated it was of the utmost importance."

"Damn! I don't have time for this. What is the stubborn female's name?"

"Says her name is Coogan. Ireland Coogan."

A loud crash of thunder shook the building, and a torrent of rain blurred Michaels's vision. He swiveled away from the window. Trying to look calm, he hoped his trembling hands weren't noticeable.

He took off his glasses and rubbed the bridge of his nose between two fingers. "Well, guess I do need a break. Send her in, Miss Dowd."

And then Ireland was there. A rain hat sitting jauntily on her thick, sable hair with its tight bun, raindrops glistening on the beige raincoat and dripping onto his office floor. She grinned at him with parted carmine lips and kicked the office door closed with a high-heeled shod foot. She slinked toward him on shapely legs.

The raincoat opened as she approached, not revealing one of her ugly suits but rather bare breasts with erect nipples that taunted him and a dark triangle below that called temptingly. Before she had flung the hat off and released the bun, his own jacket, vest, and tie already lay in a heap on the floor.

Unable to divert his gaze from Ireland, Michael discarded his trousers and felt for the intercom. He made a quick call to Miss Dowd saying he didn't want to be disturbed and to hold all calls. Then Ireland's arms enveloped him.

With one fell swoop the desk was cleared and they were on top of it. Hungrily, Michael savored the smoothness of her skin, nibbled her neck, caressed her eyes with his lips. His mouth moved slowly, finding her breasts and nipping them with his teeth. He descended her body with a trail of hot kisses, causing chills up and down her spine, his mouth finding its target. Ireland writhed and moaned in ecstasy. His tongue delved and licked until he knew she was on the edge. Then, they were one.

She quivered and encircled him with her legs. Her back arched, her nails dug into his back. They climaxed in an explosive tidal wave. Breathless, they lay on the desk smiling at each other. Without a word, they rose and moved to the couch.

Finally, Michael spoke. "Well, this is certainly a delightful surprise. Where the hell have you been? I haven't seen you in ... how long?"

Her fingers played with his gray chest hair. "Much too long. It was nine years ago when we met that New Year's Eve and took that amorous elevator ride. I take that back. The elevator wasn't moving, only we were." Ireland laughed lustily. "I thought I'd hear from you after that, but I didn't."

She traced his jaw with her finger, "It's all I could do to stay away. I've thought of you every day since. Not knowing if you'd want to see me after all this time. I took a gamble and here I am." Her mouth spread in a wide smile. "Remember that day on this very couch when I was working as your temp and you kissed me?"

"How could I forget? I felt guilty, but happy. Then you didn't return the next day and someone else was sent in your place to work for me. After our surprising meeting at the planetarium and then in the elevator, I was a wreck. I had never been unfaithful until I met you. You'll never know how hard it's been for me to stay away from you."

The tip of her tongue licked her lower lip, and she touched him. "I bet it has been hard."

"You devil." He pulled her to him. Her mouth found his with consuming fire. This time their lovemaking was slower---not as greedy---more gentle. Yet still, they were spent when it was over.

Michael chuckled. "Bet you didn't know you've been making love to a grandfather."

"Really?"

"Twice over."

Michael proceeded to tell her about Kane's birth, how Fin and family had lived with Meghan and him for a time, and then about the birth of Chiara.

"Family events have kept me busy, as has my law practice. It's helped keep my thoughts of you at bay."

"But now ... ?" Ireland's eyes questioned.

"But now, that's done, and you're here."

9

Francesca had never been close to Sylvia, Pietro's wife, but she was the only person Francesca felt could help her. Of her two sisters, only Angeline had been a confidant, but with Angeline being a nun and living in Wisconsin, she wasn't available for private conversations. Of course, Lucia never counted. She'd always been a black sheep, and since incestuously marrying their uncle years ago and fleeing to Italy she was now an outcast as well.

When Sylvia opened the door, Francesca hugged and kissed her sister-in-law, then stood back in awe. "You look wonderful." She eyed Sylvia up and down. "I've only seen that outfit in magazines."

"Do you like?" Sylvia twirled around showing off her floral-print silk dress with its mid-length full skirt, nipped at the waist with a belt.

"It's beautiful. Your waist looks so tiny, and there's enough material in the skirt for two dresses. My brother must be doing really well for you to be wearing such an expensive dress during the day."

Sylvia's sapphire-blue eyes sparkled. "Yes, Pietro's doing fantastic since he's off the booze. Back working the trucking business since Daddy passed away."

Sylvia led Francesca into a chartreuse and gray living room that had red accents.

"Goodness, you've even redone this room. Rather lively isn't it?"

"I love it." Sylvia motioned for Francesca to sit in a French caned chair with a gray velvet cushion. A table between them, Sylvia sat in a like chair on the other side and spread her bountiful skirt. She surveyed her living room with pride.

"My decorator says it's the latest thing. After all the drab colors we had during World War II, the country is finally using color again. Your brother's even gotten himself one of those garish Hawaiian shirts."

"I can't quite picture that," said Francesca. "And look at you, wearing silk stockings." She regarded her own bare legs.

"Would you like a pair?" asked Sylvia. "I have a whole drawer full."

"Thanks, but I have no reason to dress up. Silk doesn't exactly go with my lifestyle. Living over a bar is more in line with wearing flour sacks. In fact, that's the reason I'm here."

"Flour sacks?"

"No, no, my lifestyle. Or rather the lack thereof. I hope you don't mind, but you're the only person I feel I'm comfortable talking to about what's bother me."

"What's on your mind?"

"I remember hearing that you put up with Pietro and his drunken ways for a long time, and I need to know how you did it."

Sylvia shifted in her chair, took a cigarette out of a leather case and lighted it with a Ronson table lighter. "Don't tell me Fin has a drinking problem."

"He does. And it seems to be getting worse. Naturally, working in a bar doesn't help any. Still it does give us a roof over our heads and enough money to eke by on."

Sylvia drew on her cigarette and exhaled. "I didn't tolerate Pietro's drinking. Remember, I threw your brother out? I knew Daddy would support my decision. That he would take care of me and the kids if I left Pietro."

"I don't remember you ever booting Pietro out. Guess I was too young and wrapped up in school."

Francesca couldn't take her eyes off of a red Bakelite statuette next to the lighter, wondering why anyone would have such an atrocious thing in their house.

"Francesca, you don't have the choice that I had. I can only imagine what your papa would do if he knew about this. He's not crazy about Fin in the first place. As it is, it's been hard for Vito to accept where you live and that Fin is a barkeep. Of course, Vito does his own over indulging at Fazio's, but that's different. He doesn't have a problem with liquor, as Pietro did and as Fin seems to have."

"No, Papa must never know. But tell me, how did you get Pietro to quit alcohol."

Sylvia lighted another cigarette from the one she was finishing and pinched a bit of tobacco off her tongue. "I didn't. He saw the feathers after a binge."

"The feathers?"

"You don't know? It's some Italian thing. Pietro passed out in an alley where evidently an angel appeared before him. Your brother saw it as imminent death. After the visit of Gabriel," Sylvia scoffed, "or whoever, and he woke up, feathers were floating near him. That was the end of Pietro's romance with the bottle. He has never touched another drop. Of course, your papa said that the feathers belonged to a neighbor's chicken. Chicken or angel, it's nice having Pietro dry. He's still a mean bastard, but I can handle that, now that he's on the wagon."

Francesca smiled. "Seeing feathers isn't going to happen to Fin, so my hands are tied. I can't tell Fin's parents about Fin and ask for their help. His mother would go crazy if she knew. Their relationship has always been tenuous. I don't want to be responsible for making it worse. Besides, she's never liked me anyway."

Francesca took a sip of coffee that Sylvia had offered earlier. "Even though Michael doesn't imbibe, he knows Fin does. He often takes him for drinks and conversation. Still, I don't think he realizes Fin's problem. Yet, you'd think he'd be suspicious. On more than one occasion Michael secured a job interview for Fin that he missed because he was drunk. Of course, his excuse to his father was that he was sick or some other lamebrain lie." Francesca sighed. "I guess there's nothing for me to do but just live with the way things are and keep praying the drinking will stop. Despite it all, I still love him. And when he is sober, he's loving to me."

Sylvia stubbed out her cigarette and reached over and patted Francesca's hand. "I'm here whenever you need a shoulder or an ear. I could get Pietro to talk to Fin, if you'd like. Would that help?"

"No, no, I don't want Pietro to know what's going on. My brothers aren't any fonder of Fin than papa."

"Well, I know it's not easy for you, with the kids getting older and beginning to realize something's wrong. I remember how it was when Pietro went on binges."

"You're right. When Fin talks mean to me, Kane's beginning to take my side. Why just the other night, Fin was on a rampage. Nothing I did was right. I was damned if I did and damned if I didn't. Fin started for me, and Kane stuck out his foot and tripped him. We were all stunned."

Francesca giggled. "There Fin was, flat on his face. The fall seemed to sober him up somewhat. He even apologized to me for being nasty. But I never know. The incident could have gone the other way with Fin taking his belt to Kane."

10

Vito's arthritic pain often made him a worse curmudgeon than any of the fairy tale ogres his grandchildren were familiar with. When they stopped by the Savios' and Vito was on a tear, the older ones steered clear of him as best they could. trying to avoid his raging, which consisted of him trying to hit whatever part of their bodies he could reach with his cane. The younger grandchildren trembled and clutched their mother's skirts hiding behind them in fear. When caught without a protective skirt they would run away hollering, trying to avoid the swinging stick.

Their short, barrel-chested grandpa, whose black eyes peered at them from a face with its jagged scar, whose head seemed to be floating atop muscular shoulders, and who growled and swore, petrified them. All except for Kane, that is.

Kane, smarter than his cousins, learned at an early age how to get on his grandpa's good side. When Vito bellowed, all Kane had to do was disappear inside the house, go to the sideboard in the dining room, and pour a shot of whiskey.

Kane wasn't sure how he had learned that taking his grandpa a nip would make the old man his friend, but he discovered it before he was tall enough to reach the alcohol without the aid of a chair.

He had scrambled up to see a wooden crucifix carved from olive wood and polished to a luster. It hung over the sideboard's clutter of liquor bottles, decanters, glasses, and Maria's prized silver bell, given to her by Dominic. There had also been a cut-glass bowl of fruit. Kane had barely averted a catastrophe.

Thinking that by pulling the crocheted doily under the heavy dish and sliding it toward him would enable him to reach the plain everyday glasses on the other side of the dish had not been wise. He saw the bowl sliding toward the edge of the sideboard and with all his strength had only just been able to push it the back in the nick of time.

Now, being tall for an eight-year-old, he no longer needed a chair. He did need, however, to make certain his grandma was either on the second floor or down in the kitchen because he didn't want to risk getting caught.

One time, she'd discovered him pouring his grandpa's shot and all hell had broken loose. She and Vito yelled so intensely at each other that the neighbors, noisy Italians in their own right, slammed their windows to shut out the feud. Even without a row going on, Vito made a lot of noise on his own.

It was amazing Maria didn't hear the loud outbursts because it never failed. While Kane was pouring the drink, his grandpa could be heard out on the stoop, grumbling and cursing to the heavens. The minute Kane returned with the whiskey shot, Vito's grousing took a different turn. Now it was because the shot wasn't big enough. Yet, none of Vito's crotchetiness daunted Kane they had come to an understanding.

It started on a sweltering summer day when Kane arrived with his mother and Chiara at the Savio's. They found Vito sitting on the stoop swatting flies and observing Kane's cousins, Tommy, Colin, and Valentina playing cars out front on the sidewalk. Kane went to join them while his mother and Chiara went into the house.

Before long, a gush of water swirled along the gutter because neighborhood boys, at the end of the block, had opened a fire hydrant to cool off. The barefoot children began wading and splashing, the yellow tow truck hoisting a blue sedan, the red fire engine, and road grader forgotten.

"Oh, don't splash so," whimpered three-year-old Valentina, trying to protect her pink sundress. The boys kicked at the water harder just to hear her squeal.

"If you're going to play with us, Valentina, you have to play our way," called Kane, kicking water in her face.

"Yeah, Valentina, our way," chanted Colin and Tommy. "Our way." The boys gathered handfuls of water and threw it at her.

By now, Valentina was drenched. The once perky sash of her dress was untied and trailing in the dirty water. Muddy splotches dotted the bodice of a once spotless frock.

"Grandpa," wailed Valentina, "make them stop." She gathered the soggy garment around her knees. Her shoulders heaved. Her lips quivered. It was difficult to distinguish her tears from the water that was tormenting her.

"Cry baby, cry baby," the three boys chanted in unison. "Valentina's a cry baby."

An explosion from the stoop burst on them louder than a rocket blast. Vito shook his fist at the kids and waved his cane wildly.

"Outta the water! All of you! Valentina in-a the house. Tommy. Colin. To the backyard. You come here," he roared, pointing to Kane with the dangerous cane.

The children scattered to their designated spots and out of the path of their grandpa's wrath. But not Kane. His dripping feet climbed the stoop.

"Godadamn, son of a bitch," yelled Vito. Vito swung the cane and popped Kane's wrist bone, causing him to feel a paralysis and a shooting pain to his elbow. Stopping dead, Kane glared at his grandpa. The hurt hand twitched limply by his side.

"Come closer," bellowed Vito.

Kane stood stubbornly, continuing to stare. The cane reached out again and with a whack slammed against Kane's left leg. "I said, come closer."

That was it. Never taking his eyes off his grandpa, Kane reached down and picked up a small footstool his grandma had used while planting geraniums next to the sidewalk. He hurled the seat through the air straight for Vito. It crashed into the hand holding the cane.

Shock, then anger registered on Vito's face. Excitement and satisfaction coursed through Kane as he watched the stool hit its mark.

Francesca wandered out of the house just as it struck Vito. "Kane, what do you think you're doing?" Francesca grabbed him and smacked him up the side of the head. "You don't throw things at your grandpa." She slapped him again.

"Francesca, stop it," roared Vito. "Come here, Kane."

Boldly, Kane moved further up the steps, eyes blazing. Vito reached out and seized his arm. The grasp felt like a steel vise. Vito shook him violently.

This was all Kane needed. He'd had enough. With his free hand, he snatched up the cane still on the step and hit Vito soundly on the hand that clutched him. His grandpa's grip was weakened by the surprise blow. Kane wrenched himself away and ran like hell, dropping the cane behind him.

The jagged scar on Vito's face grew blood red. "Get him outta my sight."

Four days later, at Vito's request, Francesca took Kane by the hand, led him down Taylor Street and over to the Savio's on Lexington. She dragged him into the backyard to the grape arbor where Vito waited.

The summer sun beat on the purple-black grapes overhead, filling the air with sickening sweetness. Kane would never forget seeing his grandpa sitting on the bench at the back of the arbor as if he was king on a throne. A hand rested on his scepter, ready to pass sentence.

Kane tried to pull away from his mother, but her grasp tightened, forcing him to stay beside her. It wasn't that Kane was afraid, he just didn't want to get hit again. He got enough of that when his daddy was drunk. He might accept those blows, but he wasn't going to take them from anyone else.

"Are you afraid of me?" Vito asked.

Kane didn't respond.

"Come, next to me." Vito tapped the bench beside him.

"No."

"Come. Come to me."

"No."

"I give my word. I won't hit you." Vito nodded at Francesca. "It's okay. Go. Leave him."

Kane hesitated, reluctantly dropping his mother's hand and slowly advancing toward Vito. He sat down beside his grandpa, remaining wary---on guard---in case a move was made. But it wasn't. His grandpa kept his word. That day in the covered bower, in the humid closeness, Vito and Kane became simpatico.

Years later, the only things Kane remembered of that day was his grandpa saying how proud he was of him for being brave and standing up for what he felt was right, and his grandpa's words, *Remember, when a man gives his word, he keeps it. He must have honor above all.*

11

Kane wasn't eager to become a Cub Scout, but Francesca insisted. "It'll be good for you to do something constructive after school besides playing with older kids in the street. You need to be with boys your age."

She brushed a piece of lint off Kane's scout cap and handed it to him. "I'm sorry we can only afford your cap now. In a few weeks, I'll have enough money from my envelope stuffing to buy your uniform."

"That's okay, Mom." Kane crammed the cap into a pocket of his dungarees, gave her a peck on the cheek, and left for school.

Francesca watched him hop down the stairs. She couldn't believe how fast he was growing. Only eight and he was already as tall as her five feet. In a couple more years, he'd probably be able to look six-foot Fin in the eye. She dreaded that day.

It was all she could do to keep Kane in clothes now. Luckily, his cousins gave him hand-me-downs. But at the rate he was shooting up, he'd soon be taller than they and unable to wear their cast-offs. Then it would be a real struggle. It was impossible to keep him in shoes as it was. She felt guilty stuffing newspaper in the bottom of his shoes when the soles wore out, but it was the only way. And though, he would likely outgrow his scout uniform in a year, Francesca was determined he would have one.

Kane thought Cubs Scouts seemed like a sissy thing to do, but if it pleased his mom, then he'd go. After school, he wandered over to Mrs. Casale, the den mother's house, for his first meeting. It introduced the boys to scouting and gave an overview of planned activities for the year.

That evening when Francesca asked what he thought of scouting, Kane told her it was okay. He wouldn't admit that it did sound kind of fun, particularly the soap box derby, but he had reservations and doubted he'd like any of the boys in the group.

The next meeting, held in the parish church basement, was a combined one and included all the scouting dens and troops in the immediate area. It was here that Kane found a few kindred souls.

While Head Scoutmaster Conrad and others spoke to the group, Kane and two other boys, Joey Masserli and Freddy Gandini, began whispering back and forth and cutting up. The long-winded speeches were boring. After receiving dirty looks from the adult leaders and told to be quiet several times, the three boys decided to sneak out.

They tiptoed upstairs to the sanctuary. At the font of holy water, they horsed around, dipping their fingers in and flicking the wetness at each other. Soon that became tiresome, so they proceeded to a side altar with votive candles. They lit all the candles and soon the burning of wax permeated the corner.

When all the candles were lit, Kane mockingly asked, "Should we recite a little prayer?" This brought gales of laughter that echoed through the high-ceilinged church.

"Shhh." Joey pressed his finger to his lips. "We don't want to alert a priest."

"Hey, here's the box where people put money when they buy the candles. I bet there's enough in it for us to buy some candy," said Freddy.

"Are you thinking of taking it?" asked Joey.

"Why not? Who'll know?"

"But the box is locked. We can't break it open. Besides, it's a sin to steal."

While the two boys were arguing back and forth, Kane had been examining the donation box. "I bet I can pick this lock in a minute, and no one will ever know."

"Really?" Freddy looked at him in wonderment. "Do it. Bet you can't."

"No. Leave it alone. It's wrong." said Joey.

"Oh, come on Joey. No one will ever know." said Kane.

"God will."

Agitated Freddy said, "Joey, either you're with us or not. It's no big deal. Besides, there's probably not a lot of money anyway."

"Oh, okay. I give. Go ahead, Kane. Work your magic."

With everyone's approval, Kane immediately took out his pocket knife, and in a flash the lid of the box opened. Four shiny quarters sparkled at them. The boys grinned at each other.

"Wow!" said Kane. " There's one apiece and an extra for me since I'm the one who jimmied the lock."

"How did you know how to do that?" asked Joey still looking in awe at the open box.

"I don't know. I just did."

The boys pocketed the money, and Kane closed the top to look as it had before the theft. They moved on to the old altar. They stood for a minute considering the tabernacle's ornate box-like vessel. "Why don't you pick this lock, and let's see if there's money inside?" asked Freddy.

"Naw, We better leave that alone. I think that's for sick people," said Joey.

"Wouldn't it be more fun to put that out?" Kane pointed to the red-lighted lamp hanging from a cable over the tabernacle.

"Yeah. Do it, Kane," Freddy urged. You're the tallest. Get on that chair. See if you can reach the chain and pull the lamp down."

Just as Kane was reaching for the lantern, Jimmy Conrad, the head scoutmaster's son appeared. "What do you jerks think you're doing? You shouldn't be up here. Get out."

"Then why are you here?" asked Freddy.

"I followed you, and I saw what you did."

"Go away, you little shrimp," yelled Kane. "We aren't going anywhere."

"You better," said Jimmy, "or I'll go tell my daddy."

"You'll do no such thing, you little bastard." Kane, jumped off the chair.

"I will. Then your whore of a mother will be all over you," shouted Jimmy, standing his ground.

"What did you call my mom?"

"A whore. That's what."

Kane's papa might call his mom a whore when he was drunk, but no one else was going to. Kane's fist connected with Jimmy's nose.

"Ouch!" Jimmy put his nose to his shirt sleeve, trying to stop the blood.

"Serves you right for saying that about my mom. Now take it back."

Kane was ready to hit Jimmy again when voices were heard on the steps. The meeting below had ended, and people were ascending from the basement. Jimmy's father, followed by a half-sober Fin, strode into the sanctuary.

"We've been looking for you boys. What are you doing in here?" Seeing Jimmy's bloody nose, Scoutmaster Conrad asked, "What's the meaning of this? Which one of you did this to my son, and why?"

Kane stepped forward. "I did. And I'm not sorry."

Fin butted in. "Why did you hit this boy, Kane?"

"Because, he called Mom a whore."

Fin turned to the scoutmaster. "You should teach your son better manners." And with that, Fin slugged him.

Scoutmaster Conrad, with his own bloody nose, tried to gather himself from the pew where he'd fallen from the blow.

Fin grabbed Kane's hand. "Come on. Let's get out of here."

"Good idea," yelled the scoutmaster. He shook his fist at them. "Scouting doesn't need the likes of you or your bully son. I don't want to see either of you again. Don't ever come back."

On the way home, Kane felt the quarters in his pocket but said nothing. Maybe, he could buy something for his mother with them.

"Give me your cap," said Fin. As they passed a trash bin, he tossed it in. "You won't be needing that anymore."

12

"Can squirrels really cross the state of Michigan without ever touching the ground?" Kane sat with Meghan under a thick, leafy canopy where thin shafts of sun fought their way to the mossy floor.

"I suppose it's possible. The squirrels can jump from tree to tree because see how dense the leaves are overhead?" Meghan's jade-green eyes locked on the dense forest. "Such a shame, so many lovely trees are being cut down in this area for their hardwood. At least, these have been preserved. I love coming here because these trees are more profuse than the ones by the cottage. That's why I wanted to bring ye. Thought ye would like it here."

Meghan leaned back against a smooth, beech trunk watching a couple of tiger swallowtails flit back and forth and breathing in the greenness of the fiddlehead ferns and the dank smell of earth. She closed her eyes. "Can't get any closer to nature than this."

"Yeah, it's great." Kane stowed the rest of the leftover food into the picnic basket. "Everything's all packed up like you wanted. How long will it be before Mr. Bosco comes back for us?"

"We have another hour to enjoy this serenity." Meghan opened her eyes, regarding her grandson with pleasure.

It had been surprisingly easy to talk Francesca into letting Kane spend a week of his summer vacation in Michigan with Michael and her at their lake house in Union Pier. When Michael suggested the invitation be extended, Meghan was unaware that Kane had been getting into trouble, first at the scout meeting, then instigating fights at school. He had even stolen a coat for Francesca from a Sears Roebuck store. Knowing his mother needed a new one before winter set in, he had swiped the first coat he had seen from the rack, oblivious to its color or size.

Trying to leave the store, Kane was caught with the goods, and the manager learning who Kane's grandfather was, called Michael. Michael talked the manager out of pressing charges and paid for the coat. Afterward, when Michael lectured Kane on stealing, Kane kept mum about his family's financial problems.

Michael's idea to invite Kane to Michigan was to take him out of the city for a while and try to steer him on a better path. Meghan was excited by Michael's suggestion and wanted Kane to spend the entire summer, but Michael suggested she go slowly. Ever since the rift when Fin and family had lived with Michael and Meghan, the relationship between the families had improved somewhat.

It wasn't that Meghan liked Francesca any better, or Francesca Meghan. But a kind of peace hung precariously on the edge of eruption. Both sensed that with the slightest provocation war would ensue and neither wanted to be responsible for World War III. So they circled the wagons when together, which was seldom, and made the best they could of their situation.

Kane inspected a beetle attacking a fallen leaf and poked it with a stick. "I have a question, Grandma Cal. Instead of us taking the train here, why didn't Grandpa Cal let you drive me here from Chicago?"

"Well, yer grandfather took away me driving privileges a long time ago. In fact, ever since yer father was little. Early on, yer Grandpa Cal bought a car called a Duesenberg. I loved driving without the top, feeling the wind in me hair. But I have what is called a lead foot. I drive too fast. One time, I was driving and missed a curve, hit a pole, and threw your father into a ditch."

Kane whooped. "You did? I can just see him flying through the air. Did he get hurt?"

"He didn't. After that your grandfather limited me to driving without passengers. I don't really mind because living in Chicago cars aren't necessary. It would be nice to be able to drive here, though. But, at least, I have good 'ole Harry Bosco to drive me places and bring supplies when needed. Quick, Kane. Look."

Meghan pointed, across the road, to a lower branch of a sugar maple where a bird with a flaming red crest, the size of a crow was perched.

"It looks like Woody Woodpecker," whispered Kane.

"It is Woody," whispered back Meghan. 'It's a pileated woodpecker."

They watched the bird pecking at the fissured bark of the maple until it flew away.

"Come here, Kane. I'm going to teach ye to meditate."

"Really? Why?"

"Because, me love, eventually I want ye to learn how to control yer mind and travel to other places. Meditation is just the first step."

"That sounds fun. Is that what you do, Grandma Cal, when you sit in your backyard?"

"Partially. As ye grow older, I'll impart many things to you. But for now, I want ye to get comfortable, keep yer back straight, and close yer eyes."

Kane leaned against the tree next to his grandmother.

"Now, ye must clear yer mind of everything in it."

Kane giggled and his eyes flew open. "That's impossible. Too much going on in there."

"I know, but it will be helpful to ye. One day, it might even save yer life. Now, no more talking. Do as I say."

Kane closed his eyes and quietened.

"Concentrate on yer breathing, in and out ... in and out. Visualize yer breath going from yer nostrils and back into yer nose. Keep doing this. When a thought pops into yer mind, lay it aside and resume to thoughts of yer breathing."

Meghan could see that Kane was trying and was pleased. She leaned back in the diffused light and did as she had instructed Kane. After ten minutes, her eyes fluttered open. Kane was staring at her.

"Didn't ye do as I asked?"

"I tried, but I kept hearing noises from the woods ... birds chirping, leaves rustling overhead. I think I heard a branch break somewhere. My thoughts just kept going to other places."

"That's okay. Keep practicing. Ye'll get the hang of it one of these days. At least, ye've become more aware of nature. That's good. Feeling and being one with yer natural surroundings is important. Come. Let's walk down to the river. I want to pick some swamp roses for the dinner table. Maybe we'll see some other interesting things along the way."

That evening back at the cottage, Kane sat with Michael, who had arrived for the week from Chicago. "How do you like your first time here in Michigan?" asked Michael.

"I like it. Grandma Cal and I had fun today." Kane started telling Michael about his and Meghan's excursion to the Warren Woods. He wasn't sure why, but he decided to leave out the part about the meditation lesson.

"Sounds like you two had a good day. Would you like to go fishing tomorrow?"

"Oh, yes." Kane's eyes sparkled and a grin spread from ear to ear. "Will you teach me how to make the boat go?"

"Of course," said Michael with amusement.

He saw Kane eyeing the bookcases next to the fireplace. "You know, there just might be some books over there that your father read when he was your age. Let's see if we can find one for you. Would you like that?"

Kane nodded and began looking at the books as Michael withdrew them from the shelf and called out the titles: *Ivanhoe, The Call of the Wild, Tom Sawyer.*

"I think I'd like this one," said Kane. That night in bed, he opened the book he'd picked, *The Red Badge of Courage*.

Up until now, Kane hadn't appreciated books that much. Now, he became enthralled with the story of Private Henry Fleming's cowardice, his shame, and the realistic battles between the blue and gray soldiers. He turned the pages reading of the vivid encounters of Henry's internal struggles. Kane didn't stop until he'd finished the last pages, telling of the final conflict where Henry, unarmed, became the flag-bearer, bravely leading the men of his regiment through Confederate fire.

The next morning, when Michael went to wake Kane for breakfast, he found his grandson asleep with the book open beside him. Michael had fallen asleep many times the same way. He nudged Kane, who raised his head and opened bleary eyes. He immediately made a face.

"Oooh, that smell's dreadful, Grandpa Cal. What is it?"

"What are you talking about? I don't smell anything,"

"Well, I sure do."

"Maybe my sinuses are acting up. Are you getting a whiff of Grandma Cal's breakfast? She did burn the bacon." Michael chuckled.

"No. No, it's not that," said Kane, holding his nose. "It's a metallic, rusty odor. Sort of like wet pennies. Sickening. But it seems to be gone now."

Michael noticed the open window. "Well, maybe it was from an animal walking by or some odor coming from across the lake. Let's go. Your grandmother's waiting breakfast."

Kane dragged himself out of bed and to the kitchen table, but he couldn't get the stench out of his mind or from his nose. Over breakfast, he continued talking about it. Michael shook his head. All the while, Meghan remained quiet, looking at Kane peculiarly.

He was still going on about the horrific odor as he and Michael prepared the boat for fishing. Years later, Kane would remember this morning.

13

After Fin's shift at Bruno's was over, he knocked back a few drinks in a corner booth, while upstairs the family waited dinner.

"Do you want me to go get him?" asked Kane, checking the clock.

"No, let's wait a while," said Francesca. "But I'll go ahead and let ChiChi eat."

"I'm not ChiChi," declared Chiara. "Grandma says my God-given name is Chiara. That's what I should be called."

Francesca knew her mama adamantly refused to use nicknames. "Well, ChiChi's our pet name for you. But it's our secret. When you're at Grandma's house we'll call you Chiara. Okay?"

"Okay." Chiara eyed the food.

Francesca dished up a bowl of Slumgullion Stew and set it on the table in front of her daughter. "You're starving, aren't you?"

Chiara nodded and dug into her food.

Thirty more minutes passed. "Okay, let's eat. Your papa can just eat his dinner cold."

Francesca and Kane were finishing their meal when Fin burst through the door. His thick shock of sandy-brown hair was rumpled, sticking out in all directions like feathers in an old mattress. His eyes were as red as the bull's eye on the barroom dartboard. He grew irate when he recognized dinner had been eaten without him.

“Jush go ahead and eat without me won’t ya? Can’t ya wait a goddamn minute?” He stumbled toward the table.

“We did wait, but we got hungry. Here. I’ll reheat the food for you.” Francesca knew better than to make waves in his drunken condition. She picked up the bowl of cold stew.

“Jush give it to me,” said Fin. He grabbed at the bowl, knocking it from Francesca’s hand. The dish landed in pieces at their feet. Tomatoes, carrots, and meat skittered across the floor.

“Now, look what you’ve done. I’ve had enough of you and your drinking.” Francesca bent to clean up the mess, and Fin kicked at her.

“Stop it!”

Francesca rose and pushed him. “You son of a bitch, don’t kick me.”

Fin slapped her. “Whore.”

“Don’t whore me. Francesca kicked his shin.

Fin shoved her down into a chair, and exasperated, she started weeping. Then Chiara howled. Fin stood glassy-eyed, swaying back and forth over Francesca in the middle of the chaos.

“Don’t you hit Mom,” yelled Kane, beating Fin’s chest with his fists.

Fin backhanded Kane and sent him flying across the room into the wall. “Don’t tell me what to do you goddamn son of a bitch.” Fin yanked off his belt. If you don’t want this you better get out of my sight, boy.”

“Stop it, Fin. Leave Kane alone.” Francesca tried to grab Fin’s hand, but he shoved her away.

“This is between Kane and me.”

Kane rose from the floor, feeling the sting on his face, not rubbing it as he wanted to. “I’m not afraid of you. Go ahead, hit me.”

Fin slapped the belt against his hand. Then cracked it in the air.

“You damn right I will and you won’t forget it.”

“Kane, go. I’m okay,” called Francesca. “Things will be fine. Get out of here for a while.”

It wasn’t the first time this kind of scene had played out. There had been one even worse. Kane had talked back to Fin and his dad had socked him in the face, producing a black eye. Kane had clenched his fists, kept quiet, and didn't react, but his mind was in high gear. He hated his old man.

The next night Kane had retaliated. While Fin was working, Kane rigged a strong cord across the apartment steps at the top, figuring Fin would be drunk when he came home, wouldn't see it, and would trip and fall. Maybe he'd even kill himself. Then peace would reign in the family forever.

Although, the deed didn't provide death, Fin did trip and fall. He tumbled head over heels, landing at the bottom of the stairs in a heap. Miraculously, there were no broken bones, but he sustained a gash over his right eye that required stitches. The next day, his eye was swollen and more black and blue than Kane's.

Francesca had mixed emotions when she discovered the clothesline that Kane had rigged. Yet, the only punishment that she meted out was treating him like a stranger for the next week, acting as if he was invisible and not speaking to him. This hurt Kane worse than any scolding or punishment she could give.

It seemed Francesca had inherited Maria's trait for clamming up and sulking when things didn't go right. Despite being distressed, Francesca never said a word to Fin, allowing him to believe the fall was because he was drunk. She knew telling the truth would cause more trouble for Kane, and she hoped that the accident would sober up Fin for good.

Kane had a bag packed and was ready to run away in case his mom ratted on him, telling Fin the real cause of the accident. But seeing she wasn't going to spill the beans, Kane shelved his plan.

Tonight, he pulled his thin jacket from the peg by the door to do Francesca's bidding, otherwise, chaos would prevail all night with his dad crashing through the apartment like a wild animal keeping everyone awake. The best they could hope for was that Fin would pass out so they could all sleep. With Kane out of the way, perhaps things would calm down. It seemed his mere presence always inflamed Fin.

Kane went out to the fire escape and climbed to the top of the steps. When they ended, he pulled himself up by a dangling rope that he had secured with a metal clamp to the edge of the flat roof.

Black tar paper showed through the worn asphalt, rising in bubbles and waves, like a dark ocean, frothing and seething toward the shore. Aluminum ventilator fans stood knee high like the ten pins over at the West Side Lanes two streets over. A rusted metal box sat in a far corner belonging to a non-functioning air conditioning system that had never worked properly. The system had always made a clattering, tinny noise producing tepid air at best to the bar customers below. A chimney of crumbling mortar and loose red brick rose across the way.

Despite the bleakness of the roof's terrain and street noises below---car horns, squealing brakes, dogs barking, kids yelling, it was a beautiful and quiet place to Kane. He hoped his old man had calmed down after his departure and that his mother and Chiara weren't being mistreated.

Kane huddled against the chimney, feeling no protection against the cold. His flimsy jacket was next to useless, and he wished he had on another couple of layers to ward off the snow that was beginning to fall in fleecy flakes. He raised his face to the night sky sticking out his tongue to catch a few as they fluttered down like small white angels. The snowfall muted the traffic sounds and footsteps crunched below on the sidewalk.

Kane inhaled, feeling the cold sting in his lungs. He relived his vacations in Michigan, the quiet woods where he had seen deer grazing and the warm sun he had felt on his face as he swam in the lake. He had been allowed to go for a couple of summers now and had been granted permission to bring books home from Michael's library. Ever since *The Red Badge of Courage*, he had been captivated by reading.

Needing solitude to absorb his hunger for words, he had sought out a private retreat for a place to read and had discovered the roof top.

On summer nights, while it was still light, reading on the roof transported him to other worlds away from the turmoil in the apartment below. On winter nights, when it grew dark early, and he was unable to read, he practiced meditation.

In a niche behind some loose chimney bricks, he'd created a perfect hiding place for his books. There fiction and history books, that he was partial to, were hidden from buddies who might taunt and laugh at him if they discovered his new found pleasure. He wasn't afraid of their jeers. Didn't want the hassle. The works were also safe from his father, who in a fit of drunken rage, had once torn pages from a Jack London book.

Kane awoke. It must be late because he was covered in white like the Himalayan yeti. Shivering he stood and shook the snow off, then scrambled back downstairs. The house was quiet. He undressed and slid under the warm covers, knowing he would be able to get a few hours sleep before school, even though he dreaded trudging through the wet snow. By morning, he would need to put on four pairs of socks and line the inside of his shoes with cardboard. It was the only way to help keep his feet dry.

He had experienced an embarrassing moment the first time he'd done this during a snowstorm. Arriving at school, he'd gone to the restroom, removed the wet socks, and replaced them with a dry pair, then lined his shoes with new cardboard. Unwittingly, he'd wadded up the wet socks and stuffed them in a front pocket of his pants. The soggy footwear leaked through, causing it to look as if he'd had an accident.

After beating up the kids who teased him about wetting his pants, he was marched to the principal's office and suspended for two days. From then on, he wrung out the socks thoroughly and put them in his jacket pocket.

14

Chicago - 1960s

"We'll go after we visit Grandpa and Grandma Cal's. But for now, comb your hair, Kane. We'll be late if we don't hurry." Francesca tied the sash on Chiara's dress, trying to hide the worn seam at the waist.

"It's my birthday. I don't see why can't I go to Grandpa's first." Kane ran a comb through his coarse, wavy hair giving it a lick and a promise.

"Because we'll be at Grandpa's longer than we'll be at the Callahans'. Now, listen both of you." Francesca issued a warning, "You are not to say anything at either house when asked why your papa's not with us. He's working. Understand?"

Chiara pouted. "But he's not." Suddenly she brightened. "Ha, ha, Kane. You're going to get bumped today."

"No, I'm not. I'm too old." He puffed out his chest. "I didn't get bumped last year either, but you're younger. When your day comes round, you'll get it."

"Okay. Both of you, enough." Francesca pulled their jackets from the wall pegs, handed Kane his and helped Chiara button hers. "Such a silly Irish tradition picking up children and bumping their heads on the floor."

"So, you think tugging one's ears, isn't?" Kane could already feel everyone jerking on his ears twelve times and another for good measure when they arrived at the Savios'.

And that's the way Kane's twelfth birthday began. Francesca having to go to Michael and Meghan's without their son because Fin was nowhere to be found. He'd disappeared. This wasn't the first time Fin hadn't come home after a night of drinking, but it was the first time he'd been away so long.

Before it had been for a night, two at the most. Those had been peaceful times, Fin's drunkenness not marring their lives. This time, Francesca was worried. She wondered if he was okay and where he was. At the moment, she was preoccupied with how she was going to make the utility payment and other bills which were past due.

The money she made from stuffing envelopes wouldn't begin to cover them. She was surprised Jimmy Bruno, owner of the bar, hadn't been knocking at the door, asking why Fin hadn't been coming to work and telling her that they had to move since their living arrangement was conditional on Fin's job.

The bus took them within several blocks of the Callahans'. Kane and Chiara enjoyed stomping on the fall leaves as they walked along on the crisp October day. Although, the season was different, for some reason making the walk reminded Francesca of going with Fin to tell his parents that they were getting married. She had been panicky about meeting them, especially Meghan. She laughed to herself remembering how she'd asked Fin if his mother was a witch.

Francesca still wasn't sure that she wasn't, but it was a fact Meghan was a cold bitch. Living with Meghan and Michael when Kane was a baby had done nothing to quell Francesca's nerves when she was near her mother-in-law. However, she had to admit that since Kane was born, Meghan had warmed up a bit.

"Come in," said Michael, opening the door and hugging the three of them. "Happy birthday, Kane. Ready for your birthday celebration?" He looked around. "Where's Fin?"

"He had to work," said Francesca. She avoided Michael's eyes and squeezed Chiara's shoulder, a gesture to stay quiet.

"Well, come on in. Grandma Cal has everything all set up in the dining room. Aunt Kitty's here too."

"Here's me birthday boy," said Meghan, hurrying to Kane and giving him a hug. She tapped Chiara on the head and actually smiled at Francesca. After greetings were exchanged with Aunt Kitty, they all sat down at the table. Meghan went to the kitchen, returning with her traditional fruit cake with lighted candles while everyone sang "Happy Birthday."

"I don't like that kind of cake," whispered Chiara.

Francesca touched her arm. "Shhh, don't let Grandma Cal hear you."

"Now," said Meghan, "blow out your candles and make a wish."

Kane blew as hard as he could.

"Hooray! You did it with one breath." Chiara clapped, her eyes bright. "What did you wish for?"

"You know it won't come true if I tell," said Kane, eyeing the small presents sitting next to the cake.

"Go ahead. Open them," said Aunt Kitty.

Kane tore off the wrappings to find a new shirt and pair of pants in the first package, and in the other a book called *Treasure Island*. There was silence. Francesca kicked Kane under the table and frowned at him.

"Thank you everyone," said Kane, managing a smile.

"I think you'll enjoy that book," said Michael, aware of Kane's disappointment. "Kane, while Grandma Cal's cutting the cake, come with me. I want to show you something I think you'll like even better."

Kane followed Michael into the backyard and there, with a huge bow tied on the handlebars, sat a shiny red bicycle.

Kane threw his arms around Michael's neck. "Thank you, Grandpa Cal. Thank you so much. My wish just came true. I need a new bike. I'm way too large for the one papa bought me when I was six." Fin ran his fingers over the bright paint, inspecting it from front to back. "Can I go for a ride?"

"Not now. Let's have cake and ice cream first. Don't want to disappoint Grandma Cal, do we?"

The rest of the time spent at the Callahans' was fun. Kane took several trips down the street on his new bike while everyone watched. He even gave Chiara a ride on the cross bar. When it was time to go, he was sad that he had to leave the bicycle behind, but Michael promised to bring it to him by car the next day.

Unlike at Meghan and Michael's, the birthday celebration at the Savios' was anything but sedate. The minute Francesca, Kane, and Chiara walked in the door a sign, hanging from the ceiling and reading *Buon Compleanno Kane*, hit them in the face. Francesca's brothers had done their usual birthday decorating, draping red and green crepe paper streamers in the living room and along the stairs.

A decorated cake with candles sat in the middle of the dining room table. It would be cut later in the evening. The Savios' house overflowed with people. Besides uncles, an aunt, and cousins, there were friends and children from the neighborhood. Even Arriana Gabbelli was there, holding hands with Gino. Francesca couldn't believe that her brother was still seeing a woman he kept indicating meant nothing to him.

The house was alive with laughter, and pleasant aromas drifted up from the kitchen below, indicating another of Maria's mouthwatering meals. Everyone took a turn, during the day, pulling Kane's ears. But he didn't care. This was the best birthday ever. And even though he got lots of presents, nothing compared with the red bicycle.

During the evening, Francesca managed to get Gino away from Arriana long enough to talk to him in a corner of the kitchen.

"The money from my envelope job hasn't come in yet. I was wondering if you could loan me a little until the first of the month to tide things over?"

Francesca not being her usual happy-go-lucky self when around family hadn't gone unnoticed by Gino.

"What's wrong, cara? You look sad."

"Nothing. Guess I'm just tired."

"Are you sure?"

Francesca forced a smile. "It's been a long day. Don't forget it started at the Callahans'. Being around my mother-in-law would tire anyone."

"From what I know, I'm sure you're right." He patted her shoulder. "By the way, where's that no-good husband of yours?"

"Don't talk about Fin that way. He's working. Besides, why would he want to be here when he's treated worse than an alley cat? And what's with all the questions? Can you loan me a bit, or not?"

Gino's hand plunged deep into his pocket.

"Don't tell me mama's still extending your pockets."

"Hell, yes. Pickpockets are worse now than ever."

"You're something else," said Francesca, stuffing the money Gino handed her in her own pocket. "I promise, I'll pay you back."

She clasped his hand and checked to see if anyone had noticed the transaction. Someone had. When Kane had seen the two go off together, he'd followed hoping to get Gino to teach him cards.

Later that night after they returned home and Chiara was in bed, Kane told Francesca he had overhead the conversation with Gino. A tear slid down Francesca's cheek, and she admitted that with Fin gone she didn't have enough money without Gino's loan.

"I've got to pay for the lights and water. I'll just make it, but that doesn't leave much for food. It'll be tough until your papa returns. But we'll manage. I don't want you to worry. I'm sorry to burden you with this but guess you'd find out eventually."

Kane put his arms around her. "Don't worry Mom. It'll be all right." Francesca laid her head on Kane's shoulder. She hated that she'd poured out her troubles to him. He shouldn't be weighed down with her problems. He was only a child.

That night before he went to sleep, Kane was glad for his new bicycle. He needed transportation if he was to get a job and help his mom.

A week later, Fin still hadn't returned. As expected, Jimmy Bruno, who had been out-of-town, came knocking on the door and asked where in the hell Fin was. When he found out Fin had disappeared, he was ready to kick Francesca and the children out.

After much pleading and many tears from Francesca, he relented saying they could stay if she paid rent.

The amount requested was low, exactly what Francesca made stuffing envelopes. But that meant nothing would be left for food. During Bruno's and Francesca's conversation, Kane once again eavesdropped. He knew they needed more money than his neighborhood paper route brought in.

Skipping school the next day, he jumped on his bicycle and searched for his Uncle Gino. Kane found the black Caddy toodling down the street. Gino pulled the car to the curb when he saw Kane.

Always the dandy and wearing the latest style, Gino was clad in a slim-cut black pinstripe suit and thin red tie sprinkled with white polka dots. He was supposedly working at overseeing his city street-paving crew.

Kane had heard talk about the cushy job his uncle had been given by Lorenzo Gabbelli, in return for Gino squiring Arriana. Kane decided he should be as lucky someday. He wanted to wear nice clothes and have a woman on his arm. Of course, he'd rather have more of a looker than Arriana.

"I need to talk to you, Uncle G."

"Hop in," said Gino.

Kane shook his head. "I can't leave my bike here. Can we go to Leona's over on Taylor where I can lock it up?"

Gino agreed and away they went. As usual, Leona's was busy when they entered, but they found an empty table near the kitchen where Gino could sit facing the door.

After they ordered breakfast and the waitress left, Gino asked, "So, what's up?"

"First of all, Uncle G, you've got to swear you'll never say a word to anyone about what I'm going to tell you. I mean it. If Uncle Pete, Uncle Carlo, or Grandpa find out, they'd take the old man out. I wouldn't mind. I hate him for what he's doing, but Mom still loves the son of a bitch."

"Fuck, this sounds serious," said Gino. "I give my word. It'll stay between us."

In a hushed tone, Kane leaned forward and told Gino everything. How Fin was drinking all the time and how he hit his mom, and how Fin had disappeared leaving them in the lurch with no money.

"That damn Fin. I knew something smelled rotten when he wasn't at your birthday party. Why didn't your mama level with me? We've always been close."

"You know Mom, Uncle G. She doesn't want any of you to know what she's going through. Besides, the old man's not anyone's favorite, anyway. Mom wouldn't be happy if she finds out that I've told you, either. Only reason I am, is I'm trying to earn more money to help out. I need another job. I thought maybe you'd have some ideas or connections for one."

"Don't worry, kid. I'm glad to help. I respect you for steppin' up like a man and being there for your mama. Tell you what, I've been running numbers for your Uncle Pietro ever since your grandpa started doing shakedowns. I'll turn the numbers over to you. Pietro won't mind."

"But that won't work. Uncle Pietro will know something's going on if I do that."

"No, he won't. I'll tell him I'm too busy right now and need to lay off for a while. That you need some spending money, so I'm letting you step in. Besides, you need to dip your toe in the water. You'll be perfect because you know the ropes from making the rounds with me from time to time. And now that you have wheels, you'll be able to run numbers after school and your mama won't get wise."

"Gee thanks, Uncle G. You're the best."

"Now, let's eat," said Gino, carefully tucking a napkin at his neck to protect his tie before digging into the heaping plate of bacon and eggs that the waitress had placed in front of him.

15

Kane was busy. He'd gotten three more paper routes, was running numbers for Gino, and even washing bar glasses for Bruno on the weekends. With the food swiped from DeLisi Brother's Market, the family was able to stay afloat.

Francesca assumed Kane was buying the groceries and was proud of him for being ambitious and working so hard, even though it was a lot of responsibility for a twelve-year-old to shoulder. Of course, she was unaware that most of the cash was coming from what Kane earned by conveying money and bookmaking slips from the betting parlors to the mafia. Despite all the jobs, Kane's grades weren't much lower than normal because he was smart and able to get by without much studying. Yet, not smart enough to keep his nose clean.

One Sunday, he went to play baseball with friends. Afterward, he walked to the Callahans' to meet up with Francesca and Chiara. At Michael's insistence, Meghan had invited Francesca and Chiara, along with Aunt Kitty to tea. It would be, Meghan decided, a good time to teach Chiara the art of being a lady since the ten-year-old had inherited her mother's tom boyishness. Chiara enjoyed climbing trees in overalls rather than donning a dress and playing with dolls.

This galled Meghan. She needed to instruct her granddaughter on how to be a lady and teach her the manners that she lacked. Learning to pour and serve tea would be a good lesson.

After Kane arrived at his grandparents', he and Michael went into the backyard to practice pitching. They threw balls back and forth, laughing and having fun when suddenly the quiet of the neighborhood exploded into loud shouts and the sound of a car motor revving from the street.

Before Michael could stop Kane, he had picked up his bat and run around the corner of the house. A carload of teenage boys in a souped-up '57 Chevy was stopped in front of the Savios'. The boys were hanging out the car windows yelling obscenities at his mother and Chiara, who stood on the front porch.

"Guineas, guineas, Go back to your own hood. You fuckin' guineas."

Not stopping to think, Kane ran to the car and began beating it with his bat. "Dumb micks, go fuck yourself. Get outta here, or I'll kill you."

Quickly, the boys rolled up the windows. Kane and his bat were relentless. He hammered at the car leaving big dents, smashing the back window. "Fuck you! Fuck you!"

The driver floored the accelerator, and the car peeled away, leaving a patch of rubber as they sped off down the street. Kane gave chase, swinging the bat and yelling until the car drove out of sight.

When he returned to his grandparent's house everyone stood in the yard. Michael grabbed Kane's arm, causing him to drop the bat. Aunt Kitty clutched her chest as if having a heart attack and looked horrified.

"What have you done?" screamed Francesca. "What's wrong with you? Do you want to bring the cops?"

"Those micks won't be calling the cops," said Kane. "They aren't saints." He tried to break away from Michael but was unsuccessful.

Meghan started for Kane and began screeching. "Ye've got the dark blood in ye. The tainted blood."

"Hush, Meghan. Let Michael handle this." Kitty, having overcome her shock, steered Meghan and Chiara back into the house, leaving Michael to deal with Kane in a more sane way.

"Kane, what's gotten into you? You know better than to damage other people's property."

"But Grandpa Cal they were saying mean things to Mom and ChiChi. No one does that when I'm around."

"You've got to learn to control your temper, boy, before you get into some real trouble. I can't always be available to come to your defense."

On the way home, Francesca asked, "What did Grandma Cal mean when she said you had the dark blood? Was she blaming my Italian culture?"

"No, Mom. Grandma Cal told me a story once about the Vikings who long, long ago invaded Ireland. They were vicious and powerful and lived in Ireland for at least a hundred years. Not having women of their own race in Ireland, they married local girls. Grandma Cal said this caused many Irish to become impure because their blood was mixed with that of the ruthless Vikings."

Francesca laughed. "So the dark blood she thinks you have is from her side of the family and has nothing to do with me?"

"Right. It's not your fault, but I don't think Grandma Cal was saying it was hers either."

"I'm sure you're right about that," said Francesca under her breath.

16

Francesca was about to faint from exhaustion after lugging two heavy bags of groceries from the store. She dropped the load at the bottom of the stairs in order to catch her breath before tackling the steps. Looking up, she found Michael waiting at the top by the apartment door.

"Michael, what a surprise," called Francesca, watching her father-in-law descend to help carry her parcels.

After entering the apartment and placing the groceries on the kitchen floor, Francesca said, "These can wait." She motioned for Michael to sit down which they both did. "It's not like you to stop by during the day. The kids are still at school, you know."

Michael wiped his sweaty brow against the recent exertion and stuffiness of the room. "I'm glad they are because we need to have a serious talk."

"Goodness," said Francesca, " whatever's the matter?"

"You tell me. I've suspected for a while that something's amiss. I haven't seen Fin lately. I'm wondering why? Is it something I've done? Is he avoiding me for some reason? I stopped in the bar to see him, and he wasn't there. The bartender gave me no answers as to his whereabouts."

"Well, that's because Fin doesn't work there anymore. Michael ..." Francesca's lip trembled, and her eyes filled with tears.

Michael rose and went to her, handing her his handkerchief. "What is it? Is Fin okay?"

Francesca wiped her eyes. "I don't know. He's gone. I have no idea where he is. I'm sorry, but I can't keep this to myself any longer. I didn't want any of you to find out, but I have to tell someone. I'm at my rope's end. I've covered for Fin long enough."

Francesca's widely-spaced eyes avoided her father-in-law's. "I'm embarrassed to tell you, but Fin has a drinking problem. To put it bluntly, the kids and I have been living in hell. I haven't dared tell my parents. Papa and my brothers would be after Fin like a pack of hyenas, and the outcome wouldn't be pretty. I certainly don't want Meghan to know, either. It would just give her more fodder to find fault and say how weak he is. I'm sorry to lay this on you, Michael, because I know you and Fin have a good relationship."

Stunned, Michael listened as Francesca unloaded her frustrations of Fin's drinking, of him leaving them, and how, since his disappearance, Kane had been contributing money from his many jobs.

"With his help we've been able to scrape by since Fin is no longer working downstairs." Francesca dabbed at her eyes with Michael's handkerchief.

"You don't know how wretched I feel about this. I had no idea he drank so much. I'm so sorry he's done this to you and the children. I wish I'd known about this sooner, but glad I finally do."

Michael paused, taking a deep breath, holding back his own tears. "Of course, I won't mention this to the others. My dear, I want you to relax and not worry about money. I'll gladly help you."

Francesca threw her arms around him. "Oh, Michael, I hate taking from you, but you really are a life saver. Thank you."

"My sweet, there's no need to thank me. But know one thing, I'm going to find my son. This has got to be dealt with. Fin has a responsibility here. I'm going to see that he shoulders his family obligations like a man. I can't tell you how disappointed I am in him. Mark my words, things will change if I have anything to do with it."

After Michael left, Francesca felt as if a burden had been lifted. However, she worried. When Fin was found would he be angry with her for telling Michael?

Immediately after leaving Francesca, Michael called on a private investigator and some of his street contacts and set them on a search for Fin.

In a couple of days, Sidecar McGee, a derelict Michael had helped out of numerous scrapes with the law, reported Fin was on skid row and living at the Starr Hotel.

Michael was in disbelief that his son was holed up in the six-story flophouse on West Madison. It was an awful place. He'd once defended a small-time bank robber who had been found hiding in one of the hotel's many small cubicles whose walls were made of plywood and chicken wire.

But that's exactly where Michael found Fin. Like a common bum, he was dirty, unshaven, and passed out, lying on a dingy mattress surrounded by empty wine bottles of Muscatel and Boone's Farm.

Michael didn't know who to turn to for help now that he had found Fin. Then he remembered a well-known attorney and recalled hearing of his brother, Monsignor Ignatius McDermott. Father Mac, as the monsignor was called, frequented skid row helping alcoholics, junkies, and other down-and-outs. With a couple of telephone calls, Father Mac was located, and he met with Michael.

When told of Michael's plight, Father Mac said, "I'm sure you're aware that people who have trouble with alcohol are ridiculed and shamed. Families feel disgraced by their kin with the problem. So it's kept hush-hush, swept under the rug. Sometimes, even the alcoholic's own loved ones can't accept that there's a problem. They think it's a character weakness and rebuff the person or turn a blind eye."

Michael nodded in understanding. "That's exactly what I'd like to do. It *is* difficult to accept. Yet, I know Fin, nor his family, can live like this anymore. It's sad, but it seems Fin takes after my father who had a bad time with alcohol."

"I can tell you are uncomfortable divulging this about your son," said Father Mac, "but you shouldn't be. Hopefully, you'll feel differently after I explain some things to you."

"Research has recently been done in Canada. One study concluded that alcoholism isn't a character flaw but rather a disease that can be passed from one generation to another. Obviously, that's the case here."

"Interesting," said Michael. " Do you believe this study?"

Father Mac rose and went to his desk. "I truly do, and it should be treated as a disease ... by a doctor. From now on, Fin needs more love and understanding than ever if he is to get well. He also needs medical help."

Father Mac wrote something on a piece of paper and handed it to Michael. "Here is the name and address of a friend's boardinghouse where I often take men to help sober them up when they don't have the means for a rehab facility. I'm sending you there because I know that you want to keep this quiet. I advise you to contact your family doctor. He will know of a colleague who can help Fin."

So with the aid of Sidecar, Michael took Fin from the sleazy hotel and ensconced him in a clean room at Mrs. Fahey's boardinghouse. Taking Father Mac's advice, Michael also contacted Dr. Finley, the family physician. Dr. Finley said that he'd send Dr. Boyle, who was skilled in the rehabilitation of alcoholics, to the boardinghouse. Michael now waited for the doctor, as well as for Fin to come to.

When Fin finally awoke and saw Michael beside him, he bolted upright and in a stupor looked around with bleary eyes. "Dad? What are you doing here? Where am I?"

"I'm here because Francesca has been beside herself since your disappearance. And because you need help. It took me a while to find you and take you out of that god forsaken rat hole. I brought you to a clean room and bed."

Fin held his head in pain. He tried to concentrate on what Michael was saying, but after weeks of steady drinking, his mind wasn't absorbing the words and his body was crying out for alcohol.

"Look at me, Fin, and listen," said Michael in a rough voice, a tone he'd never used before with his son. Still, it wasn't severe enough to get Fin's attention.

"Dad, wait. Before you start in, a drink would help me focus better." Fin's hand trembled.

"Don't be a fool! There will be no more booze for you. You're going to straighten up right here and now. You've let me down, Fin. Most of all you've let down your family."

"One little drink? Please? All I need is one." Fin's whole body visibly shook.

"No more alcohol! I told you years ago how liquor ruins a man. I can see you're trying to prove the point. You're on the road to being just like your grandfather."

"Please, Dad. I'm feeling bad. I need a drink."

Michael was growing exasperated. and realized he was wasting his breath. There was a knock at the door.

Answering it, Michael found a reed-thin man with a kind face. "Dr. Boyle?"

"Yes, Dr. Finley sent me."

"Come in. Thank God you're here." Michael motioned him inside. Fin thrashed in distress, his tremors full-blown now.

"I don't know what to do. I've been trying to talk to him, but I know he's not hearing me. It seems he's already going through withdrawal. All he talks about is wanting another drink."

"Of course he does. That's natural. Let me take over from here." Dr. Boyle sat down on the bed next to Fin.

"Who are you?" Fin was trying to make sense of what was happening.

"This is Dr. Boyle, Fin. He's here to help you feel better," said Michael.

"Are you gonna get me a drink?" Fin's voice was weak and shaky.

"We'll talk about a drink later."

"No, I need it now. I've got to get out of here and get one. Gotta have a drink." Fin stood up but fell back on the bed.

"Here. Relax. Let me help you." Dr. Boyle brought Fin's legs up on the bed and situated his head on a pillow.

Fin's face had grown ashen, and he was sweating profusely. "I feel sick."

"Michael, will you get that wastebasket and bring it by the bed?"

Fin moaned and drew himself in a fetal position.

In a soothing voice, Dr. Boyle said, “Fin, I need to examine you.” He pressed Fin to lie flat, took a stethoscope from his bag, placed it on Fin’s chest, and listened.

Fin struggled to get up.

“It’s okay. It’s okay. Settle down now. I’m going to make you feel better. Just take it easy.”

Fin finally quit trying to sit up, but his agitation increased. He tossed from side to side.

Michael started for the bed, but Dr. Boyle motioned him away. “His heartbeat is fast but that’s due to anxiety. I’ll take care of him. I won’t leave his side until he’s dried out. When he’s sober and feeling better, he’ll be able to understand what’s going on. Right now his mind is muddled.”

“What can I do? I can’t stand to see him in so much agony. He’s got to kick this.”

Dr. Boyle put his hand on Michael’s shoulder. “You should go. It’s not going to be pretty around here for a while. After going through withdrawal, hopefully he’ll want to stay sober. Some people do, others don’t. After the binge he’s been on he’ll probably have the TD’s (delirium tremens) pretty badly. You should go. You don’t need to witness this.”

“But Doc, can’t I stay and ...”

Dr. Boyle handed Michael his coat and hat. “I know what I’m doing. I’ll call you when he’s better. And don’t worry, it will be several weeks before you hear from me. I’ll give him Antabuse after he’s through withdrawal and sobers up.”

“What the hell is that?”

“It’s a drug on the market that produces an intense sensitivity to alcohol, keeps the body from absorbing it. However, it doesn’t keep a person from craving a drink.”

“Then what good is it?”

“Well, if Fin takes a drink when on the medicine he will get a throbbing headache, might vomit and sweat, and may experience chest pains.”

This is a signal for him to stop drinking. If he doesn’t, he’ll become deathly ill. I can almost guarantee that at first, he’ll think he can get away with a few drinks, but after a few bouts of being extremely sick, his brain will get the message that he can't drink anymore. After he's ready to go home, I'll find a sponsor to take him to AA meetings. Trust me. I'll get Fin sober, cleaned up, and back to his family. After that, it's up to him."

Michael shook Dr. Boyle's hand and gave Fin's trembling body one last look. He couldn't believe this was happening. He heard Fin retch as he closed the door.

Weeks later, Kane, Chiara, and Francesca were just finishing dinner when Fin came through the door, dragging his sober tail behind him. With moist eyes, he was full of apologies, saying it would never happen again. When he finished with his expressions of regret, begging each of them to please forgive him, Chiara threw her arms around his neck and gave him a big kiss.

Although fearful that he might relapse, Francesca also hugged him, said she was happy he was back, that she loved him, and now they would go forward and forget the past.

Kane said nothing because it would take more than a few words of remorse to erase the disgust he felt for what his old man had put them through. As far as he was concerned, words meant nothing. This wasn't the first time Fin had asked for forgiveness after a drinking bout but his remorse had only lasted until his next drink.

At least for now, Kane could quit stealing food because it seemed the bartending job downstairs had been restored. No one seemed to question the reason why, but Kane, already becoming street smart, guessed someone had paid Bruno off to rehire Fin.

17

One evening after having dinner with the Savios, Kane said he should be going home. Vito told Maria he would walk with him. Kane was about to say he was twelve, not five, and old enough to go alone, but Vito gave him his *don't say anything* stare.

Maria thought it odd, Vito wanting to go with their grandson since he'd never done such a thing before, but then Vito never ceased to surprise her. Maybe he just wanted to spend time alone with Kane. So she kissed them both goodbye, and they ambled out into the pleasant night air.

"This isn't the way to my house," said Kane as Vito steered him in the opposite direction.

"I know. Just told your grandma that. Follow me. Taking you to a show."

"I didn't know you liked flicks, Grandpa."

"Not a movie. It's live. And it's our secret. No tell your grandma or your mama or there'll be hell to pay. Capisce?"

"Sure, Grandpa." Kane wondered why going to a show needed to be kept quiet.

They strolled along until they came to a row of stores. Vito turned down a gangway into an alley between them.

"Come." Vito motioned and turned into a building without a sign.

He led Kane down a dimly-lit passageway until they came to a beaded curtain hanging over an open doorway. Vito parted it, and

Kane heard the beads jangle against each other and felt them hit his back as he followed his grandpa into a smoke-filled room. Kane rubbed his eyes from the stinging haze and saw tables of boisterous men and waitresses in skimpy costumes serving drinks. What kind of place was this?

Vito led Kane to a scarred table in front of a stage, and before Kane knew it, they each had a beer sitting in front of them. Kane hesitated. Beer and liquor were what made his old man get loaded and mean. Did grandpa want him to be like that?

"Is this for me, Grandpa?"

"Si, Kane, have a little. Won't hurt you."

Kane sensed he shouldn't tell Vito about his old man's drinking and how nasty he was when he did. So he kept quiet and took a sip while Vito watched. The taste was bitter, and Kane didn't like it.

"It's notta bad, eh?"

Kane smiled weakly and took a second swallow. It was still unpleasant, yet by the third and fourth sips, he'd gotten used to the amber liquid. Still, it wasn't to his liking.

Soon the house lights dimmed and erratic-sounding music, rising to a crescendo, splayed over the room. The men yelled, whistled, and banged their fists on the tables. After a drum roll, Kane saw a shadowy form coming from the back of the stage. A woman in a slouch hat, trench coat, wearing the highest-heeled shoes that Kane had ever seen came into view.

The men hooted and hollered.

Someone shouted, "FiFi! FiFi! Take it off. Take it off."

The room noise rose to fever pitch.

Kane wondered. Take off what?

The coat slid from the woman's shoulders onto the stage, the hat followed, and the woman named FiFi bent over and shook out her long auburn hair. With a boom of the drum and clash of cymbals, she was hit by a spotlight. Throwing back her head, Kane saw gray cat eyes, outlined in black, in a tawny-skinned face.

FiFi's tongue flicked like a snake's from between her ruby-colored lips. He gasped. She wore a lacey black bra from which small, creamy orbs rose, a pair of thigh-high black stockings, and a black pair of panties no bigger than something that a doll might wear.

Kane understood why his grandpa had been so mysterious. He'd brought him to a girlie show. Kane felt uncomfortable, yet he had to watch. He was enthralled by it all. This FiFi was the most beautiful woman he'd ever seen. And what she was doing---mama mia!

She bumped her hips out from side to side in time to the music, slinking toward the front of the stage where they sat. She rotated the lower half of her body. Bump went the right hip to the side---her pelvis pushed to the back---the left hip bumped out. Her pelvis pushed to the front as if she had a basketball in that little black triangle and was shooting a goal. The music beat a steady staccato. Da da boom went the drum, accenting each bump.

The bumps and grinds hypnotized him. He thought that he must be dreaming when FiFi leisurely removed her black bra to reveal egg-shaped breasts, each covered with a red tassel. The fringes twirled---first on one breast, then on the other, then both went round at the same time, first in one direction, then in the opposite---one to the right, the other to the left.

Wow! Kane's friend, Joey Masserli, had told him about a peep show his big brother had taken him to, but this was way better than that, and to top it off his grandpa had brought him. Kane understood why his mom and grandma would be furious if they knew he was here. He could hear them both saying that he was too young, but mostly that it was sinful and evil.

Out of the corner of his eye, Kane observed his grandpa. Vito was cheering the show along with the other men. Kane had never seen his grandpa have so much fun.

Slowly, FiFi shimmied down to the floor and sat on the stage. Legs wide open, knees slightly bent, she brought her right foot toward her crotch. Her left hand grasped the heel of her shoe and removed it. Then she reversed the process taking off her other shoe. But it didn't end there. Ever so gradually, she rolled down a stocking and removed it, holding one end of it on the floor with her toes, the other in a hand with long crimson nails.

The stocking off, she laid on her back, raised her hips and pulled the hosiery seductively up and down over her black panties.

She sat up and tossed the stocking off the stage. It landed on the bald head of a man wearing a polka dot bow tie. Wiping his sweaty brow, he pulled the stocking off his head, kissed it with a flourish, and stuffed it in his jacket pocket.

The second stocking received the same undulating treatment. This time when thrown, it landed in a mug of beer on a table near Vito and Kane, causing a near riot as the men fought for possession of the nylon.

Kane's mouth was bone dry. He licked his dry lips and took a big swig of beer and almost choked when he saw FiFi stand up and remove a tassel. The roar in the room was deafening. The pert breast, with its rosy nipple, was almost more than Kane could bear. FiFi flung the red tassel into a group of men who held up their hands trying to catch it.

Kane was so entranced by the jiggling breasts that he paid no attention where it landed. Then, plop, the second one landed right in his lap. He didn't know what to do. He wanted to touch it but was afraid. Blood rushed to his head. His heart beat in his ears.

His grandpa's elbow jabbed in his ribs. "Hey, Kane. That's yours."

A voice in the back of the room yelled, "Good going, kid."

A sly grin crossed Kane's face as he picked up the fiery-red tassel. A hint of strawberries emanated from it as he stroked the silkiness. Back on the stage, FiFi's eyes seemed to be smiling only at him. And then, she was gone. The stage dark. The show over.

Vito and Kane shuffled out of the room and down the long hallway. Kane gripped the sweet reward while Vito talked and laughed with the other men as they left.

Outside, Vito asked, "Did you like that show?"

Kane was speechless. Grinning from ear to ear, he looked at his grandfather and stuffed the tassel in his pocket. The red tassel and FiFi were all Kane could think about as he walked home, that and the secret he and his grandpa shared.

18

On occasion, Vito took Kane to dinner at Bella's on Taylor Street. These were Kane's favorite times. It was a treat having his grandpa to himself and to have a glass of wine which lately hadn't been served at home.

Tonight, as always, he and his grandpa sat in a corner facing into the room. A new waiter working for Bella had once tried to seat them in the middle of the room, and Vito became furious.

"Goddammit, everyone knows that's my table," said Vito, pointing with his cane to a corner where they now sat. Bella smoothed Vito's ruffled feathers, gave him a free dinner, and the seating blunder never happened again. Even Kane was wise enough to know his grandpa never sat with his back to a door when eating out or anywhere else. He needed to be able to see the whole room, who was in it, who was entering, and what they were doing.

Tonight, Kane felt like a grownup because his feet, that once dangled from the chair beneath the red and white checkered table cloth, touched the floor. He tapped his toes, waiting for Bella to appear and take their order. He surveyed the room with its embossed tin ceiling, candles stuck in wax-dripped Chianti bottles on each table, and bunches of artificial grapes hanging in the front window.

Finally, Bella's wide girth emerged from the kitchen and wiping her hands on her apron, she hurried to greet them.

"Vito, ciao. Sorry, I just learned you were here. Good to see you. It's been a while."

Vito rose, kissing both Bella's cheeks. "Ciao, Bella. You 'member Kane?"

"Of course, how could I forget such a handsome bambino?" She tousled Kane's wavy hair.

"The usual, Vito?"

Vito nodded. "Si, always the linguini with clam sauce, and Kane wants the special tortellini Bolognese."

Bella smiled at Kane, showing the space between her two front teeth, her hazel eyes twinkling. "Coming right up." She waddled back to the kitchen.

Kane and Vito sipped their wine waiting for the food to come. Soon the tortellini swimming in Bella's special marinara and the creamy linguini were being devoured by the two.

"It's good?" Vito asked between bites. Kane nodded. "Only your grandma makes better."

After the dinner plates were cleared, Bella set a cannoli in front of Kane while Vito lit up a thick cigar. Kane ate the tube-shaped dessert filled with creamy ricotta, and scrutinized his grandpa, trying to see the brutal eyes that he'd heard others say belonged to him. But all Kane saw was a man he adored. Vito puffed on the cigar, the smoke almost hiding his thick neck and bull-like head and shoulders.

Eventually, he spoke. "Now you getting older, I want ta spend more time with you. You a smart boy." Vito knocked ashes off his cigar. "I want ta start teachin' you. Helpin' you become a strong man, so you can help carry on tradition. Your mama and grandma might not approve cause women don't understand certain things. Capisce?"

Kane loved hearing the accent of the old country when his grandpa spoke, and tonight his words were making Kane feel proud. While Vito finished his smoke, Kane busied himself, noticing people at the surrounding tables. A man and woman holding hands and gazing into each other's eyes sat nearest to theirs. Old men, jabbering in Italian, sat on the other side. In an opposite corner was a lone diner. He was dressed in an inky black suit and kept staring at him. Kane was glad when the man left.

Finally, Vito smothered his cigar in the ashtray and pulled bills from his pocket, laying them on the table. "Let's get outta here."

He waved to Bella, who had come from the kitchen and was clearing a table. "Ciao, Bella."

As they walked out the door, Kane grabbed his grandpa's hand. Normally, Vito didn't like any show of affection, but tonight he was feeling mellow. It was dusk, that time when the sky has a copper glow after the sun has just fallen below the horizon. It was a pleasant evening walking hand in hand with his grandpa.

Kane noticed a woman with a small boy coming down the walk toward them. They each had a gelato. The mother a chocolate one, the child a strawberry. Pink streams were running down the arm of the child as he licked at his.

Suddenly, a rushing sound surrounded them and a midnight-blue sedan squealed down the street shattering the serenity. The car screeched to the curb, bounced to an abrupt stop, and out jumped two men. At that instant, Vito dropped Kane's hand and reached inside his tweed jacket, withdrawing a pistol. "Hit-a the ground, Kane."

Kane immediately did as he was told, at the same time hearing a pop-pop sound, a woman's scream, and a child's loud wail.

Daring to look up, Kane saw Vito grab his stomach and double over, falling to the sidewalk beside him. Kane didn't need to think twice. He picked up the gun lying next to his grandpa's head and fired at the men as they jumped back into the waiting car.

Pop! Pop! Ping! Ping! Bullets ricocheted off a nearby garbage can. The smell of car exhaust hung in the air as the sedan sped away. The woman, now quiet, was crouched over her sobbing son, shielding him, their gelato melting on the sidewalk.

With the gun dangling in his hand, Kane knelt over Vito who was bleeding profusely. "Grandpa? Grandpa!"

19

Vito had no choice in the matter. He was in the hospital where the doctors with their cotton-soft hands, whom he had always scoffed at and despised, worked frantically to save him. He'd been in the operating room for several hours. Maria grew more panicky with each sweep of the minute hand on the waiting room clock. Francesca, Kane, and Gino attempted to comfort her, trying not to let their own fears for their papa's and grandpa's life show.

"What are they doing? Why hasn't the doctor come out? He can't die," wept Maria.

"Papa's gonna be fine, Mama," said Gino. He put his arm around her shoulders and pulled her close.

Francesca squeezed Maria's hand. "That's right, Mama. Papa went through worse than this fighting your brothers and getting sliced up when you eloped from Naples. And remember when he got shot during that poker game when we were kids?"

Maria dried her teary eyes. "I know, but I took care of him those times. This time is different. I can't see him. I don't know what's going on. Besides, he's not cut up, He doesn't have a bullet in his thigh. This is more serious."

On the other side of his mother, Kane leaned forward to get a better view of his grandma. He touched her knee. "He'll be okay, Grandma. He has to be. And don't you worry. If I ever see those men again, they'll be the ones in the hospital. Either that or in the cemetery."

Horrified, Maria's tears flowed, coursing down her cheeks.

"Hush, Kane, don't talk like that," said Francesca. "You're upsetting your grandma."

Gino gave Kane a warning look. "Yeah, button the lip. "Besides," he said quietly, "a customer leavin' Bella's told the coppers one of those men clutched his chest as he got back in the car. You must have wounded one, maybe killed him. Knowing that should make you happy."

Kane didn't acknowledge Gino's remark. He hadn't seen the driver's face but was busy remembering the faces of the gunmen. He'd seen them for only an instant, but the face of one was burned into his memory. He would never forget the shock of carrot-red hair above the spoon-shaped ears of thc hit man. The ghastly man had tried to kill his grandpa. Someday ...

It was Gino's turn to earn a frown from Francesca. "Both of you be quiet. You're not helping the situation here." She returned to comforting her mother. "Don't pay any attention to them, Mama. They're just upset and saying stupid things."

Kane and Gino exchanged glances but didn't comment further because Dr. Ferrante, the surgeon, was walking through the double doors coming toward them.

"Mrs. Savio." The doctor stood before Maria and looked down in sympathy at the tiny woman with red-rimmed eyes. "Mrs. Savio, your husband's out of surgery. He lost a lot of blood, both before and during the operation. Surprisingly though, it seems the only damage from the gunshot was to the liver and the spleen. We were able to repair the liver, but we had to remove the spleen."

"Is he going to die? Am I going to lose my Vito?" Maria began to sob in earnest. Through her tears she said, "Please doctor, tell me the truth. I need to know."

Visons of her dear friend Nella losing her husband, Vito's cousin Lenny, raced through her mind. "Please, doctor, tell me that my Vito will be all right."

The doctor knelt down in front of Maria and took her hands in his. "We've done the best we could, Mrs. Savio. But frankly, your husband's condition is very grave. I can't answer your questions. Only time and the grace of God can do that.

Vito had lain in a coma for days. Despite her sons' and Francesca's pleadings, Maria never left his bedside, sleeping in an uncomfortable chair beside him. The only time she left the room was to go to the Saint Anthony Hospital chapel and pray. The children brought her food, although her appetite was lacking. They tried to persuade her to go home and get proper rest. They would stay with their papa, but Maria wouldn't budge.

One day she was awakened by a rustle and found a young, blonde priest beside Vito's bed.

"Father, you're early today," said Maria, trying to wake up fully.

"Mrs. Savio, Dr. Ferrante felt it necessary that I visit promptly. It seems your husband has taken a turn."

Now fully aware, Maria sprang to her feet. "What do you mean? Are you saying you're here to give my husband his last rites?"

"No. I'm here to perform the Sacrament of the Anointing of the Sick." The priest's eyes were soulful.

Maria drew herself up to her full four feet tren. "Father, that means my Vito may be nearing death, and he's not. He's getting better. There's no reason for your visit. I will *not* pray as if he's leaving me."

The young priest could see he'd distressed Maria. Because he was newly ordained and was not yet smooth or subtle in handling cases such as this, he wasn't sure what to do. He needed to soothe this woman before she became more upset, so he offered a suggestion. "Shall we at least say a prayer of thanksgiving, then?" He reached for Maria's hand, but she ignored it.

"Then do you mind if I say one by myself?"

"I do," said a weak voice from the bed.

"Vito, oh my darling, you're awake!" Maria pushed the priest aside.

Vito's eyes were open and his face exhibited faint color. She held his hand and he squeezed it, then whispered, "No thievin' priest is ... " Then his eyes closed.

With happy tears Maria looked upon the priest. "Father, thank you, but my husband won't be needing you." She made a shooing motion with her hand.

The priest, tongue-tied and at a loss as to what he'd just witnessed---perhaps he'd observed a miracle, scurried from the room in disbelief.

As soon as he was gone, Maria scrambled onto the bed beside Vito, rested her arm across his chest, her head next to his, careful to avoid the tubes connected to him.

As she drifted off to sleep, she thought she heard Vito whisper, "Grazie."

She smiled to herself, remembering Vito's blasphemy, saying that neither thievin' priests with their callous-free hands could forgive him, nor could her invisible God. That was her Vito, and she loved him.

Dr. Ferrante was amazed at how fast Vito was recovering after his near-death experience. "It's a miracle."

When he voiced this sentiment to Vito, Vito stared at the doctor with fierce eyes and said, "I ain't no miracle. Fuckin' gonna take more than a bullet to off me."

Doctor Ferrante announced he would release Vito at the end of the week. It wasn't a day too soon for the nurses on the floor.

"He should have left a week ago," said head nurse, Sister Mary John, to the doctor. "That man is driving us all crazy."

Dr. Ferrante shook his head. "I want to to be sure he's out of the woods before I discharge him."

"He's fine. Can't you send him on his way tomorrow?" pleaded Sister Mary John. "If he's not bellowing at us to wait on him, he's poking our backsides with that cane of his."

"That's easily solved. Put the cane where he can't reach it?"

"We tried that, doctor, but he disrupted the whole floor with his ranting until we had no recourse but to give it back to him."

Dr. Ferrante was unsympathetic. "Guess you'll have to endure his yelling or his poking for a few more days. So take your pick."

Pietro drove Maria to the hospital. Watching her son maneuver through the morning traffic, she couldn't help but recall his first car, the black Tin Lizzy. How she had vowed then to never ride with him. How scared she'd been for him, fearing he would have a wreck or kill someone every time he got behind the wheel. It had taken a long time, but she'd finally accepted the fact that he was a good driver, especially since he'd given up drinking alcohol.

Today, she relaxed against the plush seat of his sedan as they sped toward Saint Anthony's to pick up Vito. She was anxious to be with him. It was only the second time since their marriage that they had been apart for so long.

The other time had been when Lucia, their now incestuous daughter, and Tony, Lucia's first husband, had their car accident going to Milwaukee. Maria had spent weeks in Wisconsin, away from Vito, during Lucia's recovery.

After that fatal day, Maria had unabashedly confessed to Father Joseph that she was glad Tony was dead. It was imperative she tell the priest because she freely admitted all her sins. Well, almost all of them. She still harbored deep guilt for sending Vito, so long ago, to buy condoms. *That* sinful deed she would take to her grave.

She had prayed every day, after Vito had returned with the little packages, that she would be forgiven for going against the church. But there had been no other recourse. The doctor had said she might die if she birthed any more babies, and she wasn't about to give up making love with Vito.

"We're here, Mama, and there's Papa waiting for us."

Maria peered out the car window to see Vito in a wheelchair attended by a nurse. He was tapping his cane impatiently on the sidewalk. Maria's heart raced. It had been four long weeks since he'd been beside her in bed. She'd missed caressing the ropey scars on his chest that he'd received years ago, staving off her three brothers when they attempted to keep them from sailing to America.

It had taken time, but she no longer mourned her dead brothers, nor Donato, the lone survivor who'd come to Chicago with a vendetta against Vito. But instead of killing him, had unwittingly fallen in love with their daughter, his niece, Lucia.

Much to everyone's shock and dismay, headstrong Lucia and Donato vowed to marry, despite being related. That was the last Maria had seen of either of them.

And as Vito declared, "Good riddance."

When Pietro opened the car door for his mother, Vito bolted from the wheelchair, despite the nurse's attempt to hold him back.

"It's about time you fuckin' got here," he bellowed at Pietro. He jerked away from the nurse and hobbled into Maria's arms as she alighted from the car.

"Take me home." He stopped his outcry long enough to give Maria, whose eyes were wet with happiness, a quick kiss on her cheek.

"Next time let a me die before you bring me to this god awful place and its voodoo doctors. Capisce? Godadamn nurse had to wheel me out like a fuckin' cripple."

Vito shook his cane at the shocked nurse who was crossing herself against Vito's blasphemy. "See? Look at me. I ain't lame!"

Pietro shook his head. That was Papa. He helped his parents into the car and they drove away, Vito berating the nurses and doctors in absentia all the way home.

20

Fin and Francesca lolled in the sun. It had been three months since Fin had returned from rehab with Dr. Boyle. Michael felt they needed to get away and have time to together without the children, so he had suggested they use the Michigan house for a week. Since they'd never had a honeymoon or vacation of any kind, they were making every minute count.

They picnicked in Warren Woods at Kane's suggestion, had gone fishing, and now lounged side by side on the grassy slope overlooking the placid lake. Francesca hadn't been this happy in ages.

"I'm proud of you, Fin, for staying dry. Things have been so much better. You're a different person when you're sober, the man I fell in love with. I think even Kane might be coming round, believing in your sobriety.

Fin reached for Francesca's hand. "It's not easy, but I'm trying." He drew Francesca closer to him on the grass and began kissing her ardently. Before they knew it, they were undressing each other.

In one sane moment, Francesca whispered, "We should go into the house." Fin put a finger on her lips and went down on her. After that, neither cared who saw them. With his lips, Fin caressed every inch of her, from her neck to her stomach, her inner thighs, behind her knees until soon she was weak and quivering.

Recently, their lovemaking had been over in minutes, but now they both luxuriated in the feel of being one---moaning---feeling pleasure. Francesca's back arched. Her nostrils flared, a signal to Fin that she was ready. They cried out together, staying entwined for several minutes, then rolled away from each other.

Francesca smiled, languidly. "We're shameless."

"But wasn't it wonderful?"

"Wouldn't your mother absolutely die, if she knew we'd been out here naked on the lawn making love?"

"It's sure not something that I can see her doing ... ever. But then, I don't think she and dad have been together in years."

"Really? How sad. Maybe that's what's wrong with her. Needs a good roll in the hay."

They both giggled. "Well, that's not what's wrong with us," said Fin, hugging her again, his mouth insatiably on hers.

Fin was right. Michael and Meghan hadn't made love since shortly after Fin's birth when Meghan gave her ultimatum---no more sex because she wanted no more babies. Where once Michael had hoped she'd feel differently, he had finally accepted that she would never change her mind. He had remained faithful for years until Ireland Coogan came into his life.

He had also grown to accept Meghan's strange practices. The thing that concerned him now was that she had taken Kane under her wing. He knew Vito was attempting to do the same. Let them duke it out. Both were strong-willed individuals, trying to guide Kane's life to their own way of thinking.

Michael had no inkling who might come out on top. Maybe neither would. He just hoped Kane would stay grounded and not go off on wild and unlawful tangents as he'd done in the past. He had already dented a car with a bat, stolen a coat, and shot at Vito's assailants. Those incidents perturbed Michael. But at the moment, even those worries were distant because he was anticipating dinner that evening with Ireland.

Meghan was happy. While Fin and Francesca were in Michigan, the children would be staying with her and Michael. Meghan could do without Chiara, but having Kane to herself for a week thrilled her. And it was exhilarating because during the time Kane would be be with her the summer solstice would occur. She planned to share this important event at Lake Michigan with her grandson. All she had to do was talk her aunt into keeping Chiara so she and Kane could be alone during the event.

Meghan found Kitty in the sunroom arranging roses. Chicago was having an early heat wave, so instead of brewing tea, Kitty had made a pitcher of iced tea for Meghan. It sat on the table beside a plate of lemon cookies. Kitty poured glasses of tea but resumed filling containers with her garden blooms that she would later take to shut-ins.

Meghan praised her aunt for her thoughtfulness, then excitedly told Kitty of the children's visit and explained that she wanted to share the summer solstice with Kane at Lake Michigan.

"Oh, so you're not having your usual backyard bonfire that is burned for protection against the evil spirits that roam when the sun turns southward?" Kitty swatted at a fly with her hand.

"No. We'll just welcome the dawn because I know the people at the Adler Planetarium wouldn't appreciate the blaze of a fire. Me neighbors will probably be glad I'm gone and not smoking up the neighborhood."

Kitty laughed. "You're right about that."

Meghan bit into one of the cookies and washed it down with a sip of tea. "Welcoming the solstice will be a good experience for Kane."

"Meghan, I think you should take Chiara. She'd find it interesting." Kitty finished arranging the flowers and sat down.

"I'm sure she would, but I want this to be a special time for only Kane and me. Please? Can't Chiara stay with ye?"

Kitty didn't wish to quarrel with her niece. "Of course, I'll keep the darling girl. The parish is having its annual outing to Pioneer Woods. I'm sure Chiara will find that to be fun."

"It's to ward off the evil eye and unwanted spirits," said Meghan as she watched Kane hang dried calendulas and basil on the front door for her. "Alban Hefin is what Druids call the summer solstice."

"Alvin what?"

Meghan laughed. "Not Alvin ... Alban. Alban Hefin. It means The Light of the Shore."

"Oh, so is that why we're going to Lake Michigan?" asked Kane.

Meghan was pleased Kane was showing an interest in what she had planned for them. "Yes. Being at the water is like being between worlds. Meaning it's where earth, sea, and sky meet. There is great power there. I have a deep reverence for such places."

"What's so great about the summer solstice, anyway. It's just another day."

"No, it isn't. It happens to be the longest day of the year. A time some people actually feel sad because the sun's strength is waning, and the days are getting shorter. The year is winding down. It's the cycle of life ... a time of death and rebirth."

"That's silly. There's still half a year left. It's too early to feel it's nearly over. Does this time of year make *you* sad?"

"Not at all."

"Okay, I think I get it. But what I don't get, is why we're going to camp out behind the planetarium tonight, just so we can watch the sunrise over the lake in the morning."

Meghan's voice was enthusiastic. "Because witnessing the dawn of the summer solstice signifies a new time and season, the beginning of summer. Watching the sun peek over the lake, seeing it slowly rise until it just clears the horizon is a moment of wonder."

"Sounds like a blast."

"A blast?"

"Yeah, a good time."

"Ye and yer talk." Meghan's voice was serious. "Well, more than a good time, it's a time of awe. A time for us to meditate and commune with nature in a different way from what we do in Michigan. It's serious, yet joyful. I want ye to experience it that way. Understand?"

"Yeah, sure," said Kane. He looked at his handiwork on the front door. "Hey, aren't you allergic to marigolds?"

"They don't bother me if they're dried. Come. We better hurry or we'll miss the bus. If we do, we'll be stuck waiting an hour before another comes along."

As they rushed to the bus stop, Meghan noticed how tall Kane was getting, but why was Francesca allowing him to wear those wrinkled black pants and that hideous white tee shirt? He looked like a bum. And it was too hot for that leather jacket.

"Kane, what on earth have ye done to yer hair? It looks greasy. Like it needs a good washing."

"Oh, Grandma Cal, it's not dirty. Has Brilliantine on it. It's a hair product. Helps keep my duck's butt in place." He turned around. "See?"

"It's a what?"

"Well, Mom calls it a duck tail. Says it sounds nicer."

Meghan saw it did, indeed, look like a duck's rear end. "Why would ye want to do that to ye nice hair? It's disgusting. Take that comb sticking out of ye back pocket and get rid of it. And why do ye make yer hair so high on yer forehead like a pompadour?"

"Haven't you ever seen a James Dean movie? "

"No, I haven't." Meghan's attention was suddenly drawn to a somewhat older boy with well-groomed hair, who had just walked up to the bus stop. "There, ye need to look like him."

The boy wore nice trousers, a shirt with a button-down collar, and penny loafers with argyle socks, unlike Kane's white socks and black shoes."

"Ugh, he's Ivy League. I don't want to dress like him. James Dean's my idol. In fact, Grandma Cal, you'd probably like him. I read he's into the occult. Talks to the ghost of his dead mother."

The bus pulled up and they boarded. Meghan wasn't sure what the world was coming to, but it seemed to be to no good end if boys dressed as Kane did. After several stops, they alighted from the bus and walked past the Field Museum, to the planetarium situated at the tip of Northerly Island.

No one bothered Meghan and Kane as they strode behind the building and found, what Meghan considered, the perfect spot. There were no trees so they settled near the building where they'd be protected when night fell. Then next morning, they would have a clear view of the horizon across the lake.

It was an ideal day to sit in the sun. The vibrant blue sky was cloudless. Boats sailed in the distance, and waves splashed against the black boulders at the shoreline as power boats passed causing a wake that soothed Kane. Even the fishy-smell blowing in on the gentle breeze didn't offend him. "This is nice."

Meghan had packed a picnic and both had brought books to read until daylight grew too dim. Reading outside in the sun was a good way to connect with nature, Meghan had told him. After their dinner of meatloaf sandwiches and potato salad, they searched the sooty sky, picking out the stars they knew.

Then Meghan took out the Baby Ben alarm clock in the bottom of the food basket and set it to wake them before dawn. But when it was time to sleep, she was restless and sleep eluded her. On the night of the solstice, Meghan always felt tranquil.

Tonight she experienced no peace. Even after meditating, she felt unsettled. She shivered despite the day's heat. Something about the planetarium was sending strange vibrations, making her uncomfortable. She had no way of knowing what her senses were picking up. That this was the very place Michael had become adulterous---where he and Ireland had first made love.

"Michael, I'm so excited! I've never been inside the Palmer House before. Have only walked past."

Michael pulled up the car in front of the hotel's bronze canopy, and a doorman opened Ireland's door. She looped her arm through Michael's as they entered the opulent beige and green marble lobby.

"This takes my breath away." Ireland gazed at the painted ceiling with its Greek mythological scenes and gold leaf trim. "Oh, my! There's gold everywhere. It's like a palace."

Michael reveled in her child-like awe. The bronze sconces and crystal chandeliers glittered as they crossed the lobby and ascended the stairs to the Empire Room.

"Are you sure I'm dressed okay? It looks terribly swanky." She eyed the Tiffany-designed candelabras of winged-angels on either side of the staircase, then at her simple, black sheath dress. She fingered the pearls at her throat, a recent gift from Michael.

"My darling, you look as elegant as the room. You're going to put all those doyens to shame. I'm just sorry Ella Fitzgerald is ill and her show's been canceled."

Michael opened the door and watched Ireland walk into the restaurant, hair and hips swaying seductively from side to side. The first time he saw her, she had reminded him of a brown bird. Tonight she was a beautiful swan. He was proud that she was his and couldn't help being excited. They hadn't even eaten dinner and already he wanted to hold and make love to her.

After he and Ireland were seated and their food order given, he looked at her intently. "I never thought I'd be this happy again. You've changed my life. You know that, don't you? I just wish things were different and we could be together always."

"I don't think either of us knew what we were getting into all those years ago when we accidentally met and made love. I know you were upset with Meghan that night and needed an outlet. I had no excuse, I just wanted you."

They were interrupted by the wine sommelier's arrival presenting the aged bottle of French wine that Michael had requested. The sommelier poured a taste into Michael's glass. He swirled it and took a sip. "Excellent."

When they were alone again, Michael lifted his glass and they toasted. "Here's to us and tonight," he said. "Speaking of that first time ... it was at the planetarium, remember?"

"How could I ever forget that wonderful, unexpected night." Their eyes locked like magnets remembering how they had devoured each other on the lawn over twelve years ago.

"That evening is what tonight is all about."

"What do you mean?" Ireland took a sip of wine.

"This is the anniversary of that very first time." Michael reached for her hand.

"Michael, you are so sentimental. It's a shame your wife doesn't appreciate you. But thanks to her, I'm the lucky one. I'm ecstatic that we have the entire night to be together. Why is that, anyway?"

"Well, Francesca and Fin are in Michigan, and we're keeping the kids. Meghan's busy with Kane this evening and will be until after dawn tomorrow. They'll never miss me because they're celebrating the summer solstice all night in the backyard as Meghan always does.

"What about Chiara? Where is she?"

"Kitty's keeping her. So I'm a free man. Come, let's not ruin the evening talking about that. This is our night."

"Where are we going? You're not heading in the right direction for my apartment."

"You're right. I'm not," said Michael steering the Cadillac south on Lake Shore Drive.

"Michael, are you going where I think you are?" Ireland gasped as they turned off onto Northerly Island.

"Of course I am. What would an anniversary be without going back to the scene of the crime?"

He pulled the car up in front of the Adler Planetarium, turned off the lights, and cut the motor. He got out and opened the door for Ireland, taking her hand. "Come. Let's go for a walk."

Hand in hand they strolled down the sloping lawn to the edge of the water and looked toward the city skyline. "Lake Michigan's so beautiful tonight, but then so are you," said Michael, taking her in his arms and finding her lips.

He removed his jacket and placed it on the ground. "Here, sit down."

"Are we? Should we?" asked Ireland feeling confused.

"I don't know one reason why we shouldn't," said Michael sitting down beside her. "However, I'm a lot older since the first time we made love here, so you might have to help me back up this time around."

He loosened his tie and unbuttoned his shirt. "It's quiet and no one's around. Besides, I could barely finish dinner for thinking about this."

Once again, as on that night so long ago, they wildly threw off their clothes and became one.

Behind the planetarium, Meghan awoke with a jolt.

21

Vito was sitting on the front stoop when Kane arrived. "It's about time. I come home from hospital, and I no see you."

"Sorry, Grandpa," Kane hugged the old man, kissed both his cheeks and sat down beside him. "Lots goin' on. Then Mom and Dad were in Michigan, and ChiChi and I stayed with Grandpa and Grandma Cal. I've been pretty busy."

"Humph," said Vito. "That bitch's probably feeding ya all kinds a *cazzate*! Don't listen to her. She's a full of it! "

Vito emphasized the last words by beating his cane on the step. Though he had no idea what Meghan was really all about, Vito only knew from the few times he'd been around her that she was an Irish bitch and a snob and was trying to get her hooks in Kane.

Kane put his arm around Vito's shoulder and laughed. "Cool it, Grandpa. Don't get so cranked. It's not good for your blood pressure. Grandma Cal probably thinks you're full of shit too."

A darkness crossed Vito's face, and Kane quickly changed the subject. "So how are you feeling these days? I see you're using two canes."

"I'm feelin' fine. Yeah, I'm a two stick man since the shootin'. Legs ain't as strong as they used to be. Damn arthritis tryin' to slow a me down. Ain't workin'. Can move twice as fast with two canes."

And have an extra weapon in the process, thought Kane.

"You, my boy," said Vito, looking with pride at his grandson, "were *coraggioso*. Shootin' at those men. How you know to do that? You know gats?"

Kane shrugged. "Just my toy guns, Grandpa. I didn't think about being brave. It seemed natural for me to pick up that pistol and shoot. Funny thing, I wasn't even scared. Somehow, I just knew what I needed to do, and I did it."

Vito was silent for a long time as if mulling over Kane's words. "How old you now?"

"Twelve, Grandpa."

"Hmmm, I think it's time I teach you."

"Teach me what?"

"Knife fighting. Like I learned in Sicily. After school, every day, you be here for an hour. We'll begin."

Vito stood in the middle of the backyard with his feet planted firmly on the ground. One cane lay on the ground beside him, the other was inside a hollow, metal pipe that Kane, on Vito's instructions, had driven into the ground.

Vito swiveled this way and that. "Works good Now I can turn fast as you."

Kane, his back to the alley, facing the house, waited for his first lesson. He saw his grandma peering out the window and knew she wasn't happy with what was happening.

A few days earlier, he'd heard her ask his grandpa, "What are you trying to do, make another you?" Kane didn't hear his grandpa's reply, but from his vantage point, Kane saw the frown on his grandma's face.

His mother wasn't thrilled about the training either, but she kept quiet. Both women knew they had no control over Vito. No one controlled him. He would do what he wanted.

From the empty lot down the street, Kane heard the thwack of a bat hitting a baseball and in the distance the rumble of the elevated train taking people home from work. He waited, anticipating his grandpa's next move.

Vito cast an eye on Kane and thought---like me, he's not afraid of nuthin'. That's good. He's smarter than me. That's better. With my lessons and his brain, he can be all.

"Let's begin," said Vito. "'First, always 'member never let your will be bent. If a you do, you lose power, control. Now, to fighting. Taunt your enemy. Show no mercy. And don't be afraid to kill if it means your life. When ready to stab, never pause. Capisce?"

Kane nodded knowingly, but he wasn't sure he did.

"Okay, there are several ways to kill. Never try with just a stab. Do like this---a block, quick cut, then the stab." Vito demonstrated the moves to Kane.

"When you make the stab, thrust the blade deep and twist this way and that." Vito turned his hand to the right, then back to the left. "This causes harm to man's insides. Wound bleeds less. Not look bad on outside, but is.

"Another way," said Vito, "make lots quick small cuts to the soft parts of body. Above waist or right below. Don't aim at chest or boney areas, blade might bounce. Go for arm veins, main arteries. Keep cutting 'til enemy bleeds. Strength will flow with blood. When he's weak, arm will drop. Then quick lunge, stab, and he's *morto*. Capisce?"

Kane's head swam with all the information.

"Okay, we go slow. I teach one move until you get it. Then we do 'nother. We use these as if they are real."

Vito held up two wooden knives. "Each Friday, I give test. I'll see if you learned."

The hot sun beat on the gangland graffiti scrawled on the wall lining the alley as the lessons began. Every week thereafter, Vito rarely said a word except to give initial directions for thrusting, blocking, slicing, and stabbing. At first, Kane's movements were stiff and slow, but as days passed, he became more nimble and lighter on his feet.

In the Savios' bustling neighborhood, the lessons were never private. Next door, Mrs. Giocomelli, an Italian yenta, made it a point to hang out her wash during the lessons. With clothespins in her mouth, she'd watch the proceedings.

Tony Boy and Eddie LaFont, Kane's friends, lingered in the alley, whistling and calling, "Get 'em, Kane. Go get 'em."

Just you wait, thought Kane, you won't be cheering if you're ever on the other side of my knife. Even Kane's boy cousins, Colin and Tommy, watched jealously from under a tree and put in their two cents from time to time. Kane paid no attention to the outside audience and their sideline remarks, but they grated on Vito's nerves.

When he'd had enough of the shouts and peering eyes, he'd halt the lessons, pick up his cane, and swing it wildly above his head, yelling, "Godadammit! Getta outa here!"

Every Friday, Vito tested Kane on the lessons of the week. In the beginning, Kane went home with a puffed chest from his grandpa's praises for a job well done. Soon, however, moves became more difficult, and the next weeks' assessments didn't go so well.

"Didn't I teach you nuttin'?" roared Vito, his eyes dark. He brought his fist down hard on the top of Kane's head in disgust, as if trying to drive the lesson home. Then grumbling and cursing under his breath, he hobbled away. Despite the headaches that Kane endured, he never felt defeated. He'd show his grandpa.

Weeks passed, and Kane began darting more swiftly and moving closer and closer to his grandpa as he cut and stabbed.

And each week, Vito reminded him and pointed to the inside of his thigh where an artery was located, "this can be cut if enemy kicks and leaves exposed."

Kane learned of other vulnerable spots that would stay his enemy, such as the genitals, mouth, and eyes.

While Kane and his grandpa fought, the aroma of marinara always curled out into the yard from his grandma's kitchen because when the lessons, that she despised, were over, she wanted to feed Kane. It was her way.

One Friday, when shadows were lengthier and the graffiti on the alley wall was no longer in the sun, and the baseball games had turned to football, it happened. As Vito and Kane fought with their fake stilettos, Kane saw his grandpa's wrist and arm drop.

Kane stabbed and cried, "You're dead, Grandpa!"

With that, Vito threw down his pseudo weapon, took up his canes, and headed for the house, calling, "Get two gallons of wine from the house and wait for me by the front stoop."

In a few minutes, Vito appeared, having exchanged his sweaty work shirt for a clean one and carrying a box tucked under his arm. He motioned for Kane to follow him.

Vito made his way, canes tapping on the cement and swaying like a drunken sailor, down the sidewalk toward the corner. Into the next block, Kane carrying the jugs of wine followed as Vito turned toward a house.

Primo Rolozzi and some Mustached Petes sat on the front steps, smoking their cigars and fraternizing. Vito beamed with pride, gave a thumbs up, pointed to Kane, and sat down by his friends. Primo brought out glasses from inside the house. Vito poured wine all around and raised his glass. "For Kane, *mi nipote*, and his machismo."

"To Vito's grandson," Rolozzi shouted. They gathered around Kane hugging and kissing him. They continued drinking and toasting Kane until the jugs were empty. Kane radiated happiness. He was a man!

After a while, Vito withdrew the mysterious box from its resting place on the step beside him and held it out to Kane. "For three hundred years, this been in the family. Take it. It's yours. Never forget ... it's to be used with honor."

Kane took the box, running his fingers over the top, feeling the smooth polished wood. He raised the lid and saw, nestled in worn blue velvet, an ivory-handled stiletto. He stroked the cold handle, took it from its resting place, and flipped out the blade, turning the long, slender piece of steel with its needle-like point, over and over, looking at the deadly---double-edged----finely-honed weapon. Holding up the nine-inch knife for all to see, Kane smiled. The evening star sparkled and winked in the dusky sky as Vito and his goombas raised their glasses for one last toast.

"To Kane and his machismo!"

22

When Gino and Carlo entered Fazio's, Vito was warming a stool at the far end of the bar and yelling for his usual Mickey Mouse---beer with a whiskey chaser. They acted as if they didn't see their papa and sauntered to a table in the corner under which Cato, the bar dog, slept. When the men sat down, the old dog awoke and lumbered away to the next empty table. Fazio, per usual, was wiping down the bar.

"I bet that cloth Fazio's using is as old as he is," said Gino. The brothers hooted, eyeing the dirty rag the gray-headed owner was plying. Camilla, Fazio Junior's wife, overheard the remark as she served their beers, and the lines around her blue eyes crinkled as she joined in the hilarity.

"Disgusting is the word," she said, making a face. "Junior keeps trying to throw it away, but it somehow reappears. Seems to be attached to his old man. One of these days he'll retire, then things will change around here."

She watched her father-in-law behind the bar. "He's really tired, but he won't give up. Says he'd have nothing to do all day. This is his life. He likes talking to everybody. Your papa sure doesn't like talking much, though, does he? Not even to you two."

"Well, Papa never has let us sit at the bar with him. Don't really know why, but that's Papa," said Carlo.

After Camilla walked away, Gino said, "What do you think Pietro has on his mind?"

"I don't know, but I wish the fuck he'd get here. I gotta be back at the Tip Top for my evening shift." Carlo looked anxiously toward the door.

"I haven't asked in a while, how's it going there anyway? "

"Same as always. I've never gotten used to those snobs, but they do have deep pockets and like to gamble on the dice games I throw out on the bar."

"Are you makin' a lot of extra bread bartendin'?"

Carlo shook his head.

"My poker winnings are slim too, since the Chez Paree closed," said Gino. "I still play with the boys, but it ain't the same, somehow. Need to find better games. Maybe we should go back to the track."

"Sure," said Carlo, "and lose our shirts again? You fuckin' couldn't pick a winner if your life depended on it. Remember when you bet the horse that died right out of the gate?"

"Guess you're right, but I sure loved it there. Once I got used to the smell, that is. Well, okay, but there's got to be something more. Need to come up with some scheme. Another thing, I hear rumblings 'round town," said Gino, "the Allerton might close soon. We should look for another place to live before we're booted out."

"Fine with me. Told you in the beginnin', I didn't need the fancy life. Won't bother me to move." Carlo kept eyeing the door. "Is that brother of ours ever going to get here?" He nervously played with his drink mug. "I can always go back tendin' bar and livin' at Jimmy's. I'd like that better, anyways. Never enjoyed the Allerton. Finally," said Carlo, looking up.

Pietro came through the door and rushed over. After greeting each other, they sat down and ordered more beer with the exception of Pietro. "You still aren't drinkin'?" Gino looked surprised.

Pietro shook his head. "Naw, gettin' more temptin' every day, though. But I didn't come here to talk about that." He took a sip of the root beer in front of him. "Not sure ya knows, but my truckin' business ain't legit anymore."

Gino and Carlo looked at each other. "I heard rumors it was a front. Guess they wuz true. Huh? What's goin' down?" asked Gino in a loud voice.

"Shhh, stuff it," warned Pietro. "Hasn't been legit since Sylvia's old man kicked the bucket."

Carlo fidgeted. "Get to the point, I needa get outta here. Why did you call this meetin'?" He looked at his watch.

Pietro took a swig of root beer. "Godadammit, Carlo, don't be so *impoziente*. Right now, Gino, to answer ya, it's a front for swag and chop shop operations, but I'm headed for somethin' bigger. Hey, you know Papa's finally off the street. Retired. No more doin' shake downs."

Gino nodded. "Yeah, arthritis got him pretty bad, 'specially since that shooting."

"I still feel guilty about him ever gettin' involved," frowned Carlo. "If I hadn't been a stupid kid and stole from the book, then went on the lam leavin' Papa to pay my debt, he would've stayed straight. Wouldn't have gotten shot."

"Don't beat yourself up," said Pietro. He motioned for Camilla to bring another round. "Papa liked doin' what he did. I've heard more'n once that he left the old country to save his skin. Sooner or later he woulda been sucked back in, with or without your help."

Their conversation ceased as Camilla approached with the drinks. Pietro tossed a ten-dollar tip on her tray, and Gino's eyes grew big. After Camilla left he said, "Whoa, a sawbuck. You must really be doin' good."

Pietro ignored the remark and leaned over the table closer to his brothers and talked in a whisper. Looking at Gino, he said, "I come with something big. Sigari says Ricca wants you for a wheelman."

Gino looked stunned. "Me? Well, I do like to drive. But a getaway car? For the Outfit? Not so sure about that." He smoothed his newly-grown mustache with a thumb and index finger. "Besides, I thought Sam Giancana was their driver. I'm not a violent person like he is. Why would they want me? You two are the fighters. You wouldn't think twice about killin'. Wouldn't even need to be liquored up to do it neither."

Gino looked at Pietro. “In fact, you and Carlo have never shied away from a fight. Most times you start ‘em.” Gino gave Carlo’s shoulder a friendly punch. The three men laughed.

“But what do you mean Paul Ricca wants me? Thought his parole was on condition he didn’t associate with the Outfit. Isn’t that the reason his ten year sentence for tryin’ to control Hollywood movies in ’47 was shortened?”

“Yeah, the labor racketeerin’ and extortion of the film studios, gaining control of the Projector’s Union, and threatenin’ strikes and other labor problems put him away. But don’t be a jamook, Gino. Do you really think Ricca’s not involved anymore? Ever since that sentence and then his second one for tax evasion, he’s stayed in the background. Same as Accardo who was acting boss for Ricca.

The IRS has been giving Accardo a rough time, so he’s layin’ low, too. He and Ricca still share the power, though. Don’t think otherwise. Giancana’s the front boss only. Does nothing without their say, especially whack jobs.”

Gino had been chewing on Pietro calling him a jamook. Now he piped up, “Oh, so, I’m a jamook. A lame brain, am I? Must not be too dumb if they want me to take over driving in Momo’s place.”

Carlo was growing antsy. “Get to the point, I needa get outta here. What does this have to do with me?”

“Well, seems you’ve been fingered to .... “

“Hey, hold on a fuckin’ minute. Are you a button?” asked Carlo.

“No, I’m not a wise guy yet, but soon I’ll be one. Gonna be a made man. Ceremony’s comin’ up,” Pietro looked proud. “Then, I’ll be on my way.”

Gino shook his head at Pietro’s statement. “Like I said, you ain’t afraid to kill.”

Carlo glanced at his watch. “I don’t have time for this. Let’s talk later.” He pushed back his chair and was gone before Pietro had a chance to respond.

“Well, Gino, what do you say to the offer?” Pietro drained his drink and took a cigar from his pocket. He rolled it over looking at it, drew it under his nose for a smell, pinched the end off with his front teeth, and spit the remnant over his shoulder.

"I need to think on it. Sure as hell ain't gonna be able to walk in Momo's shoes."

"Fuck, nobody could do that. Giancana's one of a kind." Pietro lit the end of the cigar and puffed a minute to get it going. "Don't wait too long to give your answer. The guys in the Outfit don't like ta be kept waitin'. By the way, I think you and Carlo need to spend more time with Kane. Papa says we need to start grooming him."

The next day, Gino was driving around the neighborhood and saw Kane pedaling his bike down the street after school. He stopped the car and said he had time to teach Kane about cards.

Now sitting at the Savios' kitchen table, Kane observed as Gino spun the cards out and made them come back with ease.

"Wow! Uncle G, you've got strong hands."

"Here, this is the right way," said Gino demonstrating.

"Think you've got it?"

Kane nodded and Gino handed him the deck. "Okay, your turn."

"Here I go. I'm washing the cards," said Kane, scrambling the deck on the table.

"Good," said Gino. Kane omitted spinning the cards out. He packed the deck and split it in two, keeping the cards horizontal to the table. Then he put his index fingers on top, and his ring and middle fingers on the sides near the back of each stack. Bringing the cards at an angle with the corners nearest him touching, he slid his thumbs to the corners, flattened his fingers on top, and rippled the corner of the cards together.

"Nice shuffle. Keep practicin'. The object is to be able to do it in a smooth, quick motion."

After a while, Kane put down the cards. "I'm tired of this."

"You can't stop, you've only done fifty. You have fifty more to do."

"But Uncle G, isn't that enough for today? Why do I have to shuffle a hundred times anyway?"

"The more you practice the slicker and faster you'll be. But don't forget to watch the clock, we've only forty-five minutes before your grandma gets home from church. You know we can't let her see what we're doin'."

"Okay, but let me rest a minute. Why don't you teach me how I can tell if someone's cheating? Then I'll shuffle some more."

"I'll agree to that. First, pick up a card and feel it real good. See if you notice anything."

Kane fingered both sides of a king. "Strange. I don't think the sides are the same. They feel different for some reason. "

"You're right. This is called a low decker. The back of the card is laminated differently from the front. You'll never see it, but when someone is dealin' from the bottom of the deck, you gotta listen real close and you can hear a whisper. Even if they're a shark, you'll be able to pick it out."

Gino took the cards and started dealing. "Listen and tell me to stop if you hear anything."

Gino dealt four hands without Kane saying a word. Midway through the fifth, he shouted, "There! Was that a whisper?"

"Good ears. Let's do a few more, then get back to your shuffling."

Kane and Gino were so absorbed in the lesson that they failed to hear Maria come down the steps to the kitchen.

"What! What is this I see?" Maria's eyes shot fire at her favorite son. "So, you're teaching Kane cards, leading him astray?"

"No, Mama ... "

"It's okay, Grandma. It's okay. It was my idea. I asked Gino to teach me." Kane rushed to hug and kiss his grandma.

"Well, I don't like it," said Maria. Gino got up to kiss her, but she turned her face away, and instead hit him up the side of the head. "First your papa's teaching him knife fighting, and now you're teaching cards. What'll be next?"

Maria gave Gino a knowing look and bopped him on the head again. "You think you've been fooling me all these years? I know you gamble."

Maria's eyes softened when she looked at Kane. " I don't want Gino's bad ways rubbing off on you, my sweet."

"Don't worry, Grandma, we were just passing time 'til you got home. No reason to be upset." Kane gave Gino a wink and replaced the cards in their box.

"I can see I'll be needing to make a special novena with the likes of this going on. Now get out of my way you two, I need to start supper. Will you be staying, Kane?"

"Sure, Grandma, that'd be nice." Kane knew cooking was his grandma's way. She was always urging, "*Mangia*! *Mangia*!" Filling stomachs was her mission and an apron her normal attire, unless she left the house.

"How about you, Gino? You staying?"

His response was lost in the clatter of pots and pans because Maria was already starting the evening meal. But she knew he wasn't going anywhere. He'd never miss a chance to indulge in her lasagna.

23

Gino caved and against his better judgment acquiesced to become Giancana's wheelman, but that's not the only thing he gave in to. Against all odds, yet knowing it was imperative for his own well-being with the Outfit, as well as his relationship with Lonzo Gabbelli, he put an engagement ring on Arriana Gabbelli's plump left hand.

Gino hoped the gesture would be enough to stave off Lonzo's pressure to marry his daughter, at least for a while. Besides getting Gino his city job of overseeing a street crew, it seemed Lonzo was now running the Outfit's gambling operation. By putting a sparkler on squinty-eyed Arriana, Gino hoped to insure his safety when he ran up large gambling debts at the mob's secret poker games around town.

While Gino was proposing to Arriana, whose guitar-shaped body he'd become blind to because it satisfied him more than any shapely broad's ever had, brother Pietro was embarking upon another type of engagement.

It was late night at the Armory Lounge that was Sam Giancana's informal mob headquarters in the Chicago suburb of Forest Park. Here in the basement of the nondescript building on the north side of Roosevelt Road, Pietro was about to become a made man.

Seeing Pietro's dedication to the mob, how efficiently he ran the chop shop and fencing operation, but also what a mean bastard he was, Sigari DeCassio, along with Johnny *The Snake* Bucelli, had invited Pietro to become a member of the Chicago crime family.

Mob eyes had been watching Pietro for several years as to his loyalty and ability to bring in money to the organization, and now the men who had submitted his name were sure that he could be relied upon. Otherwise, DeCassio's and Bucelli's lives would be snuffed out if Pietro turned out to be a bad choice.

The mobsters had dined upstairs in the restaurant before they adjourned to the basement where initiation rites were to be conducted. Usually, more than one initiate at a time was made, but this evening there was only Pietro.

The men, including Sam Giancana, Paul Ricca, Tony Accardo, *Big Tuna* as he was often called, Sigari DeCassio, Johnny Bucelli, and other capos were drinking wine around a large table.

Pietro stood. In front of him on the table was a gun crossed with a sword. They symbolized what from now on he would be living and dying by--- the gat and the blade.

Ricca rose and began reciting, "Omerta is a code of silence and honor and is not to be treated lightly. The main concept is to take the law into your own hands and to betray authority. Your allegiance must be to us. If there is deceit, there will be death. You have proved your loyalty by certain crimes which you've committed but will go unnamed here.

"Furthermore, there are rules. You must pledge to be a stand up guy, meaning you show courage and heart and will not whine or complain in the face of adversity. When we call, you will leave what you are doing and come at once. You will keep your mouth shut and your ears open. You will never steal. You must respect women and not mess around with wives, sisters, or girlfriends that belong to family members."

All the men formed a circle as Pietro, standing in the middle, recited his vows.

"I, Pietro Joseph Alighieri Savio, want to enter into this organization to protect my family and to protect all of my friends. I swear not to divulge this secret and to obey with love and Omerta."

Ricca pricked Pietro's trigger finger. "This drop of blood symbolizes your birth into our family. We are one until death."

The blood was smeared on a prayer card with the image of a saint and placed in Pietro's cupped hands, then it was set on fire as he vowed, "As burns this saint so will burn my soul. I enter alive into the organization, and I will go out dead."

With the exclusion of Pietro, the men clasped hands, forming a tie-in. Ricca said, "In honor of our brotherhood I untie the knot."

The men dropped hands. Pietro joined the circle and held hands with the men, remaking the circle.

Ricca declared, "In honor of our brotherhood, I tie the knot."

The ceremony over, Pietro was welcomed with a kiss from all on each cheek. At last, his goal of becoming a wise guy, a member of the Outfit, was reality.

24

Breakfast was over and Chiara and Fin were gone, but Kane and Francesca remained at the table.

"Mom, I really want to go to St. Rita's next year. It's a great high school."

"And expensive. There's no way we can afford to send you there. It'd be impossible even if we weren't adding to the family." Francesca patted her basketball-sized stomach.

"I bet Grandpa Cal would pay for St. Rita's."

"Grandpa Cal's already done more than he should for us," said Francesca, clearing the dishes. "And I don't want you asking him. Capisce?"

"Yes, ma'am."

"And I better not hear that you've gone to your Uncle Gino for help, either. You hear me?"

"Loud and clear," said Kane. "Well, I'm off to collect for my paper route."

The dog days of summer had hit Chicago with a vengeance. A paper-thin haze hung over the city, blocking out the sun as Kane manipulated his bike in and out of traffic. His mind worked overtime as he pedaled down 63rd until he came to Claremont and stopped in front of St. Rita's High School.

He imagined walking up the sidewalk to class---an impossible dream, but one he wanted so bad he could taste it. He lingered a while just envisioning what it could be like. He knew he had to reconcile that it wasn't going to happen, but it wasn't easy. Then his thoughts turned to his mother's pregnancy.

He hadn't liked hearing the news. It was an embarrassment. His friends hadn't mentioned Francesca's bulging stomach to his face, otherwise, they knew he'd beat them up. But he guessed they talked and snickered about it behind his back.

Sex was the main thing in Kane's and his friends' pubescent minds these days. Yet, none of them believed their parents *did it* anymore. It was unbearable to think about. There would be nearly fourteen years between him and the baby. Ridiculous!

The only good thing was they'd moved to a bigger apartment to get ready for the new arrival. The bad thing was, they now had three flights of stairs, instead of two, to climb to their rented flat, and Kane knew that would be hard on his mother taking a baby up and down. It would also be a more disastrous tumble for his father when drunk. Even though they no longer lived over Bruno's Bar, nor did Fin work there any longer, Kane suspected that his old man might be hitting the bottle again.

Michael had instigated a job for Fin at the South Water Market on South Racine and 14th Place. Fin worked early mornings loading and unloading produce trucks, coming from off-site warehouses. Kane swore he could smell booze on his old man when he came home mid-afternoon and fell into bed. But if his mother's nose had picked up on an alcohol smell, she kept it to herself.

The pregnancy, a result Kane guessed from his parents' time in Michigan after his dad's drying out, had been announced to him and Chiara only recently. Chiara didn't seem any happier about the blessed event than Kane, and he knew Grandma Cal would be beside herself when she found out.

He had realized as a young child his grandma didn't like kids. It was blatant. She rarely paid attention to Chiara or showed affection toward her. Although, for some reason Kane was an exception. Meghan adored him, as Kane did her. She would probably ignore the new baby, and he bet she wouldn't be at all pleased with the news of it.

Kane was right. Meghan was more than unhappy, she was fuming. She lambasted Fin up one side and down the other when he visited and told his parents the news.

"What do you mean you're having another child? Don't you know when to stop? I knew marrying that Italian would be your downfall. And I was right. She's ruined your life. Except for giving you Kane, she's done nothing right."

Fin let Meghan's cruel spate of words wash over him. Michael, too, kept quiet. Both were aware Kane was the only saving grace in the whole situation. Anything they might say in defense of Fin's marriage or his other children would make no difference. Although Michael wasn't exactly pleased with the advent of another child, due to Fin's economic situation, he did dearly love his grandchildren and knew Francesca was good for Fin.

Despite his son's flaws, and seeming lack of ambition, which Michael chalked up to his battle with alcohol, he would always stand by his son. Since Fin had detoxed, their relationship seemed to be stronger than before. Michael had finally gotten Fin away from bartending by securing the job for him at the produce market and was hoping, now that Fin was sober, that he might go to college. Had even told his son he'd foot the bill.

Michael had never mentioned to Meghan about Fin's drinking problem, nor would he. Nor would he ever let on to her about Fin's dismal economic circumstances. The fact is, they rarely talked about their son. It had always been that way unless Meghan thought doing so would help her social standing in any way, such as the time she insisted Fin go to parochial school instead of a public one.

Fin had always been a shining light to Michael, but he only helped his son's family in little ways. He was afraid if he made his son too comfortable financially he would be even less motivated than he already was. At least for the moment, his and Francesca's marriage seemed to be happy, and they obviously had a sex life, something his miserable marriage hadn't enjoyed for years. He thanked his lucky stars for Ireland.

Kane's collections for his paper route were going smoothly. Nearly all his customers were home, and they'd given generous tips. He had one more house before he went to meet his pals at the Rack'em Up, a new pool hall, on Damen Avenue.

The house remaining was Mrs. Romo's. Kane always saved it for last because he liked looking and talking to her. Often times, if she wasn't busy, she'd stand in the doorway, her peroxide blonde hair curling around her face, her Cornflower-blue eyes fixed on him while they had a friendly chat about school or what book he might be reading. She liked reading, too, she told him in a low, sultry voice and encouraged Kane to study hard and stay in school.

She said there were times she was sorry she'd dropped out to marry her traveling salesman husband. Mrs. Romo was curvy and reminded Kane of Marilyn Monroe. He had become obsessed with the movie star ever since seeing a rerun of *The Seven Year Itch* with his Uncle G at the Biograph on Lincoln Avenue.

The scene of Marilyn standing over the sidewalk grate, her white dress billowing up and revealing her panties, was a scene Kane thought he'd never forget. Someday, he was going to have a woman just like that.

He knocked and knocked on Mrs. Romo's door but got no answer. Disappointed, he was turning to leave when the door opened and there she stood.

"Wait, Kane."

" Oh, hi, Mrs. Romo." He did a double take. Her hair dripped with water and her pouty lips were free of lipstick. Instead of street clothes she wore a silky kimono-type robe. Wow! She is beautiful even like this, he thought.

"I just got out of the shower, and I thought I heard a knock."

"That's okay. I can come back later or even tomorrow."

"Don't be silly. I'll get your money now. But it's too hot to wait out there. Come in. I made some lemonade earlier, maybe you'd like a glass?"

Kane hesitated. She had never invited him in before. But what the heck. It was hot, and he had always been curious as to what the inside of her house looked like. Kane nodded, "Sure. Lemonade sounds good." He stepped into a light and airy living room furnished with Danish modern furniture.

Before he could say another word, she unzipped his pants and drew them off. "Relax, you're going to be fine. There's nothing to be ashamed of." She looked down. "My, I can see we're going to get along real well."

She took his hand and placed it on her breast. "Feel and explore me, while I make you feel good."

Her fingers curled around him, and Kane felt himself growing. With her other hand she guided him and showed him what to do.

After a time, she said, "Let's see how we fit." Lying back on the sofa, she spread her legs, guiding him into her. And---it was over!

Oh, no, what had he done? "I'm sorry. Oh ... I'm so sorry," he muttered, too petrified to face her, after what had just happened. When he finally did, he saw her lazy smile again.

"Don't worry, Kane, you're fine. What happened is very common the first time. Next time it'll be better. I'll show you. There are lots of things you can learn from me, if you want to."

If he wanted to? Of course he did. Still Kane wasn't quite sure how to react, so he quickly pulled on his jeans while Mrs. Romo languidly watched.

"I ... I need to be going." Kane bolted for the door.

"Oh, my goodness, Kane, wait. I haven't paid you." He stopped with his hand on the doorknob as she jumped up and crossed the room, breasts bouncing with each step. She put the money in his hand, at the same time drawing him close and kissing him, her tongue lightly brushing his teeth. "You don't have to wait until collection time before you come back, you know."

On the other side of the front door, Kane stood for a moment, trying to gather his thoughts, reliving what had just happened. Unbelievable! Sex with Mrs. Romo. Just thinking about it was making him hard again. He felt a little shaky, but elated, as he got on his bicycle and pedaled away to meet his friends at the pool hall. Happy thoughts skipped through his mind like a playful child. But he was one no longer. The last remnant of his childhood had just been stripped away.

When Kane arrived at the Rack 'em Up, his pals were in the middle of a game. "What the fuck took you so long?" asked Joey Boy as he chalked up his cue.

"Oh, I had chores to do for Mom. Got off to a late start." No way was he going to boast about the real reason. Mrs. Romo---Lana was his and his alone. What had happened wasn't to be shared. No way would he rat her out and ruin his chances of more afternoon fun. If his friends found they might try to get some of the action, especially Sal Gandini because he'd already bragged about making out with Janie O'Shea behind the school gym.

Eddie LaFont chalked the end of his cue. "Well, you sure look happy to have been so late. You must have gotten lots of good tips today."

"As a matter of fact, I did," said Kane. If they only knew the kind he'd been given. He moved closer to the table hoping his burgeoning hard-on was concealed.

Soon, Kane became a steady visitor to the Romo residence. Mondays and Wednesdays, the days Larry Romo was on the road, were the days Kane begged off from going to the gym to box with the guys. He told them that these were times he had to do errands for his mom. Instead, he hopped on his bike and headed for Lana's, discreetly parking his bike behind some bushes by the side of the house, then making his way to the back door. Lana thought it wise the visits were kept away from prying eyes.

She usually met him at the door dressed in some kind of sexy lingerie, resting against the door frame in a movie star pose, her long legs shown off in red high heels because she had discovered he adored Marilyn Monroe. He especially liked Lana in a skimpy, black lace nightie that he could see through, which by now he was no longer afraid to remove.

The first time he had knelt down to take off her shoes, she shook her her head and climbed on top of him wearing them. She was amazing!

Another nightie Kane liked was a white ruffled one. The first time she wore it he teased and asked if she was a virgin. This made them both chuckle.

They had been rendezvousing for several months, when out of the blue his mother asked, "What were you doing at Mrs. Romo's house last Wednesday?"

Taken aback, Kane stammered, "Wh ... what do you mean?"

"I mean, why were at Mrs. Romo's house? Angie Turano said that she saw your bike in the bushes by the side of the house."

Mrs. Turano, his mother's best friend, had a big nose and was always sticking it where it didn't belong. Kane quickly regained his composure. "Oh, yeah, I was visiting with Mrs. Romo. She's a nice lady. I like talking to her when I collect."

"Oh," was all Francesca said, which caused Kane to believe she'd accepted his answer and was none the wiser.

But Kane was mistaken. The matter was uppermost in Francesca's mind. She pondered. Something wasn't adding up. Kane always collected for the paper on Saturdays, not Wednesdays, and there was no reason to hide his bike when doing so. Then it dawned on her what might be happening.

The following Wednesday before school was out, like a lioness protecting her young, she marched herself over to the the Romo's house and knocked on the door. When racy Lana Romo answered in a sapphire blue negligée, Francesca immediately saw her hunch was right about the *nice lady.*

She told Lana Romo in no uncertain terms to leave her son alone, or she would have one of her brothers pay her a visit. Fear crossed Lana Romo's face as she backed into the house and quickly closed the door.

After school when Kane went to see Lana, she greeted him at the door, fully dressed and said icily, as if he was some person she barely knew, "From now on, Kane, don't come by to collect. I will mail the money." Then closed the door in his face.

Kane was no jamook. It was clear, his mom hadn't believed his alibi and had paid Lana a visit, probably threatening her if she didn't leave him alone.

Kane knew his mother could frighten people if they were mean to her family. He had seen her do it at the market when a stranger had made a nasty remark to Chiara and made her cry. Kane had been surprised at how fast Francesca had bared her claws. He made a comment about it, and his mom's eyes had grown as black as his grandpa's when he was angry. Francesca was, after all, her father's daughter.

Frustrated and unhappy, Kane was forced to accept that his days of sex and fun with Lana were over---at least for now.

25

Meghan and Kane arrived in Union Pier to close the lake house for the winter. It was only September, but Meghan always locked things up at Harvest Moon time. She didn't like going to Michigan in the winter as some people did. Michael had driven them to Michigan on Friday, and they were taking the train back Sunday night so Kane wouldn't miss school.

Kane worked all morning winterizing the inboard/outboard motorboat, draining the fuel, refilling, adding stabilizer and antifreeze, fogging the engine and everything else that Michael required. Some of the steps weren't necessary since it was to be stored inside a heated facility, but once Michael had omitted a step, and it had ended up costing big bucks because the heat in the storage area had gone out. The owner had been taken ill and hadn't discovered the problem for several frigid months. That spring, Michael had to replace the engine. Now, he erred on the side of caution. So Kane followed his grandpa's instructions to a tee.

"Well, the boat's taken care of, Grandma. Now what?" said Kane, washing up at the kitchen sink.

Meghan was in the process of cleaning out the pantry. She hated doing all this work, but Brid, her maid, had left her in the lurch by moving to Ohio in order to take care of an ailing mother. To date, Meghan hadn't found a replacement to her liking, so she was stuck doing everything herself, which she loathed. Michael was working on a big court case and wasn't available, and Aunt Kitty was involved in church activities and too busy.

For a brief moment, Meghan had considered asking Francesca to help, but decided she wasn't that desperate. Besides, she hadn't seen Kane alone since the summer solstice and suspected he'd been hanging around Vito. That wop had probably been filling Kane's head with depraved ideas. Italians! How she detested them! They couldn't be trusted, especially that Vito Savio.

"I'm thinking we should take a break," said Meghan. Warren Woods is too far, but how about a picnic in the grove nearby? Sound fun?"

"Sounds groovy."

"Good, because I've already gotten food ready. Let me pack the hamper, and we'll be on our way."

In a forest, being near the water, or any place close to nature was always calming to Kane. It was serenity at its best. As they strolled along, neither spoke. Meghan and Kane deeply absorbed the wildlife and vegetation when in Michigan.

It was blue-crayon-cool in the woods. Bright sunlight cowered from an awning of jagged maple leaves, towering oaks, and pines. Their footsteps were muffled by the forest floor of leaves and pine needles. The earthy smell was sweet perfume to the pair. Small unseen creatures rustled through the fallen leaves and scampered on the woodsy floor. A garrulous blue jay in a nearby tree whistled between his jeers, sounding like a discontented patron of Mother Nature.

"Here's a good spot," said Meghan. They had come to a glade where sunlight finagled a hazy path through the hardwoods. A gray squirrel scurried in front of them, stopping at an oak where he stuffed an acorn in a knot hole, then dashed away in search of another.

"That squirrel better be careful because I think the blue jay's eyeing his stash."

"Well, how about our food supply? Ready to eat?" Meghan asked, spreading a piece of yellowed canvas down for them to sit on.

"You can always count on me," said Kane, helping to set out three different cheeses, a creamy potato salad, and the buttered soda bread sandwiches stuffed with meat.

They were quiet while they ate. When together, even in their silences, they were comfortable and almost knew what the other was thinking. At times, they actually did.

After the picnic remains were repacked into the hamper, Meghan asked, "How's ye meditation going?"

"Not so good since we moved," said Kane. "I used to be able to meditate on the roof. But in the new apartment I can't find a comfortable place that is quiet enough."

Meghan patted his shoulder. "I know. The city's a noisy place. Someday ye'll be able to shut out yer surroundings and immerse yourself in order to visualize. Of course, it's always much easier in a green world because the life force connection here is stronger. Ye'll learn to meditate in all kinds of environments in time. Someday, ye may even travel to another dimension. In fact, I'm sure of it. For now, just keep imagining a peaceful scene with exotic foliage, a bubbling river, or whatever landscape you find restful."

"I'll try. You know, Grandma, I had the weirdest dream the other night."

"Really? What about?"

Kane strode back and forth. "Well, I dreamed I was in a field. A bull was in front of me, snorting and pawing ready to charge. Just before it did, this huge black raven appeared circling, circling above us, shrilly calling over and over until I nearly went crazy. Finally, the bull turned and moseyed away with the raven sitting on its back. Isn't that weird?"

Knowing his grandma could interpret dreams, Kane looked at her intently, waiting. But nothing. After a moment, he said, "Well, what's the meaning of my strange dream? Do you know?"

Meghan got up and brushed off her skirt. "Let's take a little walk. I need to stretch me legs." They strolled along. "Yer dream could mean several things, but at yer age, I think the bull symbolizes sexuality. The raven has many meanings, but in this instance it symbolizes protection. I'm interpreting that yer dream is confirming you are being protected from yer own sexuality."

Meghan was glad the light was dim as she felt her face grow hot. Speaking of sex was difficult for her, especially to her grandson. As for Kane, his mind was immediately filled with images of Lana Romo's naked body, which he was no longer able to enjoy thanks to his mother.

Meghan cleared her throat. "As ye know, I sometimes use the raven for insight, though in the city I seldom see that kind of bird. I also believe they can be messengers between here and the Otherworld. But that's nothing ye need to be concerned with for now."

She looked at her grandson, knowing that he was, in many ways, wise beyond his years. "Be aware, Kane. If ye continue to see that bull, he may actually be yer spiritual animal. Yer totem, that will guide ye through this life."

"That's groovy," said Kane.

"Yes, it is," replied Meghan, wondering if he'd ever quit using such silly expressions.

26

Kane decided he'd been mistaken about Fin hitting the bottle because for once his dad was sober and working. Still, Kane had little respect for his old man, but if his mom was happy, then Kane was. Up until the time Francesca went into labor, that is.

That bitter March night when Francesca began having labor pains, Fin was nowhere to be found. Wherever he was, he had gone on foot or been picked up because their old tan and white Ford Edsel was parked by the curb in front of the house.

Gino had been swayed by the car's advertising campaign in 1958, saying, *Once you've seen it, you'll never forget it. Once you've owned it, you'll never want to change*. He bought the funny-looking automobile thinking it was going to be a sought after vehicle. A car people would look at in admiration as he drove the Chicago streets.

But soon he discovered it was a dud, an embarrassment. People looked at it and heckled. So Gino turned over the keys to Francesca. She didn't drive, but Gino knew he'd be getting the last laugh on his brother-in-law.

"Nothing is too good for your husband," he told Francesca, smiling.

Fin didn't like driving the auto either and rarely did. Through rainstorms, winter snows, and birds pooping on it in the spring, the car sat idly in front of the house. Now it was needed because Francesca was in labor, crying in pain, and there wasn't a cab in sight. There was no choice other than the dilapidated monster by the curb.

Kane found the gas gauge registered full, oddly the tires seemed to have enough air, but the battery was dead. And by some miracle, after sitting for so long, the car sputtered to life after he convinced a neighbor to jump the battery. Then Kane loaded his mother and Chiara into the lemon and headed for Holy Cross Hospital on West 68th Street. He sped along hoping that he wouldn't get stopped.

The fact was, he wasn't old enough to drive, nor did he know how. He'd ridden with and watched his Uncle G enough times that he figured he could operate the car without a problem.

The Edsel was different from most cars of the time. It had a unique Teletouch Transmission shifting system in the center of the steering wheel and self-adjusting brakes. Seat belts, an advanced feature, had even been offered for safety. They hadn't been optioned because Gino thought them ridiculous.

After starting the car and pulling into the street, Kane was thankful it was late and there weren't many cars out because driving was harder than it looked.

He bumped, jolted, and jarred his family as he tried to get the hang of driving. He braked abruptly, pitching his passengers forward, once nearly throwing Chiara from the back to the front seat. Another time his mother almost hit her head on the windshield.

Finally, he screeched into the hospital driveway, squealed to a stop, and jumped out of the car, dashing to get help. But he was too late. When he and a nurse returned, his mom was holding a bawling, apple-red baby. Chiara was crying in excitement, at the same time, vowing she'd never, ever have a child because it was awful.

Later that night, after Francesca and baby were settled into the hospital, Fin was located. He drunkenly stumbled into Holy Cross to see his new son, yelling that it was the end of that stupid Edsel. No way would he ever drive a car that had doubled as a delivery room.

That very night, it was towed to the junkyard, discarded like an unwanted animal. A few days later, Fin called Gino to go get his sister and new nephew because Francesca was ready to come home from the hospital.

Franco Michael Peter Callahan had a knobby nose that was too big for his scrawny face and limp dark hair reminding Francesca of her sister Angeline's scraggly locks. But despite his homeliness, he was a cheerful baby, and Maria and Francesca doted on him. Vito wasn't taken with the baby and neither was Fin which reminded Michael of Meghan's attitude when Fin was born. Naturally, Meghan couldn't be bothered with the new addition, nor could Kane and Chiara who had more important things to occupy their time.

Chiara was busy with school work and being with her friends. Kane, on the other hand, wasn't doing much studying. He was busy running miles and sparring at a local gym getting ready for the next Golden Gloves event. But even this activity didn't keep him out of trouble as Michael had hope when he encouraged Kane to box.

During Kane's first year at Harper High School, he learned quickly that in order to survive he needed to become a gang member. There were two options---the Street Lads and the Loafers.

The Lads wore black jackets with Street Lads written across the top. In the middle of the back was a picture of a boy leaning against a lamppost, a cigarette hanging from his mouth.

The Loafers, which Kane joined, had Loafers and 59th Street written on the back of their jackets, but the center was left empty, allowing each member to pick what he wanted for the space. A few boys chose nothing, but Kane decided on a picture of a bull since the dream about the animal kept recurring.

The Lads and the Loafers weren't really enemies because they often helped each other. Sometimes when a member of a gang was running from something he'd done, the members of the gangs would switch jackets. This way the description wouldn't match for the wanted boy, and he would be safe.

Kane's favorite class at Harper High School was shop. Here he and the other gang members made weaponries such as brass knuckles, Billy clubs, and knives. Their teacher, Mr. Hopkins, knew he couldn't keep them from creating these harmful objects.

However, he was smart enough not to allow them to be taken from school, so he kept them under lock and key in a case in his office.

Kane was proud of the brass knucks he'd made with the quarter-inch spikes on the top of each knuckle, and he wanted them. By mid-term, he persuaded the other Loafers that their handiwork was going to waste.

Thus, on a moonless night, he and three gang members broke into Mr. Hopkins office and stole their weapons. The next morning, Mr. Hopkins, when asked, was wise enough to tell Mr. Pirelli, the principal, he had no idea who the thieves were. And Mr. Pirelli decided he might as well let the matter drop.

Near the end of the school year, the stolen items were put to use. One night, the Loafers ran into a rival gang, the Laflin Drifters, who were hanging out by Oscar's Food Mart on 65th and Laflin Street. The Loafers took the Drifters by surprise. The clash was brief because someone called the police, and the Loafers ran just before the police arrived to break up the fight.

However, the last weekend before summer break, the two gangs rumbled again, this time in Ogden Park. And the outcome was different.

Neither side was lucky that night. During the fight, Kane stabbed two boys with the stiletto he'd inherited from Vito, and beat them badly with his shop-made knucks. The boys weren't dead, but they were close. Both gangs were arrested, thrown into the back of paddy wagons, and hauled into the police station, with the exception of the badly wounded who were taken to the hospital.

When Chief of Police Modena discovered Kane's uncle was Pietro Savio, Pietro was called to come down to the station. Since Modena was in the mob's back pocket, Pietro straightened things out. Kane was given his weapons back and freed, but Modena advised Pietro that Kane should leave the city for the summer.

Pietro, who barely knew Michael Callahan, but was aware that he had a house in Michigan, called on him to come to the precinct. Michael arrived to find Kane sitting next to his uncle in the waiting room. Michael knew that Pietro was a mobster, yet he thanked him graciously for calling, saying he'd take over. Pietro indicated that he owed Michael, then took his leave.

Michael sat down by Kane. "Well, here I am again, bailing you out of trouble. Each time is worse than the last. I don't know what you think you're doing. You better wise up. Stop traveling this path of self-destruction. You're lucky your uncle has pull around here. Thanks to him, you've been kept out of jail."

Kane hung his head. Michael took in his grandson's black eyes, busted lip, and his facial and arm cuts. He noted the ivory handled stiletto sticking out of Kane's back pocket and the brass knuckles hooked to his belt. He couldn't believe Kane was turning out to be a thug.

Meghan would have blamed Kane's troubles on Francesca. Michael knew she would be partially right. Kane's behavior had Savio stamped all over it, but he was aware it was Fin's fault, too, for not being the father his son needed. Michael was sick at heart.

Kane lifted his arm and wiped away blood dripping from a gash on his cheek. "I'm sorry, Grandpa Cal."

"Sorry for what you did, or that you were caught?" Michael was angrier than he'd ever been. "I'll tell you what's going to happen, young man. I'm sending you to Michigan for the summer, and it won't be to fish, hike, or gaze at the moon with your grandma. It'll be to work your tail off. Maybe some hard, honest work will straighten you out."

Kane hated that he'd hurt Grandpa Cal, yet he was more worried about what Grandma Cal would think. But Kane didn't have a chance to find out her thoughts. He only had time to pack a bag and explain to his mother what had happened and where he was going.

Francesca shed tears of anger. She had prayed Kane wouldn't emulate her brothers, but what did she expect? Fin was never around, and when he was he was no father figure. She appreciated that, once again, Michael was helping her family.

In some ways, she was glad Kane would be gone for the summer. Her hands were full with little Franco who had become a sickly child. And she was bone tired from trying to please Fin who was drinking again. Kane would be one less person for her to worry about for a while.

27

Michael drove Kane to Michigan to his friend's farm. It wasn't a big farm. Harry Reese had some chickens, half a dozen dairy cows, a goat, two pigs, and a field of hay soon to be harvested. He promised Michael there was plenty of work to occupy Kane and keep him out of trouble, and there was. So much so that Kane didn't have time to miss or think about his family. He enjoyed this new experience, yet it was an eye-opener.

Being used to city life, living on a farm wasn't anything like Kane had expected. Instead of being able to sleep in as he had at home, he was roused out of his cosy bed every morning at 3:30 to feed the animals and milk the cows. The first morning, Harry asked if Kane had ever milked.

Kane eyed the orangish-red Guernsey up and down and replied, "No, but I know I can do it." He faced the cow's udder. "No big deal. All I have to do is just pull on these things." He pointed to the teats.

Harry Reese looked serious. "It's not quite that simple. Move and let me show you. First thing is, you don't pull, you massage the teats. Watch."

He sat down on a low stool, washed the milk-filled teats with warm soapy water, dried them gently, rubbed a little Vaseline on his fingers so they'd work smoothly and not irritate the cow. With the bucket between his knees, he massaged two teats, diagonal from each other while Kane observed. Harry milked and milked until all the teats were deflated.

"Okay, I've finished with this cow. You've seen how it's done. Now get to work on the others. I've got my own chores."

Kane sat down to finish the milking. Even though the cows were held by stanchions, he hadn't been told or shown how to keep a cranky cow still so it wouldn't kick him or turn the bucket over, how to keep a swishing tail from hitting him in the face, or heaven help him, what to do if a cow needed to drop a pie or urinate.

Therefore, Kane's first day wasn't as easy as he first imagined. It didn't take long to learn that he should approach a cow slowly, speak gently, and pat her in order not to be kicked or stepped on. He became aware that feeding a restless cow while he worked would keep her quiet, and he discovered the hard way after his foot was stepped on that cows are able to kick sideways, as well as from behind. Most importantly, he found that the animal arching its back meant grab the bucket to save the milk because the cow was getting ready to relieve itself. And finally, to keep the tail from slapping his face, Harry Reese advised him to tie it to a back leg. At least, Kane didn't need a lesson on how to gather eggs, or did he?

After being pecked and screeched at a few times by a broody hen sitting tight on her nest, he learned to forget those eggs. The hen wanted to keep them to hatch babies, and she didn't want him reaching under her to take them. He was taught that usually the color of a hen's ear lobes indicated the color that the eggs would be. White, of course, meant white, but dark meant brown and red indicated various shades of brown. Although, the Reese's didn't have any Silkie chickens with fluffy plumage, Kane was told their eggs could be many colors such as black, blue, and even lavender.

After learning about chickens and cows, one morning at breakfast, Elsa Reese said, "As you can see farming ain't as easy as it looks. Now eat up. You're going to need lots more food than you've been putting away. Harry says hay's ready to be cut."

She placed a plate of scrambled eggs, fried potatoes, bacon, toast, sausage, and tall glasses of juice and fresh cold milk in front of him. "You'll need lots of strength and energy in the field today."

Mrs. Reese told Kane that at haying time all the neighboring farmers and their able-bodied sons helped one another in the fields, so now it was time to work for Harry.

Kane entered the kitchen ready to go to the field, dressed in a shirt with the collar wide open and his sleeves rolled up over his elbows.

Harry Reese scrutinized him and said, "If I was you, boy, I'd button that shirt all the way, roll down those sleeves, and put this here bandana around that neck of yours." He held out a red and black square to Kane.

Kane took it, but stuffed it in his pocket. He knew it was going to be hot so no way was he going to take the advice to button up or tie on a bandana.

Mr. Reese saw Kane was ignoring his words, so he shrugged and said, "Come on then."

At the end of the first day, Kane had scratches all over his bare skin from the rough straw, and he itched like crazy. He had never been so bone weary. He dragged himself to the house and managed a weak smile and a thank you when Mrs. Reese met him at the door with a big jar of salve.

The container had no name, and its gooey, mustard-colored contents smelled worse than a skunk, but Kane didn't care. It felt like heaven when he rubbed it on himself. Now he understood why Mr. Reese had given the advice he had.

Next day, Kane took Mr. Reese's words to heart and covered up his aching body, even to the point of wearing gloves and a White Sox baseball cap that Mrs. Reese offered him.

"Don't need you to go getting a sunstroke," she said. "Won't be no good to Harry then."

During the field work, Kane stayed to himself. When the men and their sons stopped for lunch or took a break, he walked away from the group and sat by himself. The boys his age tried to be sociable, but Kane remained aloof.

Days later, after all the hay had been cut and tedded, Harry declared it was dry enough to bale. After the baling, one of the boys drove the truck while Kane and the others followed behind. Their job was to pick up the bales and toss them onto the truck's bed.

Since Kane was antisocial, he found himself stuck at the tail end of the loaders. The boy driving the truck purposely sped up so that Kane had to run with the heavy bale before he was close enough to throw it onto the vehicle. He discovered there was a certain rhythm to the process---grab the bundle with one hand, then the other, bounce it on your knee, and heave. Because of the fast moving truck, however, Kane had trouble keeping up. He felt as if he was about to die, but no way would he cry uncle. After all, he had Savio blood coursing through his veins.

The bales were trucked to the barn and loaded onto a conveyor belt which carried them up into the hayloft for storage. It was stifling hot in the top of the barn, and Kane's stomach churned at the putrid smell of the fodder, but he persevered. He hoped he was stowing the bales correctly because he didn't want to be responsible for a fire. He'd been told they could never be stacked on top of each other or stored too close together, otherwise, they would self-combust. He certainly couldn't afford to burn down the Reese's barn. If he did, no telling what his punishment would be.

The day after all the hay was baled and stored, it was time for a celebration party. All the neighboring families flocked to the Reese farm. Kane had never seen so much food. The women brought all kinds of fare---hams, fried chicken, sliced beef, many different kinds of salads and vegetable dishes. For dessert there were various fruit pies, cakes with fluffy icing, crisp cookies, and freezers of homemade vanilla and fresh peach ice cream. After the food had been devoured and everyone was sated, the party continued.

While the men pitched horseshoes, the women talked, and the kids played. Some of the boys, younger than Kane, but too old for hide-n-seek, sneaked beers and headed to the barn. Relaxing under a tree, away from the activity, Kane watched alone. He'd never seen such goings-on.

Some of the men brought out their fiddles and other instruments, and a few couples danced. During the merrymaking, Billy Chenault, one of the boys who had helped in the field approached Kane, saying he was wanted in the barn. Kane was no dummy. He had no friends in the barn, so why would they want him? He smelled a setup but decided to see what waited for him.

Inside the barn, Kane found blonde Stan Kowlowski, a Polish kid, three years older than Kane, often called *Pretty Boy* because of his Adonis-like features. Kane had won a few light-weight Golden

Glove fights, but Kowlowski was a bruiser, who had won the state championship. Kane was tall, but his muscles next to Stan's were anemic. This didn't deter Kane.

The minute he entered the barn, Stan threw a punch. "Here's for being so high and mighty. Thinkin' you're better 'an us."

"And here's for being a stupid Pollock," said Kane, taking a swing at Stan's rock-hard stomach. Kane was determined to down the heavyweight. He kept slugging, but Stan stood like a granite sculpture, amused while Kane's hands bled from pounding him. Stan's hard body sustained few abrasions.

Unexpectedly, Stan bulldozed into Kane, knocking him to the floor next to a loosened barn board. Kane picked it up and swung, hitting Stan smack in the face.

A crack, sounded and Stan's nose spewed blood. Kane slammed him again. Finally, Billy Chenault and a boy named Frank Hennessy separated them.

Stan jerked away from Frank's grasp and started for Kane. Frank grabbed Stan's shirttail. "Come on, Kowlowski, enough is enough."

"Let go of me." Stan lurched away from Frank and approached Kane, holding out his hand. "I give you lots 'o credit, kid. No one's ever taken me on before."

Billy released Kane who reached out his swollen, bloody hand and shook the offered one. Frank and Billy stood in astonishment. They'd expected Stan to give a last flattening blow.

From that evening, until the end of Kane's stay, he and Stan were buddies.

When they went to the Kowlowski farm to work the next day, both boys' bodies were bruised and aching as they drove over bumps in the field. Stan taught Kane how to drive the truck and tractor, and Kane no longer had to follow the truck and load hay bales.

Besides working, Stan and Kane partied together in the small town some evenings. There wasn't much to do except drink beer, which Stan would buy for Kane who was underage, and go to a movie. So the rest of the summer that's exactly what Stan and Kane could be found doing.

28

Maria was picking asters when Kane came through the gangway and rounded the corner of the house into the backyard. They hadn't seen each other since he'd returned from the farm in Michigan. The sweet aroma of Maria's evening meal drifted from the house, and Kane's mouth watered at the thought of his grandma's tasty food.

"Hi, Grandma." Kane gave Maria a big hug and kiss.

She noted Kane's tanned face, sun-bleached hair, and bulging arm muscles. "I've been worried about you. What's the matter with you, stabbing those two boys?"

"Sorry, didn't mean to upset you, grandma."

"Well, you did. I can't imagine what got into you. Knifing those boys. I think someone cast the evil eye on you."

Kane laughed. "The evil eye? Do you really believe in that stuff, the religious person that you are?"

Maria looked serious. "Of course, I do." She reached into her apron pocket and pulled out a twisted, horn-shaped piece of coral on a chain. "This is for you."

Kane looked in amazement at the phallic charm she placed in his hand. He'd read that the charm was called a *cornicello,* a horn worn to protect against *malocchio*, the evil eye. The superstition dated back to the ancient Romans who had called their charm a *fascinus*.

Sexual symbols were used to divert witches from casting spells that dried up liquids, including that of the male phallus. If a man was without the charm, a gesture, by forming a fist with the thumb pressed between the index and middle fingers, representing the phallus within the vagina, could be made. Either the gesture or a charm could ward off spells and prevent loss of virility.

Also, Kane had observed Gino grabbing his crotch. When Kane asked why he'd done this, Gino explained it protected against a malicious stare. Sometimes he said, he made the gesture to generate luck when he was playing in a high stakes poker game.

After Gino's clarification, Kane began to clutch his own genitals on occasion. He never knew if it worked but felt it didn't hurt anything, sometimes even felt good. He began to notice that Italian men protecting their groin was common. No one in the Italian neighborhood thought twice about it, but he wondered what non-Italians thought.

"Here hold these flowers, and I'll fasten the charm on you." Maria handed Kane an armful of gold and purple asters in exchange for the necklace.

As his grandmother secured the amulet around his neck, Kane's mind drifted to stories of how several popes had been accused of giving the malevolent stare.

Pope Pius IX had passed by an open window, looked upon a baby being held by a nurse, and minutes later the child fell from the woman's arms, plummeting to the ground and death. After that, everything the pope blessed seemed to end in disaster.

Pope Leo XIII was another pontiff that people thought cast *malocchio,* due to the numerous cardinals that died during his reign.

Remembering these tales, Kane still wasn't convinced the evil eye was real. Maybe it was just the way things were meant to happen. That thing called fate.

He fingered the talisman hanging round his neck next to his St. Christopher medal. "So you really think this will help ward off bad stuff?"

"I said, I did." Maria became exasperated with his questioning. "Now, take those flowers into the house for me and go visit with your grandpa. He's waiting for you."

Kane entered the basement kitchen, laying the flowers on the sink. Then he went to greet Vito who was sitting in his easy chair.

"Hi, Grandpa." Kane settled down in Maria's small rocker next to Vito and waited.

Finally, Vito spoke, his eyes dark as embers, studying his grandson. "Got caught, eh? Were *stenade* weren't ya?"

Vito shifted in his chair, and Kane prepared to vacate the rocker, thinking something more might follow Vito's stinging words. But the canes remained untouched beside his chair, and Kane relaxed.

"Yeah, Grandpa. *Merda* happens." Kane couldn't help grinning. He'd never said shit in front of his grandpa before. The corners of Vito's mouth turned up. He always smiles with his mouth, thought Kane, never with his eyes.

"Better start bein' more *intelligente*. And maybe that'll help," said Vito, pointing to the horn around Kane's neck. "Sumpin' else. There's a Sicilian saying: *the man who plays alone never loses.* 'member this."

After dinner, Kane helped Maria with the dishes, and Vito hobbled off to Fazio's. Not even his arthritic legs could keep him from his nightly libations.

Kane and Maria were finishing their task when Pietro descended the stairs, his black, silk suit rustling expensively, a pair of sunglasses dangling half in, half out of the jacket's breast pocket.

"*Marone*! Thought I'd make it before Papa left for Fazio's."

Maria dried her wet hands and greeted her son. "You just missed him." She felt the bulge of a gun beneath his jacket as he hugged her, but refrained from remarking. Knowing Italian women didn't question their men.

"Why are you so excited and want to see your papa?"

"Have somethin' to tell him, Mama. Wanted him to know the news first. Guess I'll tell you. Then I'll go to Fazio's and see Papa."

"Tell us what?" Maria looked up into her son's swarthy face.

"Yeah, Uncle Pietro what's going on."

"Well, I'm goin' to Vegas."

"Wow! Vegas, that's cool. How long will you be gone?"

"A long time, Kane. Me and the family's movin' there."

Maria clutched Pietro's arm. "What do you mean you're moving? And where is this Vegas?"

"Out west, Mama." Pietro tried to remove Maria's hand, but in her distress she clung tighter.

"Oh! That's far away! No! You can't leave. I want to see my grandchildren grow up. See you and Sylvia. No, no, I won't let you go."

"Can't stop me, Mama. I'm goin'. Got an offer I can't refuse. Gonna be at a fine casino called the Riviera." Pietro finally succeeded in removing Maria's hand from his now crumpled jacket sleeve and was smoothing it.

"Way cool, Uncle Pietro," said Kane, giving his uncle a thumbs up. Maria sat down at the table and buried her head in her hands, sobbing in anguish. "No ... no ...You can't leave."

It was bedlam at the Savios'. It had been two weeks since Pietro announced he was leaving for Las Vegas. In the meantime, Carlo confirmed he was going too. They were slated to leave the end of the month, in another three weeks.

Maria went into a funk deeper than the black hole. Her melancholy was more intense than the one she'd experienced when the children were young, and she'd wanted her basement kitchen built. Despite the dark mood that hung over her like an angry hound, she insisted everyone needed to come for Sunday dinner.

"After all," she whined, "we may never see each other again. I don't know what this world is coming to. My sons running off to that Vegas place, so far away." Pietro and Carlo chuckled.

"It's not as if we're going to the moon," said Carlo. "We'll be back."

"Well, you might as well be in space," huffed Maria. "Flying in that airplane. Heaven knows how the thing stays in the air anyway. It just may decide to drop. Then where will I be? Two fewer sons, that's where."

"Don't worry, Mama, they'll be fine," said Gino, giving her one of his teddy bear hugs. "They're going to find housing. They'll be back to Chicago before they leave for good. Then Pietro and family will pack up and drive out to Vegas."

But Maria wasn't pacified. She moaned and groaned as she made the pasta for the lasagna and formed the meatballs for the spaghetti.

While Maria wallowed in her misery, everyone else had fun. Francesca cornered Gino and Arriana, asking about their wedding plans. Both were noncommittal. Later, Francesca got her brother alone.

"After all the things you've said about Arriana, I can't believe you're really getting married."

"Between you and me, it's a ploy to keep her father off my back. Strange thing, though, I'm beginning to think tying the knot might not be the noose around my neck that I've often pictured."

"Well, Arriana seems nice enough, but not the type I've ever thought you'd end up with."

Francesca glanced across the room where the unattractive woman, with her squinty eyes was coloring with Pietro's two younger children. "Of course, I'm not sure what your type is. Guess I figured you'd go for someone with more flash, more style."

Gino squeezed his little sister's hand. "Well, we'll see. I'm sure not jumping into the marriage pit any time soon."

He left her and walked into the backyard where the rest of the Savio men had gathered.

"Your goin' to Vegas is good. A sign of respect. I'm proud." Vito, slapped Pietro on the back, causing wine to slosh out of his son's glass. Being crippled had done nothing to diminish Vito's upper body strength. "Yeah, I'm a proud. My son, a pit boss."

Pietro stuck his finger in his glass, wet it with wine, then dabbed a drop behind Carlo's and his papa's ears. About that time, Kane walked up and saw what Pietro was doing.

"Uncle Pete, what's that for?"

"Spilled wine's bad luck. Gotta reverse it."

After Kane received the cornicello, Meghan saw it around his neck. When she discovered the talisman came from Maria and not Vito, it didn't make a whit of difference. She wasn't to be outdone.

"Humph, those feckin' Italians." She brought forth a small leather pouch and emptied its contents.

Three gems rolled out onto the kitchen table in front of Kane. Meghan picked up a multi-colored stone. "This is a tiger's eye. It will stop that dom evil eye better than that stupid thing around yer neck. A tiger's eye protects against all kinds of danger, not just the evil eye."

Then picking up a reddish-brown gem, she said, "this carnelian will keep away anger and hateful feelings from others, and this black stone is a hematite. It will protect ye if there is a battle, which evidently ye seem to have gotten into recently. Always carry this little sack in ye pocket and ye will be just fine."

As Kane left his Grandma Cal's, he felt weighed down with good luck. He had so many charms, he felt he would never have a problem again. But that's where he was wrong.

29

By September of 1963, Alcatraz closed, Martin Luther King, Jr. gave a seventeen minute speech during the Civil Rights march in Washington, D. C., President John F. Kennedy visited Ireland, and Kane entered his second year at Harper High School.

Kane's school year began without incident until the school principal told him he needed to sign up for swimming. Mr. Montoya, the swim coach, was a runt of a man with a loud voice and a louder whistle. He was Simon Legree and Iago rolled into one.

The class was made up mostly of the Lads and Loafers. They all disliked the tyrant because he made them swim until they were so water logged they could barely walk, then they still had to do a hundred push-ups and on top of that, pull-ups. The only thing the boys enjoyed was being allowed to swim nude since they were in the boy's gym that was off limits to girls.

One day, a new black kid named Razu Smith joined their class. But after two weeks, his big toe hadn't touched the water. He always had some reason not to dive in---a sinus problem, an earache, or some other flimsy reason for not swimming. He was a small kid, a loner, and he sat quietly in a corner during the entire period fully clothed, watching the class go through their grinding routines.

One day, Mr. Montoya fed up with Razu's lame excuses yelled, "Razu, you can have a fuckin' hangnail or a broken arm, I don't give a rat's ass, but today you're going to join the class. Get out of those clothes and get in this pool. Now!"

The rest of the class treaded water, chomping at the bit waiting for him to jump in. They grinned and nodded to each other knowingly. It was obvious, the punk was a coward, and they were ready to teach him a lesson he'd never forget.

Razu ambled to the edge of the pool and slowly removed his shoes and socks. He hesitated. Then slower than it took the turtle to cross the finish line, he removed his jeans. The minute he did, the boys began to point and jeer, taunting him because he was not well endowed.

"Where is it? Where is it?" They began chanting mid the laughter.

Mr. Montoya blew his whistle, trying to bring order and stop the chaos, but the whistle's shrillness just added to the ruckus.

Then Razu pulled off his shirt. A hush engulfed the area like a fuzzy cloud. Not a whisper, not a ripple was heard. The motor for the pool's pump stopped. Mr. Montoya was stone still, his whistle glued silently to his lips.

From one shoulder to the middle of Razu's torso, and up to the other shoulder a V had been cut into his chest. Razu was a Vice Lord, a member of the oldest gang on the street.

Originally, the gang had been started as a club by black boys in a St. Charles Illinois reformatory. As the boys were released, one by one, they continued the club, and it eventually evolved into the Vice Lords. The V, was a painful part of the initiation ritual. The scarification that denoted its members was made by cutting inch-wide strips, a half-inch deep into the skin, after which the flesh was peeled down and away leaving a raw V. When healed, a big white letter on the black body remained.

With the nation in the throes of the civil rights and black liberation movement, the Vice Lords was rapidly expanding. It were fast becoming a multi-neighborhood "super gang." No one had to be told that Razu wasn't to be messed with. Never again did the Lads or the Loafers taunt him. In their eyes, he was a man among boys, a hero of sorts.

After that, things changed. Razu assimilated into the class without any trouble, but Mr. Montoya was still the slave driver he'd always been. Tired of his tyranny, the class decided it was time their coach joined in the swim. Instead of coaching from the nice, dry edge of the pool as he always did, he needed to get wet too.

The next day, when he entered the natatorium, the boys were waiting. They rushed him, picked him up, and heaved him into the water. With a big splash he sank, then surfaced and floundered, waving his hands, crying out, "Help! Help!"

"Look at that," said Kane. "He's chuckin' and jivin' us, acting like he can't swim."

"Yeah," laughed Tony Boy, "whoever heard of a swim coach that can't."

A chorus of laughter came from the boys, sitting on the edge of the pool, dangling their feet in the water, waiting for their coach to swim to the edge and quit acting the drowning clown. They knew that they would be punished when he did, but they didn't care. At the moment, they were having a good time.

But when Mr. Montoya kept gasping for breath and his head went beneath the surface for the third time and didn't come up, they realized he wasn't pulling their leg. He couldn't even dogpaddle.

Several of the guys jumped in and dragged him out to safety. But was Mr. Montoya thankful that they had saved his life? No. After he'd coughed up water and sputtered back to normalcy, he ordered the class to do a hundred extra push-ups.

Mr. Montoya was detested even more after that. Something further needed to be done. So, Razu came up with the idea of hanging him.

"Except," he said, after the boys agreed with his plan, "I can't be part of it because I'm already on probation for murder."

The boys in the class thought Razu's idea a good one, so he watched as the they made a noose, threw the rope over a rafter, secured it, then put a chair beneath it.

As soon as Mr. Montoya appeared the boys overpowered him and carried the coach kicking and screaming to the dangling rope. Without hesitation they put his head in the noose. They were getting ready to kick the chair away when Principal Pirelli happened by, looked in, and rushed inside, saving the coach from the would-be lynching.

Straightway, the boys were marched to Pirelli's office and given a dressing down, then ordered to drop their pants. From a wall of different sized paddles, Mr. Pirelli removed one that was twelve inches across, two-inches thick, and was drilled full of holes. It was known to give the worst spanking possible because the openings caused less air to drag as the paddle was brandished to the buttocks, therefore producing more sting.

Six licks apiece were administered by the principal. But that wasn't all, six months of Encore Periods was levied. At Harper, this meant hours and hours in the hated detention. Still, Kane didn't complain. Despite the fact it hurt to sit because of the red welts caused by the paddling, he was relieved that Pirelli hadn't contacted any of the parents. Otherwise, Kane's reprimand would have been even harsher. Maybe his cornicello and gems did work.

30

Looking out the window of his father's study, Fin noticed that the crab apple tree was becoming frosted with an early November snow. He and his dad had been talking of the mundane, and now Michael waited for Fin to tell him what was on his mind.

Despite the inclement weather, Fin spotted his mother in the backyard, coming from the birdbath altar. She appeared old and weary as she trudged toward the house, her head bent against the twirling snowflakes. Fin hadn't seen her in a long time. He and his dad usually met downtown since Meghan never seemed to be interested in seeing him. It dawned on Fin neither of his parents were spring chickens. They must be in their fifties now.

The back door slammed and in less than a minute Meghan appeared at the study door, her coat covered with a dandruff of white and a puddle forming around her feet from melting snow.

What had happened to her? When Fin was growing up she shouted at anyone who didn't take off their boots or shoes. And here she was messing up the floors in the way she'd always hated others doing.

"Oh, when did ye come?" Meghan glanced at her son as she took the wool scarf off her head and shook out her hair. "Do ye want to stay for dinner?"

Fin was startled to see his mother's red hair was mixed with silver, nor could he believe his ears. His mother was extending him an invitation without his father wheedling her to do so.

"No thanks, Mom, Francesca's expecting me. Little Frankie has the croup, and I need to get back with the car in case we need to take him to the hospital."

"Okay. Give me love to Kane." And with that, Meghan left the men staring at the empty doorway.

"What's gotten into Mom? She acted almost friendly." Fin tried to hide his hurt feelings at his mother's devotion toward Kane, and showing no concern for the baby's illness or inquiring about Chiara. And what about how he was?

"Search me. Your mother's your mother. She's as changeable as the weather. In case you didn't notice, she didn't acknowledge me at all. But regardless of her aloofness, she does love you in her own way," Michael said, knowing Fin's sensitivity to Meghan's uncaring attitude.

He leaned back in the overstuffed desk chair. "But let's talk about why you're here. You mentioned you needed some advice." He took a couple of big puffs on his cigar.

Fin remembered when he'd first asked Michael for his opinion on dating Francesca. Now he focused on the same desk clock that he had concentrated on back then and tried to gather his thoughts.

"Well, you're the only one I can talk to about this, Dad. Yet, I'm embarrassed, although you've never been judgmental with anything I've ever done."

"What is it, Son? Are you in trouble?"

"Not yet, but it's luring me. You see, Dad, there's this woman at Flo's Cafe. We always sit and talk a minute when I stop after work for a bite to eat. She's not beautiful, but for some reason she's captivating. I've thought about asking to take her for a drink, so I can get to know her better. Would that be wrong?"

Fin jumped in astonishment when Michael uncharacteristically slammed his fist on the desk.

"Of course it's wrong. Don't say another word. Put the thought out of your head." Michael shook his cigar at Fin emphasizing his words. "Leave ... that woman ... alone!"

Michael knew he was being hypocritical, but his circumstances were different from Fin's. "You're a married man with a loving wife, that is, if you treat her right. Besides, you know better than to touch a drop of liquor."

Michael scrutinized Fin through narrowed eyes. "Are you hitting the bottle again?"

Fin's own eyes fixed on the edge of the desk, not wanting to meet his father's. "Well, I've had a nip or two."

"A nip or two?" Michael's voice grew louder. "What the devil? What's wrong with you? You know damn well a nip will lead to another, then another, until you're trapped again. Stop it now! Do you hear me?"

"Yes, sir," said Fin fidgeting in his seat, staring out the window over Michael's head.

"Go home to Francesca and your sick child. And start paying more attention to your family, especially to Kane. That boy is headed for big time trouble if you don't. And forget that woman. Stop going to Flo's. Then you won't be tempted."

"Thanks, Dad. Guess I just needed to hear what I already knew. You know, besides being my dad you really are my best friend."

Michael came around the desk and hugged his son. "I love you more than you'll ever know. Now scoot home to that family of yours."

After Fin left, Michael leaned against the doorframe for a moment, his hand over his heart, catching his breath. He'd adored his son from the moment he'd first laid eyes on him and had never given up wanting Meghan to feel half of what he did. Yet, he knew a leopard's spots never changed.

"What was on Fin's mind? asked Meghan as they sat down for dinner.

"Oh, just some man talk. In case you haven't noticed, Fin and I enjoy each other. We can talk about anything." Except, Michael, shuddered, my affair with Ireland that I hope he never discovers. Yet, if he did, I think he'd understand.

Michael noted Meghan's mouth had tightened, and the lines around it had become more pronounced. The gesture made her lips into a thin, sullen line. He detested this expression of hers and knew when she made it, there was always something on her mind, usually something he had or hadn't done.

The conversation died and the only sound heard was that of Michael's fork clinking against his plate as he ate. Meghan wasn't eating. She stared into the distance. Michael knew the signs, the faraway eyes, the narrowed mouth, meant she was preparing to light into him about something, but he wasn't prepared for the bomb that she dropped.

"I've never confronted ye, Michael, but I can't hold it any longer. For years, I've seen a woman's outline next to yers, and it's not me. I've tried to overlook it, but I can't. Who is she? Do ye love her?"

Michael's fork stopped in midair, then dropped deafeningly onto his plate. Being used to courtroom surprises, he composed himself and said in a calm, but angry voice, "Where in the devil is this coming from? I don't know what the hell you're talking about."

"I'm talking about her. She appeared to me again this evening, her shadow beside you, and it dom well wasn't me."

"Oh, I see. You're making accusations based on something you think you saw in that damn ... whatever that thing is hanging from your neck. I think your imagination is working overtime. You know you aren't always accurate in what you see when you do that voodoo of yours."

Meghan fingered her golden beryl necklace that she used for scrying. "I don't *think*, I *did* see, and it hasn't been the first time. That woman's come to me many times over the years. I've just chosen to ignore it. But I can't any more. So, I'll ask again. Who is she? Do ye love her?"

Deny, deny, deny, Michael had always heard. "Come on, really? How could there be anyone but you? Between work and you I wouldn't have time for another woman. I can't imagine ... "

"Stop it! All those evenings ye say yer working. Yer not are ye? Ye with her, aren't ye?" Meghan twisted the napkin in her lap trying to keep her hands from shaking.

"You know, Meghan, I've put up with a lot over the years, separate beds, your controlling ways, your obsessiveness with your meditations, predictions, and incantations. What reason would there be for me to come home? Yet, I still do, don't I?"

"Well, yes, but ..."

"I'm not going to sit here and defend myself against you, it's hopeless. I'm going for a walk."

Meghan glanced out the kitchen window at the swirling snow. "Now? But we're not finished here. Besides, it's bitter out there and beginning to look like a blizzard."

Michael glanced over his shoulder as he walked from the room. " It won't be any colder out there than it is in here."

31

Friday, November 22, 1963, the world reverberated with the news of John F. Kennedy's assassination. The fatal shot was fired from a 6th floor window of the Texas School Book Depository as Kennedy's motorcade made its way down the west end district of Dallas, known as Dealey Plaza. The Italian Carcano bolt-action rifle that fired the deadly shot belonged to Lee Harvey Oswald, who several hours later, was apprehended at the Texas Theater in Dallas' Oak Cliff section.

Two days later on Sunday, Oswald's transfer from police headquarters to the Dallas County Jail was being televised live when Jack Ruby, owner of several local nightclubs, shot him in the abdomen.

That same Sunday, in the basement of the Armory Lounge, Gino flipped on the television while he waited to drive Giancana and Johnny, *The Snake*, to a job.

Gino's mind wasn't on the program because he was dwelling on his mother's harsh words when he told her he wouldn't be accompanying her to mass that day. He felt guilty telling her he felt under-the-weather instead of the real reason he wasn't going.

When a gunshot from the TV shattered the peace in the basement, Gino plopped onto the sofa, shocked at the chaos taking place on the screen in front of him. He'd just missed witnessing the shooting of Kennedy. Sigari De Cassio was pouring himself a drink at a bar in the corner and was unaware of what had happened.

"Hey, DeCassio, that guy just shot Oswald." Gino pointed to the TV screen, "Fuck! I even recognize the shooter. But when I knew him, he was called Sparky. He used to sell me and Carlo horse-racing tips back when we wuz going to the track. Boy! He hated that nickname. Never knew his real name. Guess he don't live in Chicago no more."

"Youse kidding me," said DeCassio, absentmindedly. His baldhead gleamed as brightly as the star sapphire on his pinkie as he raised a glass of scotch to his thick lips.

"They're saying his name's Jack Ruby. Why would he be such a giamope?" asked Gino. "Oswald needed to be strung up for whacking the president, not being killed hisself."

DeCassio looked at the TV with interest. "Ruby? Did ja say Ruby?"

Gino nodded.

" Shhh, don't cha know. It was part of the plan."

"Plan? What plan," said Gino moving to a chair closer to where DeCassio was now sitting and speaking in a hushed voice.

"Ruby ain't no golden boy, but he is known to be a friend of both Joe Campsi and Tony Accardo."

Gino stroked his mustache, deep in thought. "But I thought Campsi and his brother Sam were Lieutenants of Carlos Marcello, the boss in New Orleans."

"That's right, they are," said DeCassio, taking another sip of scotch.

"And youse also saying Accardo knows this Ruby guy?"

"Sure he does," said DeCassio. "As you said, Ruby used to live in Chicago. Grew up in the Maxwell Street area. He's connected. He's done both Giancana and Accardo favors. Lots of small ones, and I'd say a pretty big one, too."

DeCassio smiled as he saw Jack Ruby being surrounded by the Dallas police. "At Accardo's request, Ruby, who is thick with the Dallas fuzz 'cause of his nightclubs there, went and talked to the sheriff in Big D. He got him to consent to the Mafia's expansion in the city. And I knows for a fact, Ruby is a friend of that bigtime Dallas gambler McWillie, who happens to be an associate of Santo Trafficante's in Havana."

Gino lighted a cigarette and took a drag, shaking his head in disbelief. "Wow! Seems it's a never ending circle."

"Yeah, kid, ya got that right. But back to Ruby. Rumor is, he was recently in Cuba visiting McWillie, who is now head of gambling in Havana's Tropicana Club. It was supposedly just a friendly visit, but I'd bet differently. Ruby may not be part of the Outfit, but he's a fuckin' good friend. Even ran guns and ammo from Galveston Bay to Cuba for Castro's guerillas back when. He's no stranger to crime."

"Never heard any of this. Course, I haven't been driving for Giancana that long. Don't know much of the goings on outside of Chicago." Gino flicked the ash off his cigarette.

"Well," said DeCassio, "Ruby's a blowhard. Has a loose tongue. Don't think he's trusted too much, but seems he's been relied on enough to do this job. Maybe it's a sly way to shut him up."

"This job?" Gino's head swam with confusion.

"Yeah," said DeCassio, pointing to the TV showing the police walking off with Ruby in handcuffs.

Jack Ruby wasn't the only one in trouble that November. It started out innocently enough on the Saturday after Thanksgiving when Kane met his friends, Tony Boy, Joey Masserli, and Eddie LaFont at the Rack 'em Up Pool Hall. Kane had asked Brenda Donovan, a cute girl in his English class, for a first date that weekend, but she had gone to Rockford with her family for the holiday. So Kane decided to join his buddies in an 8-Ball tournament.

The Rack 'em Up buzzed with activity. His friends were already there, and Joey and Eddie were well into the first game. Tony Boy was watching from a high stool by the wall next to the cue sticks. The bar was full of men, and Sally, the bartender, was busy serving several tables of couples sitting near the front window. The booths were empty except for the last one in the back corner where three men sat. Because of the dim lighting and smoky haze, they were only silhouettes, and Kane didn't give them a second thought.

He greeted Tony Boy and sat down next to him, facing the door as his uncles and grandpa had taught him. He lighted a cigarette and watched the game. When it was over, Kane got up to play the winner, and Eddie went over and put money in the jukebox. The room filled with the sounds of Chubby Checker's, "The Twist" and then Elvis singing in his sensual voice, "It's Now or Never."

After the opening break, Joey won the lag, broke the balls, and shot. He pocketed all but six of the balls.

"Damn," said Kane, "you must have been practicing. Didn't think I was gonna get a turn." He chalked his cue and was preparing to take his first shot when the three men from the back walked toward the front of the establishment. One stopped and watched the game while the other two men headed toward the door. Just as Kane was ready to shoot, he happened to look up.

It had been four years, but he hadn't forgotten the man with the shock of red hair and spoon-shaped ears that had shot his grandpa. It was obvious the man didn't recognize Kane, and that was good. Gave Kane an advantage.

"Come on, shoot. Whatcha waiting for?" Joey Boy blew cigarette smoke across the table.

"Think I need a different angle." Kane edged around the table toward the man. As he did so, he passed Joey Boy and said under his breath, "Stay cool. Just keep talking but don't make a move when I do."

As Kane got to the other side of the table near the man, he threw his cue stick on the table. In a swift motion, he pulled his stiletto from under his shirt and lunged at the man whose slits for eyes bugged when Kane plunged the blade into the man's abdomen, twisted right and left, then withdrew it. The knife was sticky and blood-coated.

Kane trembled and felt sick, yet shouted, "That's what you get for trying to kill my grandpa, you son of a bitch."

"*Merda*," yelled the man as he fell to the floor. The spoon-eared man's companions turned when they heard him cry out and ran back. They seized Kane who had already returned the stiletto to his pocket.

Immediately, Joey and Tony pulled the men off Kane and the three boys started fighting the men with their fists. The Rack 'em High was now up for grabs. The women with the men sitting by the front window were screaming, their companions trying to calm them. Sally had called the police, while a couple of patrons at the bar rushed over to try and help the injured man. Some men even started fighting each other for no apparent reason. In an instant, the night exploded with screaming sirens.

It was difficult to tell if the ambulance or the patrol cars arrived first because now the police and paramedics were both inside the pool hall. The stabbed man was carried out on a stretcher, and Kane was cuffed, fighting and cussing all the way as he was led to a police car by the curb.

Kane's friends knew better than to get involved, so they shrank back into the shadows as if they didn't know him.

32

Kane's parents had been called, and Fin, leaving a distraught Francesca, rushed to the precinct after having first called Michael. Fin and his dad arrived about the same time. They didn't see Kane who was being held in a back room. Fin grabbed Michael and hugged him.

"Dad, you're the best. You'll never know how much I appreciate you coming down here for me. I don't know what I'd do without you."

"You know I'm always here for you and your family," said Michael, as he settled himself on one of the hard benches in the waiting room.

"What's going to happen to Kane, Dad? Will he go to prison?" Fin paced up and down the hallway where he and Michael were waiting to see what charges would be filed. "I can't believe Kane stabbed and killed a man."

"He's underage," said Michael, "so the case will probably be heard in juvenile court. I called Judge Coleman, my friend, in hopes he might be able to get this through the system tonight." Michael wiped perspiration from his brow. "I've been afraid of something like this. I know I don't have to tell you, this isn't the first time Kane's been in trouble." Fin looked at his dad in dismay.

"My God! I never knew that." He stopped pacing and stared at Michael.

"They were minor infractions, and I was able to get him released. Well, there was one that was more serious. One of

Francesca's brothers was instrumental in getting him off that time. That's the reason Kane spent that summer in Michigan on a farm. A kind of probation for stabbing a couple of boys during a gang fight."

"What the hell? I can't believe this. Why was I kept in the dark about all this?" Fin sat down beside Michael.

"Francesca was aware, but I'm not sure you were around. These incidents may have occurred during your drinking binges when you'd disappeared. Or if you were sober and home, perhaps she didn't want to worry you. Maybe she was afraid you'd start drinking again. The reason isn't important. This offense is more serious than the others. If Kane was an adult, it would certainly mean prison. Not sure what will happen now." Once again, Michael wiped his face. "It's like an oven in here."

"So what are we going to do" asked Fin, starting to pace again. He needed a drink, but instead he kept lighting one cigarette after another.

"There's nothing we can do, but wait." Michael looked at his pocket watch. "It's already been a couple of hours. We should hear something soon."

Finally, a policeman whose badge read Sergeant Malone appeared. "Mr. Callahan, Judge Coleman just called. He will see you in his chamber. Your grandson's filing has been reviewed and his statement taken."

"Let's go, Fin. Don't say anything, no matter what the judge might say. Let me handle this.

When Michael and Fin entered Judge Coleman's chamber, the kind-faced judge rose and shook their hands, gesturing to the chairs in front of his desk.

"Well, I have good news and bad. Because of Michael here, I was able to get a hearing waived. Kane's statement was sent to the probation department for a pre-court screening. The decision is not to forward the case for prosecution in juvenile court. Instead, the Department of Juvenile Justice reviewed everything. It has been decided Kane will be sent to the Illinois State Home for Delinquent

Boys in St. Charles for six months, then he will have probation for the next six."

With a sob, Fin's head dropped into his hands. Michael touched his son's arm. "It's really the best sentence Kane could receive. There was a slight chance he could have been tried as an adult because of the prior gang member stabbings on his record, especially since tonight's incident ended in a homicide. You should count yourself lucky."

"But I hear that place is the worst," said Fin, looking at Michael. "Everything from car thieves to murderers are there."

"Well, in this instance it looks as if the facility fits the crime. Kane *is* a murderer. After being there, I hope Kane will mend his ways."

Kane remained in a holding cell for twenty-four hours after his fate was decided. His parents waited the next evening when he was led out of the station to be taken away. As he emerged in handcuffs from the building, Francesca ran and threw her arms around him.

"My baby, my baby," was all that was intelligible through her tears, as she hugged Kane tightly.

Kane whispered in her ear. "I'll be fine, Mama. Don't worry. I'll be back in no time."

Francesca clung to him. Finally, the authorities pulled her away and shoved Kane into a waiting police car. Francesca buried her eyes in Fin's shoulder as the vehicle pulled away from the police station. She couldn't bear to watch. Fin remained resigned, numb with disbelief, smoothing her hair.

Kane might have been street smart, a member of a gang, and have brass *coglioni* as his grandpa liked to brag about, but he was still scared shitless. He did his best to hide his fear as the official vehicle drove him to St Charles, a suburb forty miles west of Chicago.

The car followed the Fox River through the quaint town's main area, after which it turned down a road lined with high barbed wire fencing. It pulled up in front of an imposing, three-story, red brick building that was the visitor and intake center for the Illinois State Home for Delinquent Boys.

The sun in the west was slipping away faster than a thief in the night as Kane was taken from the automobile and steered into the building. He didn't know what to expect when he was led to an area where a hulk of a man told him to undress.

"And take those things from round your neck," the man snarled. When Kane hesitated to remove the cornicello and St. Cristopher medal, the man regarded him with contempt. "You'll get them back when you leave. Here. Give them to me and get a move on. I need to get you settled before lights out."

Kane fingered the leather pouch with the good luck stones in his pocket as he removed his pants, T-shirt, and bomber jacket, replacing them with a gray shirt and elastic waistband pants. He was handed an extra set of clothing and toiletries.

Once again, Kane wondered if his grandparents' good luck charms had any power at all. They sure hadn't kept him from this place. Kane tried to keep his knees from shaking as he waited for the next step in the process. The whole time wishing he was still a babe in his mother's arms.

Soon, a burly guard dressed in dark blue with a gargoyle-like face appeared and led him down a long, foul-smelling hallway.

The man stared at Kane and growled, "If you wanna get along in here, kid, you be nice to us, and we'll be nice to you."

They came to a metal door with the letter "B" over an oblong window. After unlocking the entry, the guard pushed Kane into a dormitory-type room with at least twenty-four bunk beds. "'Ere's yer home, kid."

The door slammed shut with a clang and locked behind them. Kane was shoved toward the back of the room where an upper bed was assigned to him before the guard departed.

The bed below was occupied by a beefy-looking kid with a tight, square jaw, jet-black curls, and bulging eyes. "My name's Rocco, but I prefer Rock," he said as Kane climbed up on his bunk ignoring him.

From atop his bed Kane looked around at the begrimed room. The evening's fading light and the few light bulbs dangling from the ceiling were little help in making the room look friendly.

“Ain’t purdy is it,” said Rock watching his new bunk mate’s eyes rove around the dingy brick walls.

Kane didn’t reply, but fell back on the hard pillow, looked at the ceiling, and tried to quell his fear of this new grim reality.

“And you ain’t seen nothing yet,” declared Rock, still looking up at him. “Good thing you’re not blonde and thin. That’s what they like the best.” Rock looked at Kane’s muscles. “You look strong. That’s good around here. Did they tell you, lights out is 9:30?”

Kane grunted and rolled over. He’d be asleep before then. And maybe, he told himself, in the morning this would all be a bad dream, and he’d see the green walls of his bedroom at home when he opened his eyes. But neither happened.

Kane felt he’d been asleep but a minute when he awoke to a bloodcurdling cry that seemed to rattle the room. He bolted straight up in bed unable to see anything in the inky blackness. The piercing scream seemed to come from the guard station next door and was unlike any Kane had ever heard before.

The cry reminded Kane of an animal in terrible pain. It was followed by loud racking sobs. The next thing he knew there was a rustle in the room as someone entered. Soft weeping issued from one of the beds. Kane lay back on his pillow, wondering what had just happened. He shivered. Chills raced up and down his spine, and it took him a while to fall back to sleep.

33

Before daybreak, a shrill bell sounded and everyone bounded from their beds. Kane hadn't been able to see the other inmates clearly the night before, nor had he cared to. Now the sun was rising. Its early rays slanted through the barred windows, and he observed those he would be living with for the next six months. It was definitely a motley crew---different ages, sizes, and cultures. Kane jumped from his bunk and started to pull on his clothes as everyone else was doing.

"How ja sleep?" asked Rock, climbing into his beltless trousers.

"What the hell was that hideous cry last night? Scared the shit outta me."

"You ain't heard nothing yet. Wait 'til you're waked with the noise of heads banging against the wall and agonized cries."

"I don't understand," said Kane. "What's going on?"

"Shit! Can't believe you. How did someone so naive get put in here? What ja do anyway, steal candy from a baby?"

"Killed a guy," said Kane, buttoning his shirt."

"Fuck! You killed a man? And you don't know what goes on in here. Well, I'll spell it out." Rock sat down and pulled on his soft shoes. "R--a--p--e. Better watch out. The guards go after innocents like you. They'll love making you get on your knees and suck their dick."

Kane turned from Rock, gagged, then regained his composure. "No one's gonna touch me. I'd rather die than do that. Did they do that to you?"

"Hell, no. We had it out right away. They know better than to mess with Rock. I got friends on the outside that'll get'em if those stinkin' pervs ever try me."

"Well, they're not gonna mess with me, either," said Kane, wondering if his uncles had any influence here.

Rock grinned and gave him a strange look. "We'll see."

They marched in a line on the way to breakfast. The bruiser guard, named Bluto led the way. At the door of the cafeteria, he grabbed Kane's arm. "Tonight." he sniggered.

Kane's eyes radiated fierce hatred as he moved forward in line not responding.

"Looks like you're next," whispered Rock after they'd gone through the food line and sat down.

"Fuck 'em. No way." Kane sound more confident than he felt.

After a breakfast of runny eggs, burned bacon, and dry, stale toast, Cell Block B was directed to a wall in the exercise yard, handed a brush, a gallon of paint each, and told to get busy.

While they were working, Rock said, "See that corner at the far end of the yard? Where that scraggly tree is?"

Kane nodded.

"It's off limits. You'll get beaten if you go near there."

"Why?"

"Dunno know," said Rock, "but some day before I blow this joint I'm gonna find out."

By the end of the day, Kane was exhausted. The work hadn't tired him, but the emotional strain of trying to stay out of the ruthless guards' way had. They were always on the captives' backs yelling and threatening them. The watchdogs breathed down their necks every minute, wielding their authority with a big stick.

A guard named Jude seemed to get a thrill out of hitting them if they stopped for one instant or talked. Then when paint went flying from his blow, it was justification for another blow.

It was a relief at the end of the first day when the lights went out and everyone was quiet. It gave Kane time to think about what he had done. He wasn't sorry for the killing even though it had put him in this dreadful place, but he had promised revenge on the men who had tried to kill his grandpa, and he had gotten it. At least on one of them.

At the time of the shooting, Kane hadn't been sure what the other men looked like, but now he guessed they were the two who had been with the spoon-eared man at the pool hall. When he got out of this place, he would hunt them down. For now, he'd try to be a model prisoner and maybe he'd have a chance to be released sooner than six months.

Grandpa Cal had told him getting out early was a long shot, but still Kane hoped. He closed his eyes and was instantly asleep. All of a sudden he was jerked out of bed, his feet thudded onto the floor, and before he knew what was happening he was dragged toward the door. A hint of moonlight making its way into the room revealed a gargoyle face.

34

All the way through Cell Block B and down the hall to the guard's station, Kane cussed and struggled under Bluto's grasp. He was thrust into a room where Jude waited.

"Got us some fresh meat," said Bluto.

"That's what you fuckin' think," shouted Kane as loudly as he could, hoping someone would hear. Surely, there was someone higher up who would appear and stop these guys.

"Aw come on, that ain't no way ta act. This'll be fun," said Jude, unbuckling his belt.

Kane realized help would not be coming. He had to take care of these guys on his own. Jude's trousers fell to his ankles, and Bluto shoved Kane toward him. That's when Kane, with his fists, hit Jude as hard as he could in the genitals.

Jude grunted and doubled over.

"Why you miserable bitch," yelled Bluto. He grabbed Kane from behind and threw him to the floor, kicking him in the back with his steel-toed boot.

By this time, Jude had recovered and now withdrew his stick, beating Kane while Bluto continued kicking. Kane struggled to fight them, but it was useless. Jude held him down with a grip he couldn't break.

With a final kick, Bluto said, "He ain't no good ta us tonight. But it's not over. There's always tomorrow."

Get the fuck up," yelled Jude, letting go of Kane.

Kane didn't move.

"Sonofabitch." Bluto pulled on Kane's arms.

He and Jude dragged him back to Cell B, shoved him into the room, and slammed the door. Kane managed to crawl through the dark back to his bunk. It took a few tries before he was able to pull himself to the top.

Down below, Rock was awake. "Looks like ya didn't give in. Good for you. Is you hurt bad?"

Kane collapsed in pain. "I'll survive." He'd endured his old man's abuse, so he could take anything these stupid gorillas dished out. Nothing they could do would break his will. His grandpa had taught him never to let that happen. Kane would die before he'd let the guards have their way with him.

Every night for two weeks, Bluto and Jude came for Kane, and it was the same story. No matter how battered and weak Kane felt, he always summoned the strength to fight them. After each encounter, Kane crawled back to bed more beat-up than the night before.

During the day, he ached so much that he was barely able to lift his arms in order to do whatever work was required of him. If he stopped laboring for just an instant or didn't move fast enough the guards jabbed him causing him to topple over. Then more beatings ensued.

The time came after one of the nightly drubbings from Bluto and Jude that Kane could no longer hoist himself up to his bunk. He laid on the floor and moaned.

Rock never slept until his bunkmate returned, and this night, seeing that Kane would never make the climb he said, "I'll switch with you."

Rock vaulted to the top bed leaving the bottom for Kane. This incident sealed Rock and Kane's friendship, even more so, after Kane saw Rock getting a beating for making the exchange. Still, the trade remained.

On the final night when Jude and Bluto came for Kane, they didn't try to ream him. They'd given up on that. Instead, they came to give him "the quilt." Rock had told Kane about this punishment, and now Kane experienced it firsthand.

The guards wrapped him in a blanket and started beating him with Chicago phone books on the top of his head. This caused no outward bruising, only internal damage. Faces were never beaten by the guards, only bodies in places that couldn't be seen. The phone book procedure painfully jammed the head and neck down into the shoulders. The harm that the boys sustained was from internal damage that caused blood to be painfully pissed for weeks.

No one on the outside was aware of the brutality the boys endured. Social workers came once a month and visited with the boys individually and questioned them as to how they were being treated.

Even though the inmates might be in dire straits, they always replied that everything was good. With two guards standing in the room, there was no way they could ever tell the truth. If they did, they knew they would pay later. Even on visitor days, when families came, the boys remained mute regarding their mistreatment.

The first time Kane was allowed visitors after his incarceration, Gino drove Francesca in his black Coupe de Ville to see him. It was bad enough being given the third degree when they first entered the facility, but Francesca was even more disturbed when she was searched before entering the bare, dismal room with its acrid smell of lye and body sweat.

She and Gino sat at one of the tables where visiting took place and waited for Kane. When he was brought into the room, Francesca rushed to him but was roughly pushed back by a guard who said that touching wasn't allowed. So Francesca had to be content to sit across from her pale son and talk.

"I miss your cooking, Mama," Kane said with a smile, indicating more cheer than he felt.

The conversation was stilted between them, neither knowing what to say. Each time Francesca tried to speak she stopped in order to keep from crying.

Kane wished to comfort her, touch her hand. "It's okay, Mama. Don't worry. I'm fine. I'll be home soon." But his words weren't convincing to either of them.

Gino hoping to lighten the mood, smoothed his mustache and cracked some stupid jokes. Kane and Francesca found this irritating and gave him dirty looks instead of laughter. Fin asked if Gino could bring his grandpa to visit sometime. Gino replied that he'd offered to drive Vito, but Vito had refused him.

Kane was reminded that Vito disliked jails. Besides despising coppers, he'd been to a lockup once to see his cousin Lenny, and the horrible memory of seeing him hanging in the cell by his belt still haunted him. He'd vowed on that day never to visit another prison. Kane remembered hearing the story about the relative and understood.

"As for Mama, she's wearing out her knees praying for you," said Gino. "To hear her talk, the Lord will take care of you."

"That's Grandma," said Kane, seeing her in his mind, kneeling in front of her kitchen altar. "Give her a kiss for me. Okay?"

Gino nodded.

Outside the correctional center, Francesca breathed in the fresh air and broke down. Even though she'd witnessed harsh treatment of her brothers by her papa and received mistreatment from a drunken Fin, neither equaled what she knew her son must be going through.

"I hate it. I'm sorry, but I can't visit again."

As for Fin, he never visited the entire time because he had to work. The post office had rehired him after Michael, once again, pulled strings. Kane was glad his old man was sober and had a job, but he didn't care to see him. Hatred for the way Fin had treated all of them during his drunken bouts was lodged as deep in Kane's soul as an archeological ruin.

After Gino and Francesca's initial visit, the only person to visit Kane was Michael. He drove to St. Charles every week because he couldn't stand the thought of visitor day rolling around and Kane not having someone there. Each time Michael pulled his blue New Yorker into the correction facility's parking lot, he sat for a minute and fought back the lump in his throat, before pulling himself together and going inside.

He always had a note in his pocket from Meghan for her favorite grandchild. After Kane read it, Michael would put it back in his pocket so as to return it to Meghan. It seemed she picked up vibrations of Kane after his having held it. On receiving the returned note, she'd go to the birdbath for a while.

Michael no longer scorned her rituals. If they made her happy, who was he to question? Besides, she had quit talking about the woman's shadow she'd been seeing that Michael knew had to be Ireland. These days, Meghan had nothing but Kane on her mind.

One of Meghan's first letters made Kane cry.

Dear Kane, I don't understand what ye've done or why, or what yer going through, but I foresee things will soon be better. Stay strong.

Another time, she wrote:

My darling boy, don't forget meditation will help ye get through this. Will yer mind to leave yer body.

He never sent a response because inmates weren't allowed to write letters.

Kane and Rock talked and wondered about the off-limits area of the exercise yard. The more they talked, the more curious they became. Finally, they could contain themselves no longer and hatched a plan.

They decided to execute a dig during one of the baseball games that the boys were allowed to play once every couple of weeks. During the game, the guards would be busy rooting for their cell teams and be distracted. It was their best chance to sneak away unnoticed to the corner in order to discover its secret.

The next month, after the game started and they felt safe, they hightailed it to the forbidden place. With their hands, they dug in the soft earth. Kane stood watch while Rock worked, then Rock watched while Kane dug. Before long, Kane hit something hard.

"Shit! It's just stones. Why's this so secretive?"

Rock quit his lookout position to inspect the findings more closely. He nudged Kane. "Because ... "

He pointed, and Kane saw what he had unearthed weren't rocks at all. They were human bones! No one needed to tell them that the skeleton pieces probably belonged to boys who had been killed from severe thrashings or "the quilt." Otherwise, why would this be such a forbidden area?

Charlie, a boy in their own cell, had mysteriously disappeared. It was alleged he'd been released, but Kane and Rock knew that was impossible because the kid had been incarcerated for less than two weeks. He'd been taken away one night for the guards pleasure and had never returned. The boys looked at each other overwhelmed by their find.

Kane whispered, "Do you think Charlie's here?"

Rock whispered back, "I'd bet on it."

They had barely finished throwing dirt back on the criminal evidence when two guards loomed over them.

35

The guards dragged Rock and Kane to the warden's office and told of their offense. For some reason, Rock's punishment was merely getting a beating and being made to do double work for a week. Kane was not so lucky. He was dragged off to *The Hole*, otherwise known as solitary confinement, for five weeks. Despite the boys' knowledge of what they'd found when digging, there was no way they could ever tell anyone. Who on the outside would believe them?

The Hole was a dark space no bigger than a refrigerator box. There was no furniture so Kane sat on the floor. He recoiled at the rank odor of unclean bodies and their functions, housed prior to his. There was barely enough room for him to lie down. A foot-square window high in the wall gave no indication of sky or weather, just emitted a bit of light across the ceiling during the morning hours. A can served as his bathroom, and he took great care not to knock it over when he slept, otherwise, he'd be sitting and lying in his own excrement for the rest of his stay.

A bologna sandwich was shoved from the outside through a letter-sized slot within the main door twice a day. Kane surmised if he could see properly the meat was probably green. But it was eat or go hungry. So he gobbled it, washing it down with milk made from powder in a box.

With nothing to do or see, and to keep from losing his mind, Kane took his Grandma Cal's advice and began practicing his meditation. He let go of all thoughts and focused on his breathing.

His mind, like the sun going through a magnifying glass, went into a fine line of light and left his body. For the first time ever he traveled. More than once, he saw his Grandma Cal at the birdbath. When he returned to reality, he wondered if he'd actually been there with her.

When not meditating, his thoughts went to all sorts of things, both happy and sad. One was Brenda Donovan and how he'd messed up having a date with her by stabbing the spoon-eared man. As Grandma Cal often told him---certain things were meant to be. He decided the stabbing had been more important than the date, but still he thought of Brenda and tried to imagine what she would be like, wondering if she'd date him when he was sprung from this ungodly place.

Even Lana Roma with her Marilyn Monroe looks, intruded into his thoughts. He replayed every moment of their sexual escapades, almost feeling her lips and body on his. The smell of her peroxided, freshly-shampooed hair seemed real. He created all sorts of scenarios as to where she might be and what or who she might be doing it with. These things kept him sane as the days passed slowly by.

Michael arrived to visit Kane and was upset to learn he was in solitary confinement. It was the Christmas season, and the family, on both sides, had sent cards because presents weren't allowed. Michael questioned what Kane had done to be given such a severe punishment, but the warden was unbending.

Michael tried using his clout, which he hated doing, but the warden still wouldn't offer any information. Not one to give up, Michael used the holiday good-will-toward-man speech, asking if he couldn't talk to Kane through the door.

"Perhaps, I can slip the cards through the meal slot."

Still the warden stood his ground, knowing that the confinement was too dark for Kane to be able to read the Christmas wishes even if he allowed it.

"No," he replied brusquely. "He can read them on his release."

Michael returned to his car defeated. "Damn," he shouted to the air. He was distressed by the warden's stance, as much as he was by the realization that, even when jailed, his grandson couldn't seem to stay out of trouble. After he got in the automobile, frustrated at the unfolding events, he hit the steering wheel with his fist and continued to swear. He stared out the windshield at the ashy-gray sky. Only a patch of pale-blue peeked through the dreariness.

A plague of noisy grackles landed on the ground in front of the automobile, their long beaks picking at something between the gravel of the parking lot. A lone bird swooped upon the car's hood, its golden eyes staring at Michael, its iridescent feathers shining eerily.

Michael shivered and a chill ran down his back. He knew that this feeling was the same as the time Meghan had shuddered and said that someone was walking over her grave. It was an old wives' tale, and he put no stock in it, yet it did knock him for a loop. He beat on the window until the bird flew and joined the others. A fleeting thought crossed Michael's mind as to what kind of meaning his wife would attribute to the bird incident. Maybe he would ask her when he got home.

Michael sat. Eventually, he started the motor and pulled onto the road. He felt unsettled and needed comfort. At this point, the only person capable of giving it to him was Ireland.

36

Michael rolled off Ireland onto the pillow. "I needed that."

Ireland rose up on an elbow and looked at him. "It was rough, huh? Not being able to see Kane."

She stroked his cheek, feeling the bristles of his five o'clock shadow, noting more gray than dark in it. She settled beside him, and they lay quietly each thinking their own thoughts.

Michael liked coming to Ireland's apartment. Here he was able to leave the outside world behind, the day-to-day struggle of living in an unhappy marriage---his worries about the possibility of Fin falling off the wagon---about Kane and his delinquent behavior.

After their anniversary dinner at the Palmer House, Michael had set Ireland up in this high-rise on Lake Shore Drive. She had decorated the twenty-fourth floor unit with all the accoutrements she knew Michael liked. A firm mattress for his bad back, a leather armchair by the fireplace, even a humidor filled with his favorite Montecristo cigars on the table next to it. The cigars had been a surprise for him after she had discovered they were his favorites and were impossible to buy in the States.

As they lay quietly, Ireland's thoughts drifted back to the first evening they'd spent in their love nest.

She saw Michael sinking into the luxurious chair while she sat on the ottoman at his feet. He'd opened the cherry wood humidor, reached for a cigar, and had taken off the band with its fleur-de-lis logo and slipped it on her finger. "I now pronounce you ... mine forever." He laughed, sat back, and sniffed the No. 2 cigar. "You're wonderful. Where did you find these?"

"Certainly not in Chicago. Kennedy's '62 embargo with Cuba took care of that." Ireland watched as Michael lit up and sat back taking his first puff. "My cousin in London sent them to me. He works for Alfred Dunhill on Duke Street."

"Speaking of the embargo, reminds me of something I heard," he said. "Don't know whether it's true, but the story goes that the night before Kennedy signed that trade ban he sent Press Secretary Pierre Salinger to scour D.C. to buy up all of his favorite smokes. Found twelve hundred cigars, so it's said."

"Wow! That's a lot of tobacco," said Ireland. "Sorry. You don't have that many. Maybe enough to last you a while, though."

"That they will." The end of Michael's cigar glowed as he drew on it and exhaled a puff of blue smoke. "Do you know how this got its name?" He held the cigar up and admired it.

"No," said Ireland, "but I bet you can tell me."

"Montecristo's are named after one of your beloved novels, The Count of Monte Cristo."

Ireland looked puzzled. "How can a book influence a cigar's name?"

"Well, as you know cigars in Cuba are hand rolled. The workers are called torcedores. It's a monotonous job sitting all day at long wooden benches and rolling. It takes skill and because the workers have daily quotas there's no time to talk. So, to keep from getting bored there's a lector with a microphone in front of the room. Early in the day, he reads newspapers. Then, after taking a break, workers listen to books. The Dumas' novel, one of their favorites, inspired the name for my cigar. There's also a smoke named Romeo y Julieta."

"Shakespeare? Gee, it seems all kinds of things were read to them. The owners are really good to their people."

Michael pulled her into his lap. "The readers aren't hired by the owners but by the workers who pay with a portion of their wages."

"You're so smart," said Ireland, stroking Michael's cheek. "Do you know how long this has been going on?"

"It goes back to the 1860s. Some rollers couldn't, maybe still can't, read. Yet, because of what they hear they've become better educated and politically active citizens. I understand that some have even memorized passages and poems that they've heard. A few illiterates have even been motivated to learn how to read."

"Making money and getting culture at the same time, how wonderful," said Ireland.

Ireland awoke from her reverie and heard Michael's soft snore in her ear. He'd had a rough day trying to see Kane, and she was glad he'd fallen into a much-needed sleep. She tenderly kissed his cheek and got up quietly from bed, padding to the kitchen. He'd want something to eat before saying goodnight and heading back to his home in Bridgeport and Meghan.

37

The door to *The Hole* opened.

"Come on, Callahan. You're outta here," said a voice.

Kane squinted and shielded his eyes with his arm. The single bulb shining from the ceiling in the hallway seemed brighter than the sun and hurt his eyes. He struggled to his feet and tried to stand. After a few attempts, he succeeded, but his knees buckled. He stumbled blindly out the door, still trying to get his legs working. He could barely move them, not having stood in five weeks.

"You're gettin' a shower," said the voice which had finally become a face with a globular nose and long, gray sideburns.

Inside the shower room, Kane gratefully stripped off his grime-stiffened clothes that smelled worse than a heap of dead animals. He didn't stop to worry whether the guard might attack him when he stepped into the shower stall and turned the faucet on. All thoughts faded except the feel of the stinging needles of water spraying from the showerhead.

True bliss! He'd never appreciated getting clean as much as he did now. Rubbing his body with the red bar of carbolic soap that smelled like tar didn't bother him a bit. Kane stood under the warm water, letting it sluice over his body, a dense fog of steam rising to the ceiling.

Finally, the guard yelled at him to get the hell out. Drying off on a thin, rough towel, Kane peered in the cracked mirror above the sink and saw a stranger. Vacant eyes peered at him from a drawn, sallow face. His hair was longer than the facility allowed, and he'd grown a beard. A barber came in and cut both, then used an electric razor to remove the rest of the facial hair before Kane was taken back to Cell Block B.

"Fuck! Ya look like shit," said Rock, from the top bunk when Kane returned that night. "Livin' like a mole musta been hell, huh?"

"Cool your chops. I don't need you flappin' your jaw, making fun. You shoulda been in that hell hole too, you jerk. You sure must have some *real* good friends somewhere."

Kane crawled into his bed and delighted in the stone-hard pillow and scratchy blanket that he drew to his chin. "This bed's never felt so good." Kane barely heard Rock's horselaugh before he drifted off.

While Kane was in solitary, his cell block had been assigned to kitchen duty. What a relief that the rest of his stay was spent in the kitchen on KP duty, usually peeling bushels of potatoes. Also the boys were now taking classes in order not to get too far behind in their schooling. Kanc became a model inmate and student because he didn't want to spend one minute longer in this awful place than he had to.

Kane and Rock discovered they were to be freed on the same day. Even though Rock lived in Elgin, they made a pact to see each other again before walking out into the May sunshine and parting.

It was as if all of Kane's senses had become needle sharp when he emerged into the world again. He noticed a robin tugging at a worm from the warm spring earth. The trees lining the drive budded a brilliant green. And oh, the smell was luxurious. He took a deep breath and exhaled. The air was fresh and clean like his grandma's clothesline-dried laundry. Kane wanted to dance. After six months, he was finally free. What a feeling! Tulips planted along the walkway, their purple and red heads bending in the spring breeze, gave off a hint of sweetness.

Kane saw his Grandpa Cal, a grin plastered on his face, waiting for him beside a new silvery-gray Buick Electra 225 convertible. They embraced each other tightly before Kane pulled back and inspected the shiny car.

"Cool! Grandpa, you got a Deuce-and-a-Quarter." Kane wandered around the car, running a finger along the straight-cut rear fenders, bending down to admire the fender skirts, and stopping to look at the the die-cast grille accenting the front. "It's a beaut."

"Climb in and I'll show you how it rides. Everything's power: steering, brakes, even seat adjustments and windows."

"Cool! Bucket seats." Kane sniffed the new car scent after he climbed in and shut the door. He looked at Michael in awe. His grandpa sure was no dork.

"Can we put the top down?"

"Why not?"

Soon they were on the road back to Chicago, but not before Kane had made his window go up and down and adjusted the seat a couple of times. They breezed down the expressway, the wind blowing through their hair, the traffic loud in their ears.

38

Francesca was elated to have Kane home. She hugged and hugged until he couldn't breathe. At last, she let go and tenderly ran her fingers through his wind-blown hair.

"You're home. I'm so happy. But look at you. So thin. I've got to fatten you up."

"You're as bad as Grandma. She's always pushing food."

Francesca laughed. "Well, you sure need it now. Between her and me, we'll put some meat on those bones."

Franco tugged on Kane's legs and jabbered a welcome.

Kane picked up the toddler and lifted him high into the air. "Hey, buddy, get a load of you. Talking like a big boy."

"Yeah," said Chiara, "he's just like a real person."

Kane put down his little brother and enfolded her in his arms. "You look good, kid. Growing up fast," he said, noting his sister's budding chest.

Chiara's face reddened, and she turned, busying herself by straightening the silverware on the table which she had earlier laid for the welcome home supper.

When Fin walked in he shook Kane's hand. "Welcome home."

"Yep, I'm back," said Kane, dropping his old man's hand and looking around the familiar room. "See you got a new couch."

"Isn't it pretty? It's not a hand me down either," said Chiara, plopping down on the gray polyester-covered furniture. "I helped Mama pick it out."

"Nice," said Kane.

After supper, Fin prostrated himself on the sofa and closed his eyes, Francesca tucked Franco into bed, and Chiara studied at the kitchen table for her year-end exams. For privacy, Francesca and Kane drifted into the hallway and sat at the top of the stairs.

"I hope you'll behave now. Don't forget you're on probation."

"I know, Mom."

"Will you make me a promise?"

"What?"

"That you'll stay out of trouble and graduate from high school."

Kane clasped Francesca's hand. "I promise, Mom.

Kane heard his grandpa's words after the caning incident. *Remember, when a man gives his word, he keeps it. He must have honor above all.*

Kane intertwined his little finger with his mom's. "Pinkie swear."

Kane's first visit to the Savio's after his release was a joyous occasion. When he walked in, his grandma grabbed him and nearly squeezed the life out of him she was so excited.

"Your mama's right. We need to put some meat on those bones of yours." She headed for the stove to stir her minestrone and check on the braciole in the oven.

Vito took over where Maria left off and hugged and kissed his grandson's cheeks. "Coglioni. I knew you had 'em. *Sangu di me sangu*," he said, limping to his chair.

Kane smiled. He'd heard his grandpa say the Sicilian phrase meaning, blood of my blood, many times, but this was the first time he'd said it to Kane, and it made him proud.

The basement kitchen was alive with Savios. All Kane's uncles were there. Pietro with Sylvia and children, Valentina, Colin, Tommy, and Simona along with Carlo happened to be in town from Las Vegas for a meeting with the Outfit and Arriana was with Gino.

Everyone gestured wildly with their hands, talking loudly, and laughing as they welcomed Kane. His uncles hugged, kissed, and toasted him with Vito's chianti, yelling, "Good job. Salute, salute."

The only person missing in the gathering was Fin, who was not missed by the Savio men. Kane had to admit he felt a little like a hero despite having to pay for his deed with six months out of his life.

"Papa taught you well," said Pietro slapping his nephew on the back. "Shootin' that fuckin' SOB. Youse a chip off the Savio block."

The men gravitated to one side of the room where Vito sat in order to talk in private away from the women, who were finishing up the meal preparations.

"What's going on out West, Uncle Pete?"

"Kane, my boy. Vegas is the place. Ain't at the Riviera, though. Been moved to the Desert Inn. The DI as the locals call it. Moe Dalitz one of Cleveland's Mayfield Road Gang is sole owner now. The developer, Wilbur Clark, finally sold him his interest. Course Moe's ownership ain't common knowledge.

"Ya oughta see the place, Kane. Looks like a big, sprawling ranch all redwood and sandstone with a huge neon cactus sign."

Pietro tried indicating with his hands the size of the sign. "Out front's this fountain that shoots water sixty-feet in the air. Shit, there's even another fountain in the middle of the fuckin' swimming pool. It shoots water up and down in time to music. It's called "Dancing Waters."

"Wow! It sounds really cool."

Carlo interrupted. "May sound cool, but weather out there's hotter than a whore's *fica*. Good thing the fuckin' hotel's air cooled or nobody would come."

"Yeah. And we're the first in Vegas to have individual controls in the rooms for visitors to adjust their own air."

"Shit! You guys got it made," said Gino.

Pietro nodded and continued, "Damn right. A nine-story tower was just built. Got a fuckin' high roller penthouse on top."

Again, Carlo broke in and slugged Pietro's shoulder. "Can you believe this here buffone is learning to play golf on the hotel's eighteen-hole course?"

"Really, Uncle Pietro? Thought that was a rich man's game."

"Well, I ain't hurtin'." Pietro pulled a pack of Marlboros from his jacket pocket, and in the process, Kane noted he wore a shoulder holster. His uncle tapped a cigarette and lighted it.

"The DI's got somethin' for everyone, even little kids. My family loves the playground. Hell, they're even gettin lessons in manners. Sylvia says they needs 'em."

Pietro laughed and exhaled smoke through his nose.

"Forget the kids," interjected Carlo. "Them two bars are the best. The Lady Luck's got a ninety-foot bar ... longest in the state. You should see it Kane. But my favorite's in the Celebrity Room. That bar's made from rawhide and the walls are decorated with steer heads."

"Real ones?" asked Kane wide-eyed.

"Yep, they're neat."

"I'd love to see that place," said Kane.

"Ya know," said Carlo, "we could use you out there. Huh, Pete?"

"Sure could," said Pietro. "When Carlo and I wuz your age we wuz hustling. Didn't need no school ta get where we are. You don't neither."

"That's right. Why don't you quit school and join us. I know that Moe could find a spot for you. Wouldn't that make you happy, Papa, if Kane wuz one of us?"

Vito smiled and nodded assent.

Kane shook his head. "Sounds cool. I'd flee this scene in a flash, but I promised Mom I'd graduate. Maybe after that?"

"Sure. A couple more years won't hurt nothin'.

The scent of cabbage with an underlying aroma of apple pie, greeted Kane when he entered the Callahan's. They welcomed him back in their usual staid way. Aunt Kitty joined them for dinner, as did Kane's parents and siblings. After their meal, Kitty and Francesca with Chiara and Franco left. Fin went into the study to visit with Michael.

Since Kane had seen his Grandpa Cal every week, except when he was in solitary confinement, it was Meghan's turn to spend time with her grandson. They sat in the backyard in front of the birdbath, and Kane told her about his meditation experiences.

"I know," said Meghan. "I could feel yer presence more than once while ye were gone."

It was a pleasant May evening, but Meghan wore a black cape against the night air. The evening star beamed like a smart student in the night sky and birds chirped in the trees overhead. The full moon cast the backyard in an alabaster light, and somewhere a mockingbird imitated a distant Whip-poor-will. Kane reveled in the sights and sounds that he'd missed while incarcerated.

"I have something for ye, to be guarded with yer life," said Meghan. "For yer eyes only."

She reached inside her cape and drew out a three-inch thick, black book with faded gold symbols on the cover that were strange to Kane. "I know yer ready for this book of secrets. It has been handed down from generation to generation. Study and absorb what's inside."

Kane took the rough leather-bound volume, feeling it's weight, rubbing a finger over the faint secret signs on the front, noting the worn, frayed spine of bygone years.

"Don't open it now," warned Meghan just as he was ready to pull back the cover. "Before you meditate always read some of the words within."

Holding the book felt strange, as if it had a life of its own. It gave off subtle vibrations that coursed through Kane's fingertips like tiny electrical impulses. He felt magnificent power and strength within. Overwhelmed and excited by this remarkable book in his hands, Kane knew that his grandma had entrusted him with a rare gift. His eyes focused into the distance, thinking of what he had been entrusted.

Snapping back, his eyes met his grandmother's. "There's not a lot of privacy at home with Chiara and Franco around. Perhaps it's best if I keep the book here."

"So wise already. I knew it was the right time to give ye this. Of course, leave it here. But I hope ye start studying it soon."

"Oh, I will," exclaimed Kane, "I'll come over after school when I can." He could hardly wait to see all that the book contained.

"Well, when ye do, it will be locked in me middle bureau drawer. Here's a key. I have another."

Meghan handed Kane an ornate gold key that she removed from the silver chain around her neck holding the beryl.

"For safekeeping put the key in the leather pouch of gemstones I gave ye." She tucked the book back under her cape.

As they walked toward the house, Meghan's thoughts went to Vito Savio, wishing she could tell him that he wasn't going to have the power over Kane that she knew he wanted. But he'd know soon enough. Stupid dago. Kane might not ever be the long-yearned for political figure she'd dreamed of, but her hold over him was going to be stronger than Vito's. She smiled to herself.

39

Before Kennedy's assassination in 1963, Vice President Lyndon Johnson had advised him to minimize escalation into South Vietnam. But by the time LBJ took office over sixteen thousand troops had been committed to the unstable region. Although Johnson wasn't for war, he said he wasn't going to let America be beaten by what he stated was a *damn little pissant country*.

So, in 1964, shortly after his landslide election, Johnson had a congressional resolution drawn that would give him power to expand the war if he thought it necessary. Later that year, after the U.S.S. Maddox, an American destroyer, patrolling Vietnam's Tonkin Gulf was attacked twice by the North Vietnamese, Johnson sent the resolution to Congress. It passed.

Still, the president's response to the Tonkin incident was to do nothing. In 1965, when General Westmoreland, commander of U.S. combat forces, requested up to 200,000 more soldiers Johnson refused because he didn't want to send young boys into combat. The war escalated. Additional men were drafted, and many more were killed. An anti-war movement grew.

Men burned draft cards, others fled to Canada to dodge serving in Vietnam. Anti-war protesters marched on Washington and ultimately a hundred thousand demonstrators paraded in eighty cities, as well as around the world.

Besides turbulence over Vietnam, America was bursting with civil unrest. In L.A.'s Watts area a black man was stopped by two white policemen for drunk driving. A brawl ensued, and the community, due to a bad economy and discrimination, became outraged. Six days of rioting, shootings, and lootings took place causing forty million dollars of property destruction.

During this time, women removed their bras as a symbol of independence, and the Sexual Revolution kicked in when the ban on birth control pills was lifted. Marijuana and LSD came into vogue. The Beach Boys, the Beatles, and the Rolling Stones all enjoyed the psychedelics. Bob Dylan, to the dismay of Newport Rock Festival purists, played an electric guitar for the first time.

On TV, housewives watched the hourglass announcing the debut of NBC's soap, *Days of our Lives*, and CBS showed the first Peanut's special of *Charlie Brown's Christmas*.

President Johnson signed the Civil Rights Act, and Martin Luther King, Jr. was awarded the Nobel Peace Prize. Kids rode skate boards. Women's skirts grew shorter and men's hair longer. Houston built the Astro Dome, St. Louis erected the Gateway Arch, and Astronaut Edward White made the first U.S. spacewalk.

Kane settled down and tried to dedicate himself to school. He still ran with the Loafers, but became wiser when there was a rumble with a rival gang or when a store heist or car theft was planned. Staying in the background was difficult especially when he wanted to be in the forefront of the action.

It was important to keep his promise, graduate, and complete his probation without any problems. Still those things hanging over his head didn't stop Kane from wanting to try LSD when the rest of the gang experimented with it. Hearing the hallucinogenic drug could be mind-blowing, he went with the Loafers to try it one night when they gathered in Ogden Park.

Tony Boy, who had tripped several times already, told Kane he would see things differently, that everything would become sharper, more dazzling in color, more intense.

Eddie LaFont who had also dropped acid agreed. "You'll find euphoria like never before."

Kane took the sugar cube offered him, and it wasn't long before he saw his friend's faces take on grotesque shapes. Brilliant colors swirled in nonsensical contortions, taking on a life of their own until he grew dizzy, threw up, and passed out.

The next morning when he awoke covered with vomit and dew and saw his pals lying like stones on the wet grass, he was at a loss to explain what had happened. Then he remembered his trip. He felt exhausted and wanted more sleep but not in the park, so he staggered home. He was glad no one was there when he arrived. After cleaning up, he fell into a dead slumber.

When Francesca arrived home from shopping, she was relieved to see he'd returned. The two of them had come to an understanding that on occasion when Kane didn't come home he'd be staying at a friend's house.

Many times Francesca had rued her papa's old country ways and iron-handed authority. Only her mama was able to exert influence over her papa, and even then not on raising Francesca's brothers. So just as Maria had no control over her sons when they were growing up, neither did Francesca over Kane. Combined with his grandpa's strong will and Meghan's tenaciousness, Kane was going to do what he wanted.

The doctor predicted, rightfully so, when Kane was born and hadn't cried when spanked that he would be a strong boy. And since Fin and Kane had never gotten along, and Fin didn't care what Kane did, tiny Francesca wielded little influence over her towering six foot three son. At least, she knew his word was golden and his promise to her that he would graduate would be kept. She worried as to what he might be doing on those nights away, hoping he wasn't getting into trouble.

She quietly closed his bedroom door, knowing he was safe. Kane was still sleeping when Francesca called him for dinner. She knocked. When he didn't answer, she went into the room and shook him. She became concerned that he wouldn't wake up, but when he mumbled incoherently, at least she knew he was okay even though his eyes remained closed. There seemed to be no choice but to let him be.

Early the next morning, he wandered into the kitchen where Francesca was fixing breakfast. "I was worried about you sleeping so long. I couldn't seem to wake you. Are you sick? Are you feverish?" She felt Kane's forehead.

"No, no, I'm fine." He pulled a chair up to the table. "Was just really tired. Guess I needed a good rest." Never would he tell his mother or anyone else in the family that he had taken an illegal drug.

Kane was glad he'd experienced LSD, but he discovered it wasn't ecstasy at all. For several weeks, he had recurrences of seeing colors and common things suddenly turning into weird shapes. It frightened him and was relieved when the flashbacks finally stopped.

He realized he didn't need to depend on drugs to feel pleasure. Meditating and leaving his body was enough for him. Yet, Kane recognized he did have an addiction---Brenda Donovan. He might as well be a junkie he was so captivated by thoughts of her and longed to see her again.

He was glad when the school year started. He'd had enough classes while incarcerated that he was ready to start his junior year. So with anticipation, he headed to school for registration. He looked for Brenda but didn't see her, and ended up finagling information from one of her friends as to her schedule and adjusted his to fit hers where possible.

He looked forward to watching Brenda flip her long blond hair with its fringe touching just above her eyes. And oh, those eyes---rimmed with a sea-green sparkle, growing dark as moss toward the center until they became black. Honey flecks of sunlight danced within, pulling him into their undertow.

He remembered hearing the story of how a thunderbolt had hit his grandpa when he first saw his grandma, and also how his great-grandpa had been jolted in the same way in a Sicilian vineyard many years ago. Was that what had happened to him? Kane didn't care what it was, he just knew he had to be near Brenda as often as he could.

Then there Brenda was, sitting across the room, in his first period geometry class. Between classes he wanted to talk to her, but she disappeared with a group of girls down the hallway before he had a chance. Even though they had several more classes together, Brenda didn't outwardly notice or acknowledge him, yet Kane saw her stealing glances when she thought he wasn't looking. After school, he stood at the bottom of the building steps waiting for her to emerge. When she did, he caught up with her.

"Hi Brenda," he managed to sputter because suddenly he was tongue-tied when she turned and their eyes connected.

"Oh, Kane. Hi. Sorry I can't talk, I need to get home." She picked up her pace, and he hurried to catch up to her.

"Slow down. Can I walk with you?"

"That's not wise," said Brenda, picking up speed.

"What's the deal? Are you seeing someone?"

"No, but my parents said to stay away from you. You're a jailbird."

Kane's heart sank. "It wasn't really prison. It was a correctional place."

"Same thing," said Brenda almost running now.

Kane followed her, finally able to plant his linebacker's body in front of her. "Stop. Come on. Would they have to know? I can tell you're attracted to me. I saw you watching me in class. Tell me I'm wrong."

His eyes fixed on her. Maybe he could hypnotize her. "Please. Go get a Coke with me."

Brenda seemed to be wavering because a slight smile crossed her face. Maybe his tactic was working.

"Okay. Yes, I do like you, or did. But I have to respect my parents. Sorry. Now get out of the way."

Kane stood firm, wishing he could sink his nose in her blonde tresses. "It's only a Coke. Come on. We won't stay long. Old man Wiman at the drug store doesn't care who's with who. Your parents will never find out."

"Move. I've got to go."

"Okay. See you at school then," said Kane, stepping aside to let her pass.

She hesitated. "Well, I am thirsty. But ... I ... Oh, okay just this once. But it can't be for long."

Kane was on cloud nine when he walked home after their drugstore drinks. He knew it wouldn't be the last time they'd be together. His will was stronger than Brenda's. It wouldn't be long before she was his.

When he walked in the door, Francesca was sitting at the kitchen table. Her eyes red as the setting sun, a sure sign she'd been crying.

"Mama, what's wrong?"

When Francesca tried to tell him she burst into tears. Kane couldn't understand her. He put his arms around her shoulders, trying to comfort her.

She laid her head on his shoulder. "He's dead. Oh, my god, he's dead." Her sobs seemed to fill the entire universe.

40

The mahogany casket, lid open, sat on a bier in the middle of the parlor. Inside the casket's satin-lined interior, Michael was laid out in his usual three-piece navy suit, a Montecristo cigar peeking from the breast pocket, his hands holding a rosary. A cross hung above a small table at the head of the casket where incense and candles burned. The smell of wax and the scent of woody musk, along with the scent of carnations and lilies, permeated the room with a heavy sadness.

Meghan sat at the foot of the burial box, a figure in black, a diaphanous veil covering her head. Her trembling hands, hidden beneath the folds of her cotton brocade skirt, held a lacey handkerchief. As friends and colleagues of Michael's filed by and offered sympathy, Meghan accepted their condolences by nodding.

It was only two days earlier that Michael had given Meghan a peck on the cheek and left for his office. Some hours later a woman's voice called saying that Michael had been taken to St. Joseph Hospital on Lake Shore Drive and had been pronounced dead on arrival. Since then, Meghan had gone through various points of anger---at herself, at the doctors who couldn't save her husband---at the woman who had called, but mostly at Michael for doing this to her. How could he leave her?

After the phone call, she went outside and sat for hours in front of the birdbath in a disbelieving stupor before wandering back into the house. Why hadn't she seen it? Those grackles Michael had mentioned in front and on his car. A harbinger. Yet, what could she have done? It was written in the stars.

Upstairs in her bedroom, she screamed and threw things. The antique hand mirror Michael had given her twenty years ago shattered on the floor. A china figurine of a Victorian woman, that Michael said reminded him of her, joined the mirror. She swept her arm across the bedside table knocking everything off, causing the alarm clock to break into tiny metallic pieces.

She went to Michael's closet and yanked all his clothes from the rod until suits, shirts, and ties were piled in the middle of the floor. Then she fell onto the garments, smelling his Old Spice aftershave, sobbing and howling like an animal caught in a trap. Her heart had been ripped out. Why? Why?

By the time, Fin and Francesca with Chiara, Franco and Kane arrived, Meghan was in the kitchen with Aunt Kitty, their eyes red and puffy, wetting the tea. Meghan shunned their hugs and words, except those of Kane, and him she held close. As stoic as ever, she offered refreshment. While the others accepted, Fin refused, going into his father's study and shutting the door.

He sat behind Michael's desk, ruffling the pages of the book he'd been reading, then raised the humidor's lid inhaling the well-know scent of his father and best friend, after which he laid his head in his hands and sobbed bitterly.

Meghan peered through her veil at the people who had come to view Michael's body and pay their respects. She heard some of his pals telling stories and laughing about something in Michael's life she had never known. She realized how little she'd truly known her husband. Half the people in the room she'd never seen or heard of, and who was that?

A woman, dressed in mourning with hair pulled back in a tight bun, leaned in, kissed Michael's cheek, straightened the cigar in his breast pocket, and whispered to him. The woman offered her hand to Meghan.

A chill crawled and hair stood on Meghan's nape. With all her senses, she knew that she was the woman. She ignored the offered hand, wanted to do more than that. She wanted to spit at her, blast and accuse her, yet knew this wasn't the time or place for a confrontation, nor would it bring Michael back. Meghan watched as Ireland disappeared out the front door.

Ireland hadn't been able to resist coming to the wake for one last goodbye. It was incredulous. Michael dead. She stood on the sidewalk, seeing his other life for the first time---his house, the swing at the end of the porch---Meghan. She stumbled toward the bus stop in tears, remembering all the good times they'd had---making love on the lawn of the Adler Planetarium, romantic dinners at the Palmer House, listening to his intriguing stories.

But the last memory was the most vivid and the one she held dearest---making love before he was to go to his office that morning. He had just kissed her passionately, telling her how much he adored her, and then he clutched his chest and without warning died in her arms.

The family was gathered and a priest said a prayer over Michael. After which, the hearse drove from the house transporting the body to the Nativity of Our Lord on West 37th. The family followed. Kane, newly licensed to drive, drove Meghan and Aunt Kitty in Michael's, barely broken in, Buick convertible. Fin was behind the wheel of the family's second-hand tan Dodge with the others.

Father Lyons met the casket at the church door. He covered the coffin with a white linen pall, said a prayer, sprinkled holy water, and walked with it to the front of the church. The strains of "Be Not Afraid," swelled from the organ. All through the funeral mass, Meghan sat rigid as cast-iron, her tears dried up. Aunt Kitty wiped her eyes from time to time. Michael had been a wonderful friend and family member.

Francesca grasped Kitty's hand and cried quietly. She had loved Michael, almost like a second father. Franco was too young to understand, but Chiara wept over losing her Grandpa Cal. Fin sitting beside her looked straight ahead, his red-rimmed eyes blank hollows. On the other side of Fin, Kane sat, squeezing the bridge of his nose, holding back tears. Then, he caught a whiff of whiskey. His old man was drinking.

41

Several months after Michael's death, Fin disappeared, and Francesca knew he was on a bender. She had been suspicious ever since the funeral that Fin might be sneaking nips. However, she couldn't be sure since he hadn't missed a day of work or been belligerent or acted drunk.

Fin had been inconsolable, quieter than usual, and moody since losing his father. The two had always been close but their bond had become stronger after Michael found Fin on skid row and helped him dry out. Francesca was saddened that Fin had fallen off the wagon, but she knew he was in deep mourning. Hitting the bottle was an escape, a way of burying his sadness. She prayed this drinking bout would not last long and wasn't telling of things to come and that he'd be home soon.

Meghan, breaking a vow to never visit Francesca again, gamely climbed the steep flight of stairs to her son's humble abode. When Francesca opened the door, she felt as if she was seeing an apparition, albeit a winded one. She hadn't seen Meghan since the funeral some months ago and was taken aback seeing her standing on the threshold.

Meghan's flaming-red hair which before had been streaked with gray had turned completely silver. Her face was colorless, and her once svelte frame carried a few extra pounds. Despite deep dislike of her mother-in-law, Francesca felt sympathy. She realized Meghan, in her own strange way, had loved her husband.

Both women stood looking at each other, neither knowing quite what to do next, Meghan still gasping to catch her breath and Francesca at a loss for words.

Finally, she found her tongue. "Meghan, wha ... what a surprise. Come in. How are you? Here sit down."

She rushed to move yesterday's newspapers from the couch and pick up a throw pillow off the floor, tossing it into a nearby chair.

Unexpectedly polite, Meghan murmured what sounded like "Thank you" and entered the small room, trying to ignore the clutter. She settled where Francesca indicated and set her purse primly beside her.

"Uh ... would you like some tea?" Francesca asked nervously, not sure why the woman was sitting in her living room.

"I have no time for tea. I need a favor." Before Francesca could ask what kind of favor, her mother-in-law came to the point. "I want Kane to live with me."

Francesca froze at the request, which sounded more like a demand. She was bewildered. "Live with you?"

"That's what I said. Are ye deaf?"

Obviously, Francesca's compassion for her mother-in-law had been misplaced. Michael's death hadn't mellowed the woman a bit, and Francesca's animosity toward her mother-in-law returned stronger than ever. "No, I'm not deaf! Forget it! Kane isn't going to live with you. He belongs here with his family."

"I am family, and I need someone with me now."

"Well, what about your Aunt Kitty ..."

"Absolutely not! She has her own place. Kane's the logical one. I can give him a lovely home." Meghan looked around the unkempt room.

Francesca could barely tolerate the woman's *holier than thou* attitude. With Fin drinking again she knew it would probably help keep peace if Kane wasn't there when Fin straggled home after another binge. It would also ease the money situation with him gone, but then again, without Kane's paycheck from Buddy's

Garage, where he was now working, she would be struggling to make ends meet.

Despite that, she didn't want Kane to live with Meghan.

"No! Never! Kane belongs here, not with you. If you're lonely, he can visit. But live with you? No! That won't happen." Francesca's eyes burned like hot pokers into her mother-in-law.

"Fine." Meghan sniffed with contempt, rising and ignoring Francesca's fiery glare. "I'll come back tomorrow after school and see what Kane has to say." She drew her body up stiffly in defiance and strode to the door. "We'll just see."

Before Francesca could respond, Meghan was half out the door. "I'll talk to Kane tomorrow."

That night after dinner when Chiara had gone to her room and Franco was tucked in bed, Francesca told Kane about Meghan's visit. "I can't help that your grandma's lonely, but I forbid you to go. With your papa gone, I need you here. I don't even want you talking to your Grandma Cal tomorrow."

"But Mom, I need to listen to what she has to say. Grandpa Cal would have wanted that." Kane's soulful eyes begged Francesca.

Francesca felt guilty at the mention of Michael. He had been good to them, paying their rent and buying groceries when Fin had disappeared. Finding Fin and getting him to dry out. Getting him employment away from the bar. Helping to keep Kane out of jail.

"Oh, you're right. Go ahead. Listen to what she has to say." Francesca rationalized she'd be doing it for Michael.

Kane thought about his Grandma Cal's invitation. He was torn. It was peaceful being at home without his old man's abusive words and actions. At the same time, he did feel sad for his Grandma Cal being all alone. Yet, her house was far from ideal because she didn't live close to Harper High. It was miles from Bridgeport, and public transportation between his Grandma Cal's and school was minimal. Kane didn't want to attend a different school. After being away for six months, he was entrenched once again with the Loafers, plus he was slowly worming his way into Brenda's heart. It was his junior year, and he wanted to graduate from Harper.

"I don't want to go to Grandma Cal's. But if I did you'd have one less mouth to feed. I know you're worried about money, Mom. But I'll still give you my weekend's wages from working at Buddy's, if I do decide to go."

The next day when Kane and Meghan talked, he voiced his concerns and feelings about leaving home. He didn't mention Brenda or the gang, just said he didn't want to leave his friends at Harper. Unlike when Fin had begged not to be forced to change schools, and Meghan had stubbornly insisted he go to St. Barnabas, now she readily acquiesced. She would do anything for her grandson.

"Don't worry, you can stay at Harper. Transportation won't be a problem, I'll give you Grandpa Cal's Buick."

Kane couldn't believe his ears. A car of his very own? Of course, it wasn't a Ford Mustang or a '57 Chevy like Tony Boy's, but still it was wheels. The Buick did have fender skirts, and he could add rims and a gun handle shift knob.

"Grandma Cal that's bad," he said.

He felt a tinge of regret leaving his mother, but could hardly wait to soup up the ragtop. Though it wouldn't be the fastest car around, it was his. Wait 'til the Loafers saw it, and Brenda. Having a car would surely turn her head.

"Bad? I thought you'd be happy," said Meghan.

"Of course I am. Don't you know? Bad means awesome."

"Oh." Meghan frowned until the lines of her forehead deepened into furrowed rows. "I don't understand you kids. The way you talk and dress. Look at you, wearing those baggy green work pants and combat boots. And you could certainly use a haircut."

She eyed Kane's attire and long hair with scorn and remembered how nice Fin had always looked in his Barnabas uniform.

"By the way, I'll also giving you an allowance. It will be enough for gas and some fun each month." She hesitated, "Is that bad too?"

A car and an allowance? He wouldn't even miss the dough he was making at Buddy's Garage. Kane was riding high.

"Yeah, Grandma Cal, that's really bad," he said, hugging her.

The car did, indeed, turn Brenda's head. They dated after school and sometimes on Saturday nights, although Kane never picked her up at her house. She always met him on the corner a couple of blocks away. He never asked what excuse she gave her parents for being out. All he cared about was that she was with him.

Sometimes they would head to Harry's Hamburgers near Midway Airport on Cicero where lots of teens congregated in the parking lot. At Brenda's urging they frequently went inside, put money in the jukebox, and danced to her favorite songs, "A World Without Love" or David Bowie and Mick Jagger singing, "Dancing in the Street."

Brenda and Kane especially liked slow dancing to "Let It Be Me." Then they could be close and feel each other and no one said anything about it. Even though Harper wasn't a parochial school, the chaperones at school dances didn't let the dancers rub up against each other as they could on the floor at Harry's.

When Brenda stayed overnight at a friend's house she was able to stay out later. Then Kane's favorite place to take her was the passion pit. They drove to the Sauk Trail Drive-in theater, named for the Indian trail between Illinois and Indiana. Kane parked near the back of the gravel-covered lot, close enough to the concession stand so they could enjoy the smell of popcorn, still far enough away to give privacy for making out.

He and Brenda rarely cared what was showing or happening on the screen. What transpired behind the fogged up windows in cold weather was more fun than in the summer when discretion was needed because the car windows were rolled down and people could see in.

Kane wished the Buick didn't have bucket seats so they could lie down, but he would climb into Brenda's seat so they could be close. Brenda willingly let Kane slip his hands under her sweater and fondle her breasts, but she fought his hand beneath her skirt when he tried the maneuver.

She didn't mind when he pressed his groin against hers as they kissed, while they searched each other's mouths with their tongues.

But when their smooching built up too much heat Brenda always broke away before her feelings got out of hand. She would push Kane to his side of the car, and he would lean against the window frustrated.

"Why not?" he would ask, his groin throbbing. "You know I love you."

"I know. I love you, too. But ... "

Each time they were together Brenda seemed to be more relaxed, more excited by him. Kane hoped someday she would give in.

Other than being with Brenda, one of Kane's favorite things to do was to pile his car with Loafers. For a short time an indoor race track operated at the International Amphitheater at 42nd and Halsted. From the bleachers, it was exciting to watch the cars whiz by on floors slick as icy winter roads.

On occasion, Kane even raced the Buick. His adrenaline flowed when the flagman signaled to start, and he gunned the car and took off. It was exhilarating to race down the 440 foot track with its additional 660 feet of shut-down and be able to exit to the outside through one of the two open doors in the brick wall. It was a heady experience being able to stop outside unscathed and not end up, as a few cars did, plowing into the large bales of hay piled against the brick wall when the exit was missed.

Even though the indoor track closed after a few months, perhaps due to the dangerous carbon monoxide build up, it was fun while it lasted. After the closure, the boys often raced in the alley behind the amphitheater or went to the suburbs to find more desolate roadways.

In warmer weather, if girls were riding with the boys, a Chinese fire drill was always fun, but an irritation to other motorists. Kane loved Brenda's tinkling laugh when they all poured out of the car at a red light and ran around the vehicle, sometimes opening the trunk to retrieve an imaginary item, then piling back inside the car, usually after the light had changed to green. Car horns blaring at them made it even more fun. They would speed away honking back and guffawing. They cracked up hysterically when one of their own wasn't fast enough and was left standing in the middle of the street as they peeled away.

42

Kane living with Meghan turned out well. Some nights he joined her in front of the birdbath, and Meghan felt closer to Kane than she ever had toward Fin. She was proud of Kane for studying the book she had given him and learning to meditate as he had. Being with her grandson filled an emptiness she hadn't even known she possessed.

Kane loved his Grandma Cal and enjoyed being with her too. He noticed she seemed happier than he'd seen her in a long time and felt his being there was the reason. It was also nice not having to share a room with Franco. However, Kane wished Bridgeport was closer to Harper, and he did miss his family.

He especially didn't like being away from his mom, who he knew depended on him, but being at his Grandma Cal's was peaceful and calming. He could relax and forget the harshness of his life, mainly the friction between him and his old man.

Fin had returned from his drinking spree, and Francesca now urged Kane, who was digging in his boot heels, to move back home. She assured Kane, Fin was sober and working hard at the post office. Kane was surprised by this, but it seemed the person in charge had given Fin a pass for his absence due to Michael's death.

Kane's junior year at Harper High was winding down. Summer was a month away. He was looking forward to working more in Buddy's Garage, seeing Brenda, and hanging out with his friends.

Regardless of whether his old man was or wasn't drinking, Kane didn't want to be in a household where dissension reigned. Drinking or not, his old man was always on his back about something. And the times Kane had gone home to visit, his old man seemed nastier than usual, at the same time, jealous that he was living with Meghan.

Kane waited for Francesca outside the church. The weather was pleasant. A slight breeze ruffled the leaves of the oak tree overhead as Kane studied the worshippers filing from Sunday mass.

Francesca had trouble getting Kane to go with her to church, so instead of asking she had simply requested the he join her afterward for lunch. He wanted to see his mom but dreaded this meeting because he knew, once again, she would make another pitch for him to leave his Grandma Cal's.

At last, Francesca appeared and Kane greeted her with a kiss, then they walked toward Pompei, one of their favorite restaurants.

Pompei's founder, Luigi Davino and Vito had immigrated from Naples the same year. Luigi had opened the bakery, which originally was called Renata's. Eventually, although he spelled the name differently, Luigi had changed the name to Pompei because of its nearness to Our Lady of Pompeii.

Every chance Maria got, she liked to tell Kane how she'd once baked for Renata's to make extra money in order to furnish her basement kitchen. And she never failed to add the story of how Kane's Uncle Carlo, after delivering her baked goods one Saturday, had lost all the money she was due.

"He lost it in a sinful dice game coming back home. Let this be a lesson to you." Maria shook a finger at Kane. "Gambling is a sin. No good can come from it."

But just as Carlo and his siblings had done as kids, Kane let his grandma's words go in one ear and out the other. It was no secret how much she loved playing Bingo for money.

In the 1920s, the Davino's family-run bakery expanded to include pizza---Chicago's first. Since then, it had broadened its menu to include other Italian dishes. But sausage and sweet pepper pizza was what Francesca and Kane always ordered when they went to the red brick restaurant with its windows overlooking busy Taylor Street.

Francesca had gone to school with Alphonso, one of Luigi's three sons, and now Al, as Francesca called him, grinned ear to ear as Kane and she entered the noisy eatery. The stocky, olive-skinned man greeted Francesca with a warm hug. He led them to a table beneath a picture of Luigi shoving a pan of bread into the oven.

During the meal, Kane waited for his mother's plea to leave Meghan's, but so far there had been no mention of it. The conversation had been the mundane, mostly of Kane's school activities.

After they wiped the last traces of pizza from their lips, Kane geared up for the speech he knew was coming. But he was spared, at least for the moment. Alphonso appeared with a plate for each of them of tiramisu soaked in espresso and liqueur---the Davino's secret family recipe that was legendary.

"On the house," he chortled, winking at Francesca and squeezing her shoulder before leaving.

"He likes you," teased Kane.

"Never mind that," said Francesca, "I want to talk about you moving back home. You've been at your Grandma Cal's way too long. We all miss you. I hardly ever see you anymore, and your grandpa and grandma have been complaining about the same thing. Papa's been very unhappy about his nipote's infrequent visits."

Francesca plunged her spoon into the cake, took a bite, and gave a thumbs up to Alphonso who was watching and waiting for her reaction.

"Did you tell Grandpa that I've been staying at Grandma Cal's?"

"Of course not, you think I want to start a war? I just said you've been very busy with school."

Kane knew his grandpa would be furious if he found he'd been living with Meghan and even more so knowing Kane had been absorbing Irish tradition. He'd long ago learned his grandparents always tried to outdo the other and wanted his total attention and allegiance.

Kane despised being caught like a fish on a hook dangling between the two. He'd missed seeing his Savio grandparents more often too. He had to admit the aroma of simmering marinara was more appealing than that of boiled cabbage.

The bustling Savio household, where something was always happening, was certainly more fun than the quietness of the big house in Bridgeport. Still, he enjoyed being with Meghan.

Francesca took the last bite of her dessert. Her eyes didn't leave the empty plate, and Kane was aware she was holding back tears. His old man didn't care whether he returned home or not, but he hated disappointing his mom.

"Okay, I'll come back. Soon as school's out."

After breakfast a few days later, Kane worked up his courage. "I'm going back home end of the school year, Grandma Cal. It's where I should be. Mother needs me."

"What about me? I need ye, too," snapped Meghan so stunned that she almost dropped the morning's dishes that she was clearing from the table. "I thought we were getting along. That you liked it here."

"I do, but ... "

"Ye can't go. I want ye to help open up the house in Michigan. There's no way I can do that by meself."

Once again, Kane was being pulled---this time between his mother and grandmother.

43

In the end, both Meghan and Francesca got what they wanted. Francesca relented, although reluctantly. She would allow Kane to help his grandma Cal for the first half of the summer. Afterward, he promised to return home for good. Meghan hadn't been pleased with the compromise and had put up a fight arguing with Francesca. But Francesca stood firm saying that Kane was her son and he belonged with his family.

After a heated back and forth between the two women, Meghan realized she had to take what she could get and hoped Kane might change his mind. Kane wasn't happy about leaving Brenda for so long. On the other hand, he was eager to go to Michigan when he discovered his Uncle Gino, would be nearby at Giancana's summer house with other men from the Outfit.

"I don't like you driving your car to Union Pier," said Francesca when Kane told her of his plans. "Why can't you and your grandma go on the train?"

"If I take the car, then I can run errands and drive Grandma Cal where she needs to go, instead of having Harry Bosco do it. Besides, Uncle Gino's going to be near there. I can go visit him."

Gino was Francesca's favorite brother, and though he wasn't the best influence for Kane, she was glad that Kane was going to spend time with her side of the family. So nothing more was said. Nor, did Kane say anything to his Grandmother Cal about his uncle being in the area.

After being in Michigan a week, Kane was eager to see Gino. He fibbed and told Meghan, he was going to New Buffalo the next day because some of his school friends were there. Meghan didn't object, in fact, she was glad to be alone.

Ever since she and Kane had arrived she'd been surprised by her sad feelings. She felt Michael's presence in every room and half expected him to come through the door with his smelly catch of fish or see him sitting in his favorite wingback chair reading a book. For some reason, she needed to grieve alone.

As soon as Kane drove out of sight, Meghan went to her herb garden and picked some of the aromatic, yellow-flowered agrimony. Some force had compelled her to include the long spikes, often called Cocklebur, in her Michigan garden. At the time, she had wondered why she'd been drawn to propagate the prickly plant among her other herbs. Now she guessed it was a subconscious, innate sense that she would one day need it.

Since it was June, the plant had just come into bloom. Meghan was glad the seed-vessels with their hooked stiff hairs that clung to clothes and stuck fingers weren't as developed as they would be later in the season.

Back in her kitchen, Meghan discarded the stem and made tea with the rest of the flower. Granny Malone had taught her that the drink, besides being good for many medicinal purposes, was good to relieve sorrow and unpleasant memories. Taking the brew to Michael's easy chair in the living room, she sipped the steaming concoction.

After a few cups, her mind turned to Michael and their marriage and how she'd never been able to open up to him. "I'm sorry, Michael," she whispered. "I hope ye know. I love ye."

She closed her tear-filled eyes. The memories of her spurning Michael's goodness, his early adoration, and patience came in harsh waves. Soon, just as the golden sun slips from behind gray clouds and warms the earth after a storm, she began to feel peace, her guilt diminishing.

She went to the pantry and found some cloves, ground them up, and sprinkled them over the threshold of the front door inviting the spirit of her departed to come in. Perhaps tonight he would join her. If not, at least her remorse and tension were gone.

Wispy clouds floated aimlessly in a lapis lazuli sky, and bees hummed around the roses in front of the clapboard house as Kane walked to the side yard at Giancana's.

Gino reclined on a grassy slope under a shade tree, drinking wine with De Cassio, Johnny, *The Snake*, Carmine and several other of Giancana's loyal henchmen. Kane's exploits were well known among the men---the gang rumble and knifing, killing his grandpa's would-be assassin, spending time in the slammer.

They welcomed Kane with open arms, pouring him wine while they talked. Kane listened intently to their conversation---a plan for a nightly heist of a local, top-end jewelry store.

Giancana, recently freed from prison for refusing to testify before a Chicago grand jury investigating organized crime, chewed on the end of his cigar, his eyes hidden behind sunglasses.

"Hey, kid, why don't ja ride along. Get a new experience under youse belt. See what a good wheelman youse uncle is."

"Wish I could, but I can't stay that long."

"Ah come on." Gino smoothed his mustache, lit a cigarette, and refilled his wine glass. "Your goin's a good idea. What's gonna happen if you're late? Ya ain't on probation no longer. Call your grandma. Tell her you'll be back after dinner. It'll be an early job. This town rolls up its streets when the sun goes down."

Kane wanted to go with the men, so he crossed his fingers and called to ask if he could stay later. Meghan was so tranquil after several cups of agrimony tea that she readily agreed.

It was the perfect night for a break-in. The new moon, a slit in the starless sky, gave off a shred of light, and New Buffalo's badly-lit shopping area was as dark as the heavens. Still, Kane thought Giancana and his men were brazen to pull up in front of Larsen's Jewelry as if they were regular customers instead of thieves.

"Come on, kid. Come with us," said Giancana. "We gonna show ya how easy this is."

Without trepidation, Kane followed the men to the alley behind the store, while Gino stayed behind the Caddy's wheel ready to speed off with them in case of trouble. Kane watched as

Johnny, *The Snake*, and Carmine climbed to the top of the building and removed the skylight quicker than the flick of an eyelash. They lowered themselves down into the store with a rope hooked on a brick chimney. Before long, the back door opened and a bag of stolen goods was shoved into both Kane and Giancana's hands. When Carmine and Johnny exited, they carried a bag apiece.

They've brought out so much loot they must have cleaned out the entire store, thought Kane. He was so engrossed in the whole procedure he hadn't heard the car drive up behind them.

Gino yelled, opening the car doors, "Get in." He ran back to the driver's seat, the men scrambled into the car, and the vehicle squealed away.

"What's da hurry? I don't see no fuzz," spat Carmine, cuddling his bag of loot like a baby.

"Not yet," replied Gino, veering down a dirt road just at the edge of town and parking behind a billboard advertising Nick's Fish Market. Gino turned off the headlights and cut the motor. "But I seen 'em down the street. In a couple of minutes they woulda been on top of us."

"Good going, Gino," said Giancana, reaching from the back seat and slapping him on the shoulder. "See what I mean, kid? Your uncle's the best."

"Should be. You taught me. Didja know, Kane, Momo here was wheelman for Capone?"

"Didn't know that." Kane regarded Giancana with admiration.

Giancana's eyes locked on Kane's. "Gotta start somewhere. Ya know, kid, you kept your cool back there. That's strength. Real strength."

Meghan's bedroom light had already been extinguished when Kane returned. Later, lying in bed, Kane thought about Giancana's words. He knew his uncles were grooming him, wanting him to join the Outfit after graduation. They had told him more than once that what they did was a business, their work. He thought of Pietro, living the high life in Las Vegas. He had a plum job. It was possible for Kane to have that, too. With a long finger, the thought of it seductively beckoned.

A couple of weeks later after breakfast, Meghan asked Kane to take her shopping on the other side of the lake. Kane's face fell in disappointment. "Did you forget? I'm meeting my pals for a baseball game today?"

Meghan sensed Kane's displeasure. "Oh, all right. I'll call Harry Bosco to take me."

Kane anticipated another fun day with his uncle, wondering if the guys might be planning a hit or another heist somewhere.

In the meantime, Meghan got ready and waited for the handyman to come pick her up. After waiting thirty minutes past the agreed time, Meghan dialed his number but got no answer. He must be on his way, she thought. Ten more minutes elapsed, and still no Harry. Meghan became furious, yet determined. The freckin' man had forgotten her. She wanted to go shopping, and shopping she would go. Slapping a sunhat on her head, she strode down to the lake, stepped into the rowboat, and started rowing herself across the five mile stretch of water to the other side.

Kane was disappointed. It had been a quiet day of bocce ball with his uncle and the others. Still, he'd stayed too long. When he left, the horizon blazed a streak of fire as the edge of the sun slipped from view.

By the time Kane returned to the cottage, he was surprised to see the house was dark. It was unlike Grandma Cal to be shopping so late.

The ringing of the phone greeted him as he walked into the backdoor. The next minute the receiver dangled from the wall phone, and Kane was back in the car speeding to the other side of the lake.

44

Kane drove the twenty-one miles to Michigan City, his mind in a fog. When the voice on the other end of the phone said his grandma had been taken to Franciscan St. Anthony Hospital because of a fall and that he should come right away, he hadn't ask anything more. He'd been in such a panic, he'd dropped the receiver and was gone.

Now, here he was foolishly driving to the hospital not knowing what he was going to find when he arrived. His mind raced. Had his Grandma Cal broken a bone? Did she somehow hit her head and receive a concussion? Grandpa Cal was barely in the ground. Surely, he wasn't going to lose his grandma too.

When Kane pulled up to the medical facility on Homer Street, he felt as if he had been driving for hours instead of minutes. He sprinted inside and stopped at the desk where a blonde nurse, whose badge read, Emma Byrne, was nonchalantly filing her nails.

"My grandmother. Where is she?"

The woman in white inspected her nails and grinned, showing a row of tobacco-stained teeth. "I can't tell you unless I know her name."

Kane took a deep breath. He hadn't realized how upset he was. "Oh, sorry. Meghan Callahan."

"Mrs. Callahan. Hmmm." Emma Byrne put down her emery board and checked names, one by one, on a chart in front of her.

Kane tapped his foot anxiously.

After what seemed an eternity, the pen stopped. "Here she is."

"So what's the room number?"

"I'm sorry I can't tell you."

"What do you mean, you can't tell me?" Kane was growing more and more agitated.

"Because, a notation here says that Doctor Franklin wants to speak to you before you see the patient. Let me call him. Have a seat, please. There."

Nurse Byrne pointed to chairs lined against the wall opposite her desk as she picked up the telephone.

Kane was becoming more distressed by the minute. If the doctor wanted to see him, it must be bad. He hated hospitals with their strong antiseptic smell, hushed voices, and the constant dinging of machines. His mind reverted to when his grandpa had been shot, and the family had waited for news of Vito's condition. Here Kane was again---waiting. He didn't want to sit down. He needed to go to his grandma, but the nurse, her ear to the receiver, glared at him and motioned again to the cold, hard seats as she mumbled into the phone.

Nervously, Kane did as instructed, his mind working overtime imagining all kinds of scenarios. Nurse Byrne had replaced the receiver fifteen minutes ago and still the doctor hadn't appeared. So where was he?

At last, a ruddy-faced man wearing a garish tropical-print shirt and khaki pants, his sneakers squeaking on the terrazzo floor, rushed toward Kane. "I'm Dr. Franklin." He stuck out his hand and sat down beside Kane.

"Excuse my clothes. I was getting ready to barbeque when I got called in."

Kane nodded, thinking who cares? Get on with it.

"I don't want to alarm you, but before you see your grandmother there are a few things you should know. Your grandmother fell in Taylor's Hardware Store this afternoon."

What difference did it make where the accident happened? Why couldn't this man get to the point?

"Did she trip? Is something broken?"

"No, she didn't stumble. She became dizzy and hit the floor."

Kane felt momentary relief.

"Your grandmother's had a light stroke. Her right arm and leg are paralyzed. She may never have use of them ever again. The good news is, her speech has not been affected. And it seems, your grandmother is made of steel. Other symptoms of this kind of stroke such as blurred vision, a horrendous headache and the like don't seem to be present."

A stroke? Paralyzed? No, it can't be. Kane's eyes filled with tears. He stared at a bright orange flower on Dr. Franklin's shirt. "You're wrong. You've got to be wrong."

"I'm sorry, son. I'm being honest with you. She doesn't know the diagnosis yet. I thought it important that family be with her when I broke the news. This is not the first time I've treated your grandmother. She's a hard woman to deal with." The doctor smiled. "At least, when she learns of her condition, she can't throw anything at us since she's right handed."

The doctor was correct about his Grandma Cal being difficult, but the man was mistaken if he thought not having the use of her right hand would keep her temper from flaring.

When Dr. Franklin and Kane entered Meghan's room, her face lit up.

"Kane. Thank heaven yer here. Get me out of this place."

Walking to the bed, Kane kissed the top of his grandmother's head. He tried to sound lighthearted and relieve his own fear at what her reaction would be on hearing the diagnosis

"What is this? I leave you for an afternoon and you wind up here."

Meghan looked at the doctor. "I'll be goin' now. Me grandson's here to take me home."

"Hold on a minute, Meghan," said the doctor. He pulled a chair up to the side of the bed and laid his hand on her left arm. "You're not going anywhere. We need to discuss your condition."

He leaned closer to her. "Your fall was more than vertigo. You had a stroke."

"A stroke! Ye's an eejit! I had me a spell of dizziness. Broke me arm and leg. Now set them, so I can go home."

"I'm not an idiot, Meghan. Your arm and leg aren't broken. They're paralyzed. Possibly for good."

Meghan's chin lifted. Before the doctor knew what had happened she delivered a resounding slap with her good hand making his ruddy cheek ruddier.

"That'll be showin' ye who's goin' to be paralyzed and who's not. Now, I'd appreciate ye gettin' the paper work done, so I can leave this dom place." Her green eyes burned with fury.

Stunned, Dr. Franklin rubbed his jaw. Kane knew better than to comment on her action.

"Of course, Meghan. I'll see to it right away," the doctor said, still feeling his face as he rushed from the room. "You'll be out of here in no time."

On leaving the hospital, Dr. Franklin presented Meghan with a form, which she signed with a shaky left hand that released him of any further liability since she was leaving against his better judgement, and also a wheelchair. It didn't seem to be normal procedure to bestow a wheelchair on every patient, but evidently the good doctor was trying to rid himself of Meghan as quickly as possible.

The gift did nothing to alleviate Meghan's harsh words that hadn't let up since she'd heard the doctor's diagnosis. She had flung loud, angry verbiage at the empty doorway of her room, and the diatribe had echoed down the hallway dogging the doctor, causing chaos on the floor. Patients awoke and started ringing their call buttons, some yelling outright for nurses, who scuttled from room to room trying to restore calm.

Meghan was still lambasting the doctor as she was pushed to the car by a nurse. Kane noticed the hand imprint of his grandmother's rock-hard smack still on the Dr. Franklin's cheek. It was obvious he wanted to avoid another blow because he backed away and stood out of Meghan's reach, letting Kane and the nurse help Meghan into the automobile.

Back in Union Pier, it hadn't been an easy task getting Meghan out of the automobile and into the house. Once inside, she demanded Kane not take her to the bedroom. He tried to persuade her to go, but she remained mulish, so he left her sitting in the middle of the living room while he went to the kitchen.

In spite of the late hour, he called his mother and told her what had happened. Francesca said that she would contact Kitty to get everything ready for Meghan's return, and that she would come on the afternoon train to help him bring Meghan back to the city. He hung up the phone and over his grandmother's protests began pushing her wheelchair.

"I don't care if it is 2:00 in the morning," Meghan spat at Kane when he wheeled her into the blue and white bedroom and tried to help her into the four-poster. She swatted at his hands with her good one, her eyes dots of coal. "Leave! I have work to do. Let me be. Get out of here."

There was no arguing with her. Kane figured he'd just have to let her fall asleep slumped in the chair. "Whatever you say, Grandma Cal. Call if you need me."

"Don't count on it." She shouted after him.

The kitchen clock read 6:00 a.m. Kane, unable to sleep, was eating a bologna sandwich when he heard a crash in the living room, and Meghan rolled to the kitchen, manipulating the wheelchair clumsily with her one good hand. She hit both sides of the doorway as she entered and banged headlong into the red Formica table, overturning Kane's glass of milk.

"Gee, thanks." Kane eyed the mess. He jumped up, grabbing a dishtowel to wipe up the splattered milk created by the reckless driving. "Now, that you've learned to move that thing, you should practice not running into stuff."

"Harrumph," snorted Meghan.

Kane stopped the clean-up and turned at the retort. He saw the steely-glint of accomplishment shining in his grandma's eyes. His voice softened a bit.

"Well done. Now you better get to bed and get some rest. Shall I help you?"

"What do you think?" snapped Meghan over her shoulder as she jounced out of the kitchen, again bouncing off the doorway. Kane heard the wheelchair scrap nosily along the front of the dining buffet and the rattling of the glassware on top, then the clang of metal as Meghan hit the fireplace tools before her bedroom door slammed.

"Shows what willpower and mind control can do," he said to himself as he checked to see if there were more spatters to mop up. He'd always known his grandmother had guts, but by damn, that woman had fortitude. She was amazing!

The next afternoon, Francesca appeared at Meghan's bedroom door to find her mother-in-law sitting in her wheelchair, staring at a limp hand.

"What are ye doin' here?" asked Meghan, hearing a noise and turning to see her daughter-in-law.

"I'm here to help Kane get you back to Chicago."

"The hell ye say. Kane! Kane!"

"No need to call Kane. He's not going to help you. You're going."

"Forget it! I'm perfectly fine to stay here. See. I'm already getting around." For emphasis, Meghan turned her chair abruptly moving forward, colliding with the dresser, knocking over and shattering a ceramic owl sitting on top and rolling into the closet door.

Francesca made no comment, thinking that Meghan would see she wasn't as capable as she thought. But Francesca should have known better.

Meghan ignored the mishap. "Soon I'll be up and out of this feckin' contraption."

"Yes, I see. You're a marvel," replied Francesca.

The sarcasm didn't escape Meghan, but she disregarded it. "I'll be walking again. Just ye wait. Ye'll see."

"Maybe. But it'll be back in Chicago. With therapy and a competent doctor," said Francesca, pulling Meghan's suitcases from the closet.

"Wrong. I'm not going anywhere. Kane will help me. Right here!"

"No. he won't. He's going home with me. You can protest all you want, but you're going, too. Kitty will be waiting for you along with your doctor." With that, Francesca began pushing Meghan's chair to the living room. Meghan dragged her good foot trying to stop the movement.

"Dom you!" screeched Meghan. "Stop! Stop it!"

"You stop it! You're going." Notwithstanding the human brake, Francesca managed to get Meghan out of the bedroom. After which, she returned to finish packing her mother-in-law's suitcases.

Kane was busy getting the house ready to close up, turning off the water, pulling down the shades, and taking out perishables from the refrigerator and boxing them to take back across the lake. Meghan watched the busy activity around her, shrieking like a banshee that she would be staying. Neither Kane nor Francesca paid her any attention.

Meghan struggled to move her chair. "Dom it all," she cried, but she had no recourse but to sit. Francesca had put on the brake and Meghan couldn't release it no matter how hard she tried. She sat becoming more and more irate for not getting her way.

45

In the summer of 1966, when Kane returned to Chicago from Michigan with his grandmother, the nation was seeing a rise in inflation due to the funding of the Vietnam conflict. Like all Americans, Chicagoans had misgivings over the increased number of troops President Johnson was sending to fight.

More and more body bags were being shipped home, and more and more protests were taking place in the windy city, as well as around the world. But the Loafers paid little attention to the number of troops or the battles being fought until they heard about their idol. Then they sat up and took notice because heavyweight champion Muhammad Ali refused to go fight the Viet Cong, saying he was a conscientious objector.

This caused discussions among the gang. It was mandatory for them to register with the Selective Service at eighteen and be eligible for the draft at nineteen. They questioned whether they would serve if called or whether they'd flee to Canada as some were doing.

Eddie said that there was no way he would serve. What was the war about anyway? Kane and Tony weren't sure how they felt or what they'd do if called up. One thing they did know was that they were excited about the space program.

That year, when Neil Armstrong and David Scott blasted into space on the Gemini 8, the sixth mission of the first docking in orbit to the unmanned Agena, the Loafers congregated in Ogden Park. Big Joe pulled his stolen transistor radio from his bomber jacket's pocket and set it on the grass under a tree so they could all listen to the blast off. Some of the guys voiced their dream of being astronauts.

"You ain't got the smarts," said Tony Boy when Mouth, the loudest of the group, declared his aspiration. "Science was your worse subject. Besides, you gotta go ta college. Not something you'll be doin'."

"Well, maybe I could be a mechanic. Work on the ships."

All the guys laughed. "Yeah, sure," said Big Joe, "they'd hire youse right away. Youse who don't know a screw from a bolt."

Mouth slugged Big Joe. "Shut up. Youse don't know what youse talkin' bout."

The two boys wrestled. Tony Boy yelled, "Stop it! There's a problem. The ship's tumbling end over end. The mission's being aborted."

"But it's supposed to go for three days," said Louie, looking up from where he was sharpening his switchblade on a rock.

"Don't be a jamook," said Kane." They're in trouble. What if they can't get back?"

"Hey, let's go over to Bice Hardware and see if they're showing anything on that TV in the window," said Big Joe, picking up his radio.

On the sidewalk, in front of Bice's, the boys watched breathlessly as Armstrong and Scott splashed down into the Pacific, ending their ten hours in space. Amid the gang's cheers at the safe landing, Big Joe asked, "So Mouth, still want ta work the space program?"

"Naw," said Mouth, "too dangerous."

That fall at the beginning of school, students were abuzz with the recent brutal murders of eight nurses at South Chicago Community Hospital committed by Richard Speck. Brenda told Kane about briefly meeting one of the slain girls on the "L" while riding into the loop to buy school clothes.

"It was only a week before the killings. When I heard what happened, I was jittery and scared silly for a couple of days. There I'd been, talking to her. And bang, she was dead. I sure feel better since the monster was caught." Brenda nestled closer to Kane in the booth at Harry's Hamburgers.

"Yeah, no need to worry any more. He'll rot in the joint."

Hot on the heels of the Speck murders, Texas was in the spotlight. Charles Whitman climbed to the top of a tower at the University of Texas, where he was a student, armed with three rifles, two pistols, and a sawed-off shotgun. Before his shooting spree ended he'd killed fourteen people and injured thirty-one.

"Shit!" said Tony Boy. "He had an arsenal."

"What was the sense of it? Them people harmed no one. They didn't deserve to die," said Eddie.

"You're right," said Tony Boy. He's a jamook. Didn't even know his victims."

"You're the jamook. Whitman wasn't an idiot," said Kane. "He and Speck are both sick. No one goes around killing people for no reason." It's not like me or my uncles getting revenge when needed, thought Kane.

However, the Loafers main conversations revolved around what affected them. They noticed small black letters on their cigarette packs that read: *Caution: Cigarette Smoking May Be Hazardous To Your Health*, but the warning was ignored and their smoking continued. Brenda tried to talk Kane into throwing away his weeds, but, as most teenagers, he didn't believe the words applied to him. Something that did, though, was the rising cost of gas.

"Thirty-two cents a gallon is fucking robbery," Kane wailed.

His money was tight since he'd moved back home and no longer received an allowance from his Grandma Cal. Now he worked at Buddy's Garage every day after school, instead of just on Saturdays, in order to have enough cash to run his car, meet the guys at the Rack 'em Up, and date Brenda on weekends.

He tried to scrape up enough to treat Brenda to a movie at least once a month. His favorite had been *The Good, The Bad, and The Ugly*, a Spaghetti Western with Clint Eastwood. But Brenda complained so about enduring the bloody story that Kane splurged for a second movie that month and took her to see *Dr. Zhivago* so she could swoon over Omar Sharif. More times than not, however, since Brenda's parents had finally accepted Kane, they cuddled on the couch at Brenda's house, when her parents were out to dinner or a party, and watched the family's new colored TV that was fast becoming a household standard.

Gino, knowing Kane was strapped for cash set him up doing a little auto service and collecting from a couple of wire rooms where illegal sports betting was conducted. Kane was a whizz at hotwiring cars, so stealing them was easy. After which, he'd drive the stolen car to a chop shop. Gathering the gaming money was a snap, too, since math was his best subject.

Neither job interfered with his garage work or dating Brenda because both required after midnight hours. Kane realized the jobs given him by Gino were actually from "Joey Doves" Auippa. Giancana had stepped down and gone to live in Mexico. Auippa was now top boss. Auippa liked Kane and wanted to bring him into the family after he graduated, and Kane had decided it was exactly what he wanted to do.

One weekend when Brenda was in St. Louis with her parents, Kane met the gang at the Rack'em Up. Since the knifing of the spoon-eared man, Gino had confided in Kane that the establishment was one of the meeting places that Vito's would-be assassins might still hang out. So every time Kane went to shoot pool, he hoped to find the other two men who'd gotten away with trying to kill Vito.

Today was no different. As usual, he checked out the back booth when he entered. He'd yet to see the perps, or anyone else in the dark corner, but today was different. Today there were a couple of familiar faces. Not his grandpa's would-be assassins, but Bluto and Jude from the St. Charles Correctional Center. What were those mother fuckers doing in here? Kane wished Rock was available to help give them their due, but Tony Boy and Eddie, who were waiting for him, were just as good.

"My man," said Kane, slugging Eddie's shoulder.

Tony Boy gave the peace sign. "What's up?"

"Well, it's not peace. Come here," said Kane. He motioned his friends to the wall where the cue rack hung and was out of sight of the prison guards. "I need you guys to help me."

Kane had long ago told Tony Boy and Eddie about the misery the two guards had dealt him during his incarceration. His friends were just as ready for revenge as he was.

"With my plan those mother fuckers won't bother nobody ever again. But I can't get caught. I don't want to go back to that hellhole. And you sure don't want to go there either. So we gotta be real careful."

Eddie and Tony nodded in agreement, both rubbing their hands together anticipating the confrontation ahead.

Kane squatted down and the boys put their heads together.

"I can't let those bastards see me. It's up to you two. You gotta get them outta here and into the alley. They're users. All you have to do is ask if they want to buy some stuff."

Kane left. A few minutes later, Eddie and Tony Boy meandered to the back booth.

It wasn't long before Kane, hiding in the alleyway behind a Dumpster, heard voices. They grew louder, and soon Tony Boy and Eddie rounded the corner with Bluto and Jude following.

Tony Boy led them to the Dumpster. "It's hidden back here. Gimme a minute. You guys watch for the fuzz."

He disappeared behind the garbage bin. Eddie kept the two men occupied with small talk, diverting their attention from what was about to happen. Without a sound, Kane and Tony Boy stole up behind the brutes.

Tony Boy took Jude and Kane, Brutus. Grabbing them from behind with metal pipes to their necks, they clamped the pipes violently against the men's throats. Crack! Crack! Before a cry could be heard, two necks were snapped like twigs.

Eddie stood in admiration, watching the men's eyes bulge, their mouths hang agape. The boys quickly dragged the burly men behind the odorous receptacles. Eddie kicked one in the stomach.

"What did ja do that for? His bacon's been had," saidTony Boy.

"Just makin' sure," replied Eddie.

Kane peered from behind the Dumpster to see if anyone was around. "Come on. Coast is clear."

Tony Boy whistled and one by one, they sauntered back into the pool hall and resumed their game.

Some days later, Gino ran into Kane and brought up the murder of the two men from the correctional center being found behind the pool hall's garbage containers.

"Know anything about them guys?" Gino looked intently at his nephew.

"If I did, would I tell?" said Kane.

Gino slapped him on the back and laughed. "You're learning fast."

46

Kane's senior year was going smoothly. He studied just enough to pass all his subjects, didn't get into any gang related trouble, and he and Brenda were closer than ever.

During the year, Kane had racked up lots of Encore Periods. Students were allowed to make up the detention periods when they wanted, and some usually had a deficit at the end of the school year. Before final grades could be given, however, the shortfall needed to be expunged. Kane was too busy having fun and working to give a second thought to how many he had accumulated.

Two weeks before graduation Mr. Pirelli called Kane into his office. The principal was working behind his desk, tortoise-rimmed glasses perched on the end of his nose, reading a file. He glanced over the top of the eyeglasses when Kane came sashaying through the door.

"Have a seat, Kane." Mr. Pirelli, indicated a chair and pushed his specks to the top of his head. "I've been going over your record here. Seems it fell through the cracks, and for the first time, I'm seeing you have a big deficit of Encore hours."

Kane shrugged. "I guess." He was slouched in his chair in front of the principal's desk, his elbow on the armrest, head leaning on his fist.

"No guessing about it. From the looks of this," Mr. Pirelli pointed to the folder he'd been studying, "you won't be able to graduate."

Kane came to attention. "Not graduate! But, sir, I have to."

"Perhaps you should have thought about that before you racked up all these hourly detentions."

"Well, I can make them up. No problem."

"But there is a problem. There's not enough time to make up all your record shows that are outstanding before commencement."

"But if I go to detention during my free period, after school, and all day the next two Saturdays until graduation. Won't that work?"

"You can be here twenty-four hours for the next two weeks, that would not make a dent. Outstanding hours mean no graduation."

"Please, sir. Can't you make an exception? I ..."

"No exceptions. If I make one for you, then others will want the same."

Kane leaned toward the desk, his hands clammy. "I'm begging you, sir. Please. I promised my mom I'd graduate. I have to."

"If you work diligently, you will be able to finish by January."

"But it has to be now. With my class. I can't let my mom down. Please? If you let me graduate, I won't breathe a word. Nobody will know what you did. I'm not going to college. So what difference does it make?"

"It is the principle of the matter." Again, Mr. Pirelli indicated Kane's record. "It is a school rule. Something you need to rectify before a final grade is given, and in your case, a diploma."

For the next forty-five minutes, Kane and the principal conversed. Once Mr. Pirelli's secretary knocked and motioned to get his attention through the glass in the door, but he made a sign for her to leave them alone. Finally, Kane and the principal stood up.

Mr. Pirelli shook his head. "I cannot believe I am doing this, but you talk a good game. Okay. If you make up the detentions as you suggested, I will erase the rest of them. Now go down the hall and get measured for your cap and gown."

Kane pumped the principal's hand. "Thank you, sir. I promise that until the last day of classes, I'll make up as many detention periods as possible. Thank you."

The Savio clan was crowded into the bleachers of Harper gymnasium awaiting commencement services to begin. Pietro and family had remained in Las Vegas, but Carlo had made the trip and was sitting with Gino, where Father Dominic, in his collar, and Angeline, in her habit, also sat. Chiara and little Frank were parked between their parents.

Even Meghan had made an appearance. Fin gasped when he saw his Aunt Kitty, with the help of Meghan's nurse, come in with his mother. He knew Meghan hated the idea of having help, yet she wasn't able to cook her meals, dress herself completely, walk up steps, or drive, so Myra had become a live-in much to Meghan's chagrin.

Despite dragging her right leg, Meghan was now able to get around on flat ground with the help of a walker. Fin had heard talk that his mother was the miracle of the therapy department. The therapists marveled at how far she'd advanced. Yet, with all Meghan had gone through, it hadn't softened her a bit. If anything, she was frostier than ever to those who crossed her path, except for Kane.

At the moment, chin lifted to the air, she tried to brush Myra away, indicating that she did not need help in climbing up to their seats. In the process, she nearly fell to her death. But Kitty and Myra, an amazon in white, kept a tight hold on her, keeping her upright.

When the ordeal was over and after much to-do, the women settled in their seats. Fin was happy Aunt Kitty had chosen to sit next to him. She wriggled herself on the hard seat arranging her skirt like a mother hen fluffing on the nest. She rolled her eyes Meghan's way, kissed Fin's cheek, at the same time, patting his hand with a damp one.

With no air conditioning in the gym, an oppressive shroud of air hung thick. A thundering rain storm the night before had caused the day to be hot and sticky. People in the bleachers were irritable because of the uncomfortable temperature, and no one louder than Vito.

"Godadammit! Air's ain't movin'. I'm smotherin'."

Sweat rolled down his face. His shirt, fresh before leaving home, clung to his back and wet circles had appeared under his arms.

"*Lamentarsi. Lamentarsi.* Complain, complain. Everyone's hot." Maria fanned her program in front of Vito trying to cool him, her own face shining with perspiration.

"Basta!" Vito pushed her hand away. "You're only movin' hot air. Makin' it worse."

"Stop your bellyaching, Papa," said Francesca, sitting on the other side of him.

Vito beat the bleachers with his canes, disturbing everyone in the immediate vicinity.

"Let's get this show started, so we can get outta this hell."

The woman in front of Vito turned at the commotion and glared at him, "Will you please stop that?"

Her words only caused him to bang his canes louder, his eyes piercing her. Not wanting to cause a scene, the disgruntled woman turned back around. Vito raised a cane ready to jab the woman's back, while still pounding the other next to his foot.

Francesca grabbed his arm. "Papa. Don't you dare."

Giving his walking sticks one last disgusted bang, the noise stopped. Vito fumed, wiping his sweaty brow with an already soaked handkerchief.

"Just think," said Chiara, her eyes shining at Fin, "in a couple of years it'll be me up there."

Just then the processional music sounded, and the Class of 1967 filed onto the gym floor wearing red caps and gowns.

"There's Kane." Four-year-old Franco elbowed Chiara. "Look! He's wearing a dress. He looks funny."

"Shh. Be quiet," said Francesca, giving Franco a nudge.

The speeches were much too long and everyone was growing more and more restless in the unyielding heat. Francesca, holding Vito's hand gave it a hard squeeze several times when she saw he was about to speak out or do something disruptive. Finally, the speeches ended.

The seniors moved across the stage to receive their diplomas. When Kane's name was called loud cheers and whistling rang out from the Savio clan.

Kane shook Mr. Pirelli's hand and accepted his diploma with his free one. Then switched his cap's tassel from left to right, and because he was anxious to see his name on the parchment began unrolling the paper as he exited the stage.

He did a double take. The diploma was blank. That son of a bitch Pirelli had gone back on his word and tricked him. He hadn't graduated him after all. Kane wanted to punch the principal's lights out for being a liar. Instead of Kane following the person in front of him back to his seat, as the class had practiced, he walked faster until he bolted out the exit door.

"Look! Kane left. Where's he going?" yelled Franco.

"Hush, I don't know, but I'm going to find out," said Francesca.

She hastily stepped over the feet of her family, in order to get to the aisle and hurried down the steps and out the exit after her son.

47

Outside, Francesca saw Kane cutting across the school yard, sprinting toward the parking lot. First, she saw his cap fly through the air. Next, his gown landed on the asphalt as he went.

"Kane, stop! Stop! Where are you going?" yelled Francesca.

Kane didn't turn around, just kept going. Wishing he had a baseball bat, he paused long enough to pick up several big rocks. He was going to beat the shit out of Principal Pirelli's bright-red Mustang.

"Kane. Kane."

Just as he got closer to the principal's automobile Francesca finally caught up with him. "Basta! What do you think you're doing?"

Kane whirled around. Francesca saw the rocks, and she grabbed his arm as he let go of one. The missile missed its mark and clanged into a chrome hubcap.

"Basta! What's wrong with you?"

"Let go of me." Kane tried to jerk away, but Francesca's adrenalin had kicked in and her grasp was solid.

"I said, let go of me. I'm gonna beat fuckin' Pirelli's fuckin' car into a fuckin' piece of junk. That's what I'm doing."

"You'll do no such thing. Why are you so mad?"

"Because ... " Kane broke away from her and fell to his knees. "I'm sorry, Mama." He sobbed. "That *pezzo di merda* Pirelli. I'll kill him."

"Quit talking like that. Why do you want to kill him? What's he done?."

"He's a *stronzo*. A fuckin' asshole. He promised." Kane threw his diploma at Francesca. "Look! I didn't graduate after all."

Francesca picked up the diploma. All of a sudden, she burst out laughing.

Kane's eyes grew darker. "It's not funny. Why are you laughing?"

"*Mio figlio prediletto*. My dear, dear son." Francesca bent down beside Kane and put her arm around his shoulders. "Don't be upset. Everyone's diploma is blank."

"What do you mean? Didn't anyone graduate?"

"Of course. All of you did. Weren't you told that when you check in your cap and gown after the ceremony that you'd get your real diploma? The school does it this way to guarantee everyone returns their garments." She looked back at his regalia scattered on the ground.

It took a minute for his mother's words to sink in. In elation, Kane picked her up and twirled her around. "Whoopee! I graduated, Mom. I graduated."

"Yes, you did, and I'm very proud of you."

Bella had closed her restaurant for Kane's graduation party. Through the years, every time Kane returned to Bella's he relived the night Vito was shot. He saw his grandpa lying on the sidewalk, bleeding. Could feel the gun in his hand and how natural it had felt to fire it. Two of those bastards were still running free. But today was a happy occasion, so Kane put the image of the fateful night out of his mind, and took Brenda's hand as they walked inside.

The aroma of garlic filled the room, and there was Bella, in her usual tomato-stained apron, barely able to reach around her ample girth. She grabbed Kane, hugging and kissing him.

"So proud of you, Kane. Such a fine young man you've made." She raised up on tiptoe, her sturdy arms encircling his broad chest. "And who's this bambolina?"

Kane presented Brenda, after which they made their way through the room decorated with red, green, and white balloons to greet the family. In a far corner, a combo played and in the other sat Vito and Maria with Francesca.

Gino nodded and winked in affirmation at his nephew when Kane introduced Brenda. Afterward, she and Kane headed over to Vito.

"Now Papa," said Francesca when she saw the pair coming their way, "please don't embarrass me."

Reaching down and kissing both grandparents, Kane introduced Brenda. Maria smiled and welcomed her.

The first words to tumble from Vito's mouth were, "You Irish?"

Brenda's dimples deepened, and she extended her hand. "Yes, sir. Irish and German. It's nice to meet you."

Vito's hands remained on his canes. He sucked his teeth in displeasure.

Francesca quickly interceded, "Papa's tired, you'll have to excuse him."

She hoped that Brenda hadn't sensed Vito's disapproval. Kane seeing his grandpa on the verge of condemning the Irish, quickly guided Brenda to meet the rest of the family.

"Papa, I know Kane's your favorite grandson. So why do you have to act that way?"

"You know my feelings. Irish. German. Damn 'em all," muttered Vito still leaning on his walking sticks and glaring at Fin standing across the room. "The family's mixed up thanks to you and Pietro. Too much already."

"Kane's not marrying the girl, Papa. She's just a friend."

"He shouldn't be tempting *destino*."

"There's never been any talking to you. Just sit there, Papa, in your cloud of prejudice. I'm going to join the party." Francesca pirouetted onto the dance floor, motioning for Pietro to join her.

Maria stroked Vito's hand and felt it stiffen when he saw Meghan enter the restaurant. She pushed the walker and dragged her leg with Kitty and Myra following.

"How lovely everything looks," said Kitty, noting the balloons, checkered tablecloths, and the Italian flag hanging over the bar.

Meghan sniffed. “The least they could have done was have some orange balloons and an Irish flag. After all, the best part of Kane is Irish. And just look at *him*,” sneered Meghan glowering Vito’s way. “Sitting there like he’s a king, waiting for his subjects. The gall!”

“Stop it, Meghan,” whispered Kitty, moving in front of the walker, “someone might hear you. After all these years, can’t you just let it go?”

“I don’t give a dom if I’m overheard. Now get out of me way. I want to see me grandson.”

A vein in Vito’s forehead protruded, his scar grew beet-red, and his breathing labored as he watched Meghan approach Brenda and Kane and give them both big hugs.

“What the hell! Look, at that *cagna*,” he bellowed. She shouldn’t be here.”

“Hush! She has every right to be here. Kane’s her grandson, too.”

“Don’t remind me,” snorted Vito, “but why do I have ta be in the same room with that ...

“No more name calling, Vito. Remember your blood pressure. Sit there and be quiet. We’ll go home soon. Close your eyes and you won’t have to see her.”

Vito flipped his chin Meghan’s way and uttered, “*Va fangool.*”

Maria shook her head at him and said in a warning voice, “Vito.”

Taking Maria’s suggestion, Vito shut Meghan from his sight. Soon the redness in his face faded, and his breathing returned to normal.

48

After graduation Kane continued working at Buddy's Garage. He'd taken a course and was now certified to install car radios, which had increased his wages. Yet, he didn't want to be a grease monkey the rest of his days. He looked at his uncles, wearing custom-made suits, silk ties, and driving fancy automobiles. That's the way he wanted to live, not with dirty fingernails working on cars. His uncles' way of life was what he desired, and he was ready to tell Gino as much.

Then Brenda announced she was leaving for Missouri in January to attend secretarial school, so Kane decided to delay telling his uncle of his decision. He wanted to spend every minute that he could with her before she left to live with her sister for the year.

Shortly before her departure, Brenda finally allowed Kane to do more than French kiss and cop a feel. It had happened before Christmas when her parents were at a holiday party. Kane and Brenda were settled on the sofa at her house. The Jackie Gleason Show with the June Taylor girls, in their short red velvet and white fur costumes were dancing, but Kane and Brenda were too busy kissing to notice.

Unexpectedly, Brenda pulled away and started running her fingers through Kane's wavy hair. With her other hand, she unzipped Kane's skin-tight jeans, reached in and rubbed him. He looked at her in surprise and saw a gleam in her eyes. Her mouth curled in a smile. And she didn't resist when he lifted her plaid mini skirt and found to his astonishment that she wore no panties.

It had been pure bliss. Yet, pure agony after Brenda left. They'd made a vow to remain true to each other while she was away, and since Vito had instilled in Kane that honor in all forms was important, he remained faithful. Kane reveled in the brief periods of ecstasy when Brenda returned for long weekends and lived for the holidays when she'd be back for good.

But then, he got bad news. Brenda wrote that she wouldn't be home the coming Thanksgiving and Christmas after all. She would be staying in order to celebrate at her sister's with her parents, aunts, and cousins. After the new year, her parents were taking her to Mexico for a vacation. She would return to Chicago the end of January.

With Brenda gone, a piece of Kane was missing. Movies had become an escape, so on weekends when his buddies were with their girlfriends, he often sat in a darkened theater, losing himself for a couple of hours. He didn't pay attention to what was showing, he just went. This had been true the night he went to see *The Graduate*. After the movie ended and the lights went up, he sat for a few minutes, then stumbled out of the Hi-Way Theater.

The story of Mrs. Robinson seducing Benjamin reminded him too much of Lana Romo, his own Mrs. Robinson, and caused him to ache for Brenda more than ever. He vowed not to spend another year without her. It was time. On her return, he was going to surprise her with a marriage proposal. Then he'd join the Outfit, become a wise guy, and they'd be set for life.

Without Brenda to take up his time when not at the garage and with Fin working overtime at the post office during the Christmas rush, Kane hung around the house more than usual. He noticed Chiara acting strangely. His sister, usually chatty, appeared moody and withdrawn, closing herself up in her room away from the family. Once bouncy and cheerful, now his sister was often cross for no reason.

Kane mentioned these changes to his mother. Francesca told him that it was hormones. Teenage girls were temperamental.

Difficult to get along with. Still Kane worried about Chiara. Something didn't seem right.

The day before Brenda's return, Big Joe stopped by the garage.

"What are ya up to? Why aren't ya in school?" asked Kane, coming out from under the hood of a Ford where he'd been changing the oil.

Big Joe, a year younger than Kane and a grade ahead of Chiara, said, "I'm cuttin' today. Need ta talk to ya."

"Yeah, what about?" Kane took a rag hanging from his pocket and wiped his greasy hands.

"I want ta know what you're gonna do about Johnny DuFour?"

"What the fuck you talkin' bout? Why should I do anything?"

"You haven't heard? He's after Chiara."

"Well, I sure don't like the guy, but if Chiara does ... "

"It's not like that. Around Thanksgiving, Jimmy Huse and Gordy Mews came upon DuFour tryin' to rape Chiara. Somehow, DuFour got her under the bleachers after a football game. Huse and Mews happened to duck there for a smoke and found them, DuFour on top of Chiara, his hand over her mouth, trying to unbuckle his belt. Lucky for your sister Mews and Huse arrived when they did. Would a been bad if they hadn't. Now word is, DuFour's still after her. Just waitin' ta get her alone."

"Mother fucker! I'm gonna strangle you. Why didn't anybody tell me about this? Why didn't you come to me sooner?" Kane's eyes were blacker than the oil on his shirt. He shook with rage and started for Big Joe.

Big Joe held up his hands. "Cool it! I just heard bout it. Thought you knew."

"If I knew, do you think DuFour would still be walking around? Come on," shouted Kane running for his wheels.

Big Joe didn't have time to close the car door before Kane laid a patch, and the Buick squealed from the garage in the direction of Harper High School. Kane sped down the street not stopping for red lights or stop signs. The speedometer moved up to seventy-miles an hour as Kane raced around vehicles in his way.

Big Joe braced himself on the dash. “Shit! Burning rubber’s one thing, but you’re gonna get a ticket drivin’ like this ... or crash us.”

Ignoring Big Joe, Kane pressed down harder on the accelerator. The Buick spun on two wheels around the corner of Wood Street and screeched to a stop in front of the school. The boys ran from the car, leaving the doors wide open.

When they got inside, the hallway was empty. Kane whispered, “It’s nearly break time. I want you to go get your little brother and you two pass the word that no one is to come to the third floor john today for their smokes. But don’t let DuFour know. I’ll be waiting for him.”

Kane pulled his spiked knuckles from his back pocket and raced up the stairs two at a time. Hiding behind the restroom door, Kane heard the bell ring, and it wasn’t long before Johnny DuFour entered. Kane jumped him immediately, wielding the knuckles.

“You fuckin’ son of a bitch, I’ll teach you to go after my sister. I’m gonna cut your balls off.”

Johnny tried to shield his face, swinging to defend himself. “I’m sorry. It was a mistake.”

Kane was relentless with the knucks. Having nothing but his fists, Johnny yanked the towel container from the wall and threw it at Kane. The rack missed its mark and fell to the tile floor with a loud clang. Johnny was getting beaten to a pulp.

“I’ll leave her alone. I promise.” His punches were futile against the knuckles.

“You damn well fuckin’ will because you’re gonna die,” yelled Kane, pummeling him.

In the course of fighting, the boys moved to the far side of the room where a window was open. Kane managed to get Johnny’s head outside and his neck on the sill, then he slammed the window down on Johnny’s throat. Johnny’s eyes protruded and his arms and legs thrashed. He tried to kick Kane.

Kane persisted to press down on the window. “Die asshole.”

Word had spread among the students. Loving a good fight, many were gathered outside the washroom, their ears to the door, listening. They were placing bets as to who would come out the winner.

In the meantime, a teacher walking by asked what was going on. After being told, she ran for Mr. Pirelli. In a matter of minutes, Principal Pirelli, himself a big man, burst into the restroom followed by the muscular football coach. It took both of them to pull Kane off Johnny who fell to the floor in a heap, holding his throat. His face mangled---a bloody raw mess, almost unrecognizable. He tried to speak but could only make hoarse, squeaking sounds.

With the arrival of four Chicago policeman on the scene the students scattered. Chicago's finest rushed inside the restroom. Kane was cuffed, dragged down the steps, and thrown into the back of a paddy wagon. The doors banged shut. With sirens blaring, the vehicle sped away for the area precinct.

Inside, Kane was aware this time was different from his other arrests. Gino had driven Aiuppa to Detroit, Pietro was in Vegas, and his Grandpa Cal was dead. No one was here to help him. He was eighteen and would be tried as an adult and probably be sent to Joliet prison. It would be a hundred times worse than the correctional center. All Kane knew was, he'd rather die than go to the pen.

49

At the police station Kane called his parents since there was nowhere else for him to turn. He didn't tell them why he'd been arrested, just told them to please come as soon as possible. Both had responded and now waited to see him.

Francesca, not being able to sit, paced. "I can't imagine what he's done this time. What are we going to do with him?"

"There's nothing we can do," said Fin, reaching and pulling her down beside him, holding her hands. "Hopefully, this crime isn't serious because Kane's no longer a minor."

Fin's eyes clouded. "I know I haven't always been there for Kane, but we can't blame ourselves for what he's done. The boy's just got bad blood."

Francesca jerked her hands away. "Oh, so you're saying this is my fault?"

"I never said that."

"You didn't have to, I know you've never liked my family and their lifestyle. But if we're putting blame on someone, I could say that your mother is on the list too. What kind of example has she been?"

"Children! This isn't the time for arguments." Aunt Kitty hobbled through the door in time to hear their exchange.

Fin rose and hugged her. "What on earth are you doing here?"

"Well, it seems the whole family is needed for this one, and since Meghan's not able, I ... "

"Come. Sit." Francesca indicated the spot beside her. "What do you mean, everyone is needed?"

"I stopped by your house to visit. Chiara had just gotten there. School was dismissed early because of Kane nearly killing that boy. After hearing Chiara's story, I knew you two would be down here."

"Kane nearly killed someone? Again? Damn him." Fin drew Francesca closer.

"I can't blame Kane for wanting to defend his sister," said Kitty. "That boy tried to rape Chiara. But Kane will be the death of us all, trying to take things into his own hands."

"Rape!" Francesca cried. Her and Fin's eyes locked experiencing a moment of déjà vu.

It was that wintry night all over again when they were teenagers, and Fin had rescued her from Masimo's clutches, preventing Francesca from being raped. Saving Francesca had brought the two of them together. At the time, they had realized the prejudices of their parents against the other's culture meant nothing.

"Well," said Fin, "I can't denounce Kane for this one. That DuFour kid deserved to die. Too bad Kane didn't finish the job."

"Now, now," scolded Kitty, "don't talk like that. Yes, that boy should be punished, but Kane certainly was wrong too. Still, he needs our support and love. Despite all his offenses, he has a good heart."

"You're so right." Francesca kissed Kitty's cheek. "Thank you for being here. It sounds as if we need legal help for this, though. What are we going to do? With Michael gone ..."

Kitty interrupted her. " You'll have it. After talking with Chiara, I immediately called Michael's former partner Pat O'Brien, a criminal defense attorney. Speaking of ... here he is now."

A stoop-shouldered, rotund man with a head of thinning silver hair came through the door. Kitty made introductions, and after assuring Fin and Francesca that he would do everything he could to help, he left to go over the case and talk to Kane.

Kane had literally been kicked into the holding cell. The officer's shoe in his back had barely been felt, on his already sore and bruised body. His lip was bleeding, and his right eye swollen from a swing of Johnny's that had connected. Managing to remove himself from the hard, cold floor, Kane sat on the edge of the metal cot and tried to imagine what his fate would be.

He wasn't sorry for trying to kill Johnny. He'd do it again. He only regretted that he hadn't finished the job. Johnny was slime and shouldn't be allowed to live. The one pang that Kane did feel was knowing that he wouldn't be able to have the life he'd dreamed of with Brenda. When she returned tomorrow from Mexico, they would be looking at each other through bars. That is, if she even wanted to see him.

He reached for his cornicello, the red twisted horn hanging from his neck. It was gone. It must have gotten yanked off during the fight, or had it been taken when he was booked?

He was beginning to discount the talisman's dependability anyway. Yet, looking back at all he'd been through, there was a lot he'd gotten away with too. Lying back on the cot, his mind drifted to his distant cousin, Lenny, hanging himself in a jail cell. Kane knew that he'd rather be swinging from a rope, too, than being made someone's wife in prison. He brushed the thought away and let his mind drift into another realm as Grandma Cal had taught him. Once again, he was banking on the gods that somehow, someway, would keep him from going to prison.

It had been several hours since Pat O'Brien's arrival, and still they waited. Francesca saw that Kitty was exhausted, so both she and Fin insisted she go home and rest.

"You've done so much just by being here and calling Mr. O'Brien," said Francesca.

"We'll contact you when we know something," said Fin. He escorted Kitty outside and delivered her to a taxi. On his return, Pat O'Brien was talking to Francesca.

"I've spoken to Kane. "He's fine, but I'm sorry, he's not being allowed visitors. His arraignment will be in the morning at 10:00. I hope that the judge will set bail at that time, and Kane will be able to go home." He shook Fin and Francesca's hands. "Try not to worry. I'll see you both tomorrow."

After a month of gray skies, the sun had burst forth in lemon bliss. Sitting in front of the birdbath, Meghan took this as a good sign. Since her stroke it took her twice as long to shuffle outside to meditate, so she didn't go as often as she once had. But this morning was important. Kane would be going before the judge, and Meghan was determined to send good vibes his way.

She shivered. Since her illness, she had suffered from the cold even when others didn't. With a shaking hand, she unbuttoned her coat and reached inside her dress, withdrawing the beryl, rubbing it, closing her eyes, and letting her mind go to a fine point. She remained quiet for a while, then her eyes flew open. She had seen Kane not behind bars, yet in a kind of hell, nonetheless.

What it was she didn't know, but it concerned her. She struggled to her feet. Gradually, she pushed her walker up the wooden ramp that Kane had built for her, connecting the birdbath and the house.

Maria noticed Vito hadn't touched his morning coffee laced with anisette. "You're worried about Kane, aren't you?" Vito just continued staring into his mug.

"Didn't you contact the boys? Can't they help?"

Vito grunted. "I tried. Pietro and Carlo are in the mountains at some goddamn meeting. Gino's not around neither. So, *niente*. No help."

Maria came up behind Vito's chair and kissed the top of his head. "It'll be okay. Kitty called. Said that Kane has a good lawyer. A man named Pat O'Brien. He worked with Fin's papa."

She walked to her shrine in the corner, picked up her rosary, and knelt.

Vito's eyes fixated on his mug. "*Marone*, a fuckin' mick. Kane's doomed!"

50

The courtroom was abuzz with cases waiting to be heard when Fin and Francesca entered. Kane was in a holding area at the side of the room. Francesca started to go to him, but Fin held her back.

"You can't touch him." He led her to a seat while Francesca, never taking her eyes off Kane, mouthed, "I love you."

Then it was time.

The bailiff announced, "All rise. The Superior Court of Cook County, State of Illinois, is now in session, the Honorable John Jay Smithers, presiding."

The black-robed judge entered, sat at the raised bench, and rapped his gavel. "Everyone please be seated."

Many cases were heard before Kane's. In the meantime, Francesca picked at her fingernails, growing more and more edgy.

At last, the court officer announced, "Case #65233, The People against Kane Joseph Callahan."

The bailiff escorted Kane from the prisoner holding section to stand in front of the judge. Attorney O'Brien stood on one side of him and the prosecutor on the other.

The whole process took about seven minutes. Kane plead "not guilty," as instructed by his lawyer.

Francesca strained to hear what was being said but only caught a word here and there. What she did hear caused her to cry out, "No!"

Bail had not been granted. Kane was to be kept in jail. His case would be heard in three weeks.

51

It was the longest three weeks the Savios and Callahans had ever spent. Pietro and Carlo were visiting from Vegas, and Gino had returned to Chicago from his meeting. Despite Vito threatening his sons as to what he would do to them if they didn't help Kane beat the rap, they said that their hands were tied. A new regime controlled the police station and in the courts. At the moment, the police weren't in the mob's pockets, nor were the judges. They had no leverage. So in the ensuing weeks, everyone was on tenter hooks, awaiting the day of Kane's trial.

Francesca was a nervous wreck, yelling at Chiara and Franco about any and everything, until both children ran to a nearby park to get away. Chiara suffered from guilt that Kane was in jail because of her. She chastised herself for letting herself be lured under the bleachers.

Still, she was better off than her mother so was able to console little Franco, since Francesca's mind was consumed with nothing but thoughts of Kane. Chiara tried to answer Franco's questions as best she could because he didn't understand what was happening. He kept asking where Kane was and why wasn't he home? As for Fin, he buried himself in overtime at the post office and had begun drinking on the sly.

Maria upped her church visit from once a day to twice. Even Gino stopped a few times at Our Lady of Pompeii and fell to his knees. Daily, Vito limped to Fazio's, beating the stained bar with his arthritic fists, demanding Fazio Junior to keep his beer glass and whiskey shot filled.

Kitty and Meghan commiserated over more than their usual cups of tea. Kitty refrained from reading the leaves, fearing what she might see. Meghan still saw Kane in harm's way during her daily meditations.

When Brenda returned from Mexico and discovered Kane was in jail, she was heartsick. Over her parents' objections she went to see him, pledging her love, vowing she'd be there for him no matter what the outcome. For his part, Kane put on a brave face when his parents visited and said nothing to Brenda about marriage. He knew that marrying her wouldn't be fair because of what lay ahead.

Judgement day arrived. The air was raw. A gray sky emitted snow flurries that swirled, then melted as soon as they touched the ground. By the time court convened, the snow was mixed with freezing rain pellets that coated the ground with a glaze of ice. Cars slid into each other and pedestrians tried to keep their footing. The atmosphere inside the courtroom was as unsettled as the weather outside.

Because of the elements and knowing the stress Kane's sentencing would surely cause them, Gino hem and hawed when his parents asked him to drive them to court. But they insisted. After a perilous trip, Gino ushered them into the courthouse. They entered the overheated and stuffy venue just as Meghan, Myra, and Kitty arrived.

Vito and Meghan shot poisonous looks at each other, silently blaming the other for the reason they were there. Vito, not able to restrain himself, opened his mouth. Maria covered it with her hand to stifle whatever was about to spew forth and gave a threatening look. "Not today, Vito."

The families took seats across the aisle from each other, sitting behind the bar where the prosecutor and Pat O'Brien sat at their respective tables. Francesca and Fin arrived a few minutes later, sliding in beside her parents. Big Joe, having once again skipped school, sat with other Loafers in the last row. Brenda, her face white with fear, sat behind Kane's parents.

Finally, a door opened near the bench and a uniformed and armed bailiff chaperoned Kane, wearing a navy turtleneck and gray dress slacks, to the defendant's table. The judge entered and took his place on the bench.

The bailiff strode in front of the bench and proclaimed, "Please rise. The Court of the Second Judicial Circuit, Criminal Division, is now in session, the Honorable Judge Richard Coleman, presiding."

Once everyone was seated, Gino whispered to Vito. "That's the judge who sent Kane to St. Charles. Was a friend of Michael Callahan's. Maybe, this is a good sign."

"Humph! Goddamn micks are everywhere," grumbled Vito.

"Shhh." Maria punched Vito's arm. "Be quiet and listen."

Judge Coleman rapped his gavel. "Good morning, ladies and gentlemen. Calling the case of the People of the State of Illinois versus Kane Joseph Callahan. Will the defendant please rise and state his name and age."

"Kane Joseph Callahan, age eighteen, Your Honor."

"Mr. Callahan, you have waived your right to a trial by jury and have agreed to accept my sentence. Is this correct?"

"Yes, Your Honor."

"Your attorney and the prosecutor met with me earlier. After reviewing all relevant information and your prior record, I have come to a decision. Before I sentence you, is there anything you would like say?" A hush fell over the room.

"Your Honor," said Kane, "I would like permission to speak privately with you."

Francesca clutched Fin's hand. "What does this mean?"

Fin shook his head.

Attorney O'Brien tugged on Kane's trousers and said under his breath, "What are you doing? You can't do that."

Judge Coleman hesitated, scanned some papers in front of him, then considered Kane closely, who ignored his attorney's cautionary tug and stood resigned, his gaze fixed directly at the judge.

"Your request is highly irregular, Mr. Callahan. However, I will grant your request before pronouncing sentence. Bailiff, please escort the defendant and his attorney to my chamber. The court is in recess for thirty minutes."

In Judge Coleman's chamber, Kane sat squarely in front of the judge's desk with Attorney O'Brien, in disbelief, by his side.

Judge Coleman cleared his throat. "Kane, speaking to a defendant this way is rarely done. The only reason I'm breaking with procedure and allowing this conversation is as a courtesy to my friend and colleague, your now deceased grandfather. He was an upstanding lawyer and had great respect for the justice system, as well as love for you. So speak to me. What do you need to say that's so important?"

"Your Honor, I don't expect any favors. I don't deny what I did. And frankly, I'm not sorry. Johnny DuFour tried to rape my sister. He deserved what he got. What would you have done in my place, if it had been your daughter?"

Judge Coleman leaned back in his chair and made a tent with his fingers. "I'd have been outraged just as you. And probably felt the urge to strangle the lowlife. Yet, I am not one to take the law into my hands, as you did. There are other ways to handle these sort of things."

Judge Coleman leaned on his desk toward Kane. "Young man this is not the first time you have acted rashly. I remember sending you to the correctional facility in St. Charles several years ago. It seems you didn't learn your lesson there. You still need discipline. Let me ask, do you agree that you acted recklessly? That it was wrong to handle the situation as you did?"

Kane didn't take his eyes off the judge. He hesitated only a second before responding, "Yes, Your Honor. I do."

"That's all I need to know. Do you wish to say anything more?"

"No, Your Honor."

"Then it's time to go back to the courtroom."

The judge nodded to the bailiff by the door, and they reentered the courtroom.

After order was called, and the bailiff announced that court was back in session. Kane, once more, stood before the judge to receive his sentence.

"Kane Joseph Callahan, I sentence you to five years in the state penitentiary."

Kane's shoulders slumped, and his head fell toward his chest.

Disorder rang out in the courtroom. The gang members in the back booed.

"No, no!" Francesca cried out before covering her face and sobbing. Fin stared at the back of Kane's head as if in a trance.

Vito shook his fist and yelled, "Son of a bitch. *Va fangool*!"

Meghan, her usual prim self, looked like a deflated balloon. She clasped Kitty's hand tightly and cried, "This is wrong. So wrong."

Brenda wept softly.

"Order! Order in the court! Order!" Judge Coleman banged his gavel several times. "If you cannot control yourselves you will be removed from the courtroom."

A hush fell as everyone grew quiet.

"I'm not finished with sentencing Mr. Callahan. One thing that matured me, Mr. Callahan, at your age was joining the Navy and going to war. Today a conflict rages in Vietnam. If you agree to join the service for five years, I will waive your prison sentence. What will it be, prison or Vietnam?"

A look of relief crossed Kane's face. This was an offer he couldn't refuse. "Vietnam, Your Honor."

With a rap of the gavel, court was dismissed. Fate had kept Kane from joining the Outfit. He was going to Vietnam.

ACKNOWLEDGEMENTS

My deepest appreciation goes to my publisher James Kelly of Mammoth Star Publishing for his friendship, guidance, and all he did to help see this book to fruition. Special thanks go to: Paulette Kinnes, editor, Platinum Editing Group; to my friend/editor/reader, Trudy Gurn; to Deborah Costella, Donelle, Naven, Gail Lipperalli, Nancy Nelson, and Stephen Allott for their great critiques and undying support; and to all my readers who enjoyed my first book.

47961515R00148

Made in the USA
San Bernardino, CA
12 April 2017